Praise for D

ROSES OF BLOOD ON BARBWIRE VINES

"A marvelous dark fantasy—filled with ruthless vampires, flesh-eating zombies, and enough action to leave you breathless. Intense, gruesome, funny, and fast-paced—it has all the ingredients needed to satisfy even the most jaded fan of horror fiction."

—Jonathan Maberry, Author of *Dead Man's Song*

"Crackles and moves like chain lightning, violent and horrifying. Not just in your face, but down your throat and in your head. The dead just don't walk, they slither and crawl and feast as the fate of humanity hangs by a single gored thread in this wild, surreal orgy of sex, blood, and death."

—Tim Curran, Author of *Dead Sea*

"Violent and visceral and yet unexpectedly beautiful and erotic, Snell's debut novel is a startling vision of the remains of the human race trapped between two of the greatest evils ever to scar the face of the planet … mankind's days are numbered."

—David Moody, Author of the Autumn series

"Non-stop action from first page to last. Vampires with automatic weapons! Mutant zombies with tentacles! This blending of dark fantasy and hardcore horror spills enough blood to drown the world."

—Garrett Peck, co-author of *Grave Cravings*

"An epic battle of the undead … Snell's nightmarish tale is dark and powerful, an original fantasy tale of terror that preys on our most primal of instincts."

—Geoff Bough, *Revenant* Magazine

"A bone-jarring, hellish trek into the morbid and bizarre, Snell's trenchant novel serves up oceans of gore and an unimaginable body count, and yet beneath the ghastly layers, there's plenty of character development, sharp dialogue and a perceptive view of human—and inhuman—nature. An often brutal—often darkly elegant—page-turning read."

—Walt Hicks, Hellbound Books

Also By D.L. Snell

Hourglass (Publish America)
"Pale Moonlight" in *The Undead* (Permuted Press)
"Skin & Bones" in *The Undead: Skin & Bones* (Permuted Press)
"Remains" in *Elements of the Apocalypse* (Permuted Press)
"Bullet Solitaire" in *Raw Meat* (Carnival of Wicked Writers)
"King of the Mountain of Corpses" in *Potter's Field 2* (Sam's Dot Publishing)
"Meat Drippings" in *Fried! Fast Food, Slow Death* (Dead Pages Press)

Roses of Blood on Barbwire Vines

A Zombie/Vampire Novel

For my mom, because she donated a lot of blood, and for Crystal, because someday we'll find our own island.

This book is a work of fiction. People, places, events, and situations are the product of the author's imagination. Any resemblance to actual persons, living or dead, or historical events, is purely coincidental.

Published by Permuted Press (http://www.permutedpress.com).
Cover art and illustrations by Stephen Blundell.
Edited by John Sunseri.

ISBN-13: 978-0-9789707-1-0
ISBN-10: 0-9789707-1-3

Introduction

I don't know if anyone's noticed over the years, but I'm a big fan of horror. There's actually a very reasonable explanation for why I am transfixed by the sight of a teenage girl being cut in half with a chainsaw, or a gang of bikers being devoured piece-by-piece in the Monroeville Mall. It's not that I like violence. It's that I like being disturbed. Movies, books, plays—they're all supposed to make you feel something. Make you feel anything.

Comedies play on your sense of humor, dramas evoke strong emotions, and so on. Savvy? Each person has their own preference. Each genre connects with individuals differently. My genre is horror. Anything that makes me lose my appetite, or lose sleep, or feel nauseous—that's what I love. Of course, there's a problem with overexposure in any genre. Over time, you get used to it. It's hard for me to find a movie or a book that actually freaks me out these days. I have a bad rap for putting down horror movies. People all around me are cringing or screaming, and I'm waving my hand in a so-so motion and shrugging. I actually fell asleep during the remake of *The Omen*, mostly due to boredom, partially due to other things.

It wasn't always this way. There was a time, in the distant past, when the library scene in *Ghostbusters* sent me running from the room on whatever flimsy pretext I could come up with: "I just remembered I have to go outside and sample the atmospheric moisture levels," I'd say. Well, not really, I was too young to come up with anything that articulate—truthfully, most of my excuses involved having to go 'pee-pee.' It bothered me that I had to leave a movie I otherwise loved (except for that scene where Dana gets pulled into the kitchen—I had to go pee-pee very often then too).

Eventually, I got over it—I still hadn't made the distinction between fact and fiction, but I did rationalize the scenes and decided that the ghosts weren't out to get me, personally. They just wanted the characters in the film. That was the start of something beautiful.

It wasn't long before seeking out the most disturbing imagery and circumstances became a kind of hobby with me. My cousin made me watch *Alien* thinking it would scar me, but I loved it. (Incidentally, it did scar my younger brother, who for a year afterward was convinced—no joke here—that there was an Alien embryo in his chest getting ready to burst forth and kill him. I carried on the tradition and showed *Alien* to my young cousins last year, thinking it would scar them, but I made the mistake of thinking anything made before 1997 looks realistic to kids today. I've never seen a seven-year-old laugh that much at something that once terrified half of America. So much for suspension of disbelief.)

But what is this? We've been talking movies and we are definitely not in a theater right now—we're probably in a bookstore or a living room, aren't we? Ye Gods, I've wandered. I suppose it's because when you add that visual element it makes it a lot easier to communicate horror. Horror novels are a tricky proposition! You have to be a true wordsmith. You're limited to just one form of media. You have to tread carefully.

I offer sincere congratulations to Mr. Snell for this most recent effort. Scenes out of your worst nightmares are recreated, piece by deliciously gory piece, within these pages. I have rarely been exposed to this level of wonderfully disturbing imagery. I've already read this book twice now, and I know I'll be reading it again in the future.

Reader, you haven't experienced zombies like the ones in this book before. I won't ruin a thing for you, but you're in for a treat. George A. Romero's zombies are cute, cuddly little kittens next to these aberrations. And the vampires? They aren't those cultured, lace-wearing wussies that Anne Rice made famous. These are dark, vicious killers—predators in the truest sense of the word. Take either one of these things and you would have the material you need for a grade-A work of horror fiction. Put them together, and the potential increases exponentially. Snell has exploited every last bit of this potential.

Believe me—I laughed out loud during the remake of *The Texas Chainsaw Massacre*, but *Roses of Blood on Barbwire Vines* destroys the old formula. You'll see things you never thought you'd see, hear things you never thought you'd hear said, and accompany some of the most darkly engaging characters you'll ever meet. Do yourself a favor. Put a low-watt bulb in the lamp next to your bed, lock the bedroom door, keep a weapon close to hand, and enjoy.

Cheers,
Z.A. Recht
Author of *The Morningstar Strain: Plague of the Dead*

Prologue

Kent readied his handgun as Troy and the zombies ran upstairs. His flashlight seemed like a movie projector, the monsters merely illusions, just actors in costumes—torn suits, ripped skirts, intestines trailing behind. Except no actor or make-up artist could manufacture the pure hunger in these creatures' eyes, nor the smell of excrement and death.

One of the corpses groped for Troy. Kent shot it, surprised at his aim, and a black bouquet budded from the zombie's head.

Troy made it to the landing and both men retreated into the apartment. Kent shut the door on the zombies. Their dead bodies crashed into it. It was cheap, hollow. It wouldn't last long.

In the corner, the women screamed and the little boy, Payton, cried. Two battery-operated lanterns lit the room against the night.

Kent grabbed Troy's dirty t-shirt and yanked him close, spitting as he yelled, beads gleaming in his beard. "What the hell did you do?"

Troy shrugged and tried to pull away, breathing hard, reeking of canned tuna. "It was Jackson, man! He lost it! He cleared the junk and just—he just walked out! He left the door wide open!"

Kent almost asked why—his brain was working too fast, his heart a cannon in his chest and ears—but he knew exactly why Jackson committed suicide. Five people had been cooped up in this small apartment for months. Their water was low, their food was low, and they fought constantly; they picked at each other's scars, warts, and sores. Kent and Jackson had actually come to blows a few weeks back, all for a cigarette. After a long silent period, Jackson finally cracked. Now everyone would be cut on the shards.

The zombies had already splintered the wood. Two minutes, tops, and they would be inside.

"What're we going to do?" Troy asked, yelling over the pounding and the kicking and the cracking of wood. He was a good kid, about twenty-three, a soccer player who preferred rugby, but he asked the stupidest questions.

Kent glanced around the room, trying to think, trying to plan. They had piled all the big furniture in the lobby downstairs to create a makeshift barrier, a scab against the zombie scourge. Troy had picked that scab. Little good the couch and bookcase did downstairs. Kent could have used them to block the apartment door. Now the front room was nearly empty except for their bedding, some coloring books for the kid, and a box full of tools they'd scavenged. And, of course, their guns. A few pistols was all. Insufficient lead.

The bedroom contained nothing, except the bloodstains on the carpet and the chill that lived in the walls. No one went in there anymore. Not since the men cleaned up Josie's suicide.

Kent couldn't come up with a plan—it was too damn noisy! And he had been a roofer, not an architect, not someone who planned or designed. But he had to protect the women and the kid. They were about the only sun in this place, and he had already failed his own woman, Josie. His kisses and reassurances hadn't patched the hole she'd been digging in herself. Their arguments over stupid shit like who hogged the blankets hadn't helped.

Payton yipped as a mangled hand busted through the door. It was hopeless. They were dead.

"Wait!" Troy shouted, holding up his hand. "I hear something!"

Kent did too. An approaching motor. The rattle of automatic gunfire.

They both went to the window and looked down at the street three stories below, a pinball machine of wrecked cars lit by the moon. Bodies rotted in the gutters. Zombies wandered everywhere.

A bus hurtled through them.

It sported plates of steel armor, a plow, and a crown of razor wire, with a machinegun emplacement on top. A man in a leather trench coat fired the gun. Other passengers shot through ports along the sides of the bus; walking carrion lay down, an easier meal for the crows.

Ramming other cars aside, metal crunching, tires shrieking, the makeshift tank pulled a U-turn and then reversed toward the apartment building. It left smears and clumps of dead flesh in its wake.

"What the hell are they doing?" Troy asked.

Kent shook his head. But as the bus sped up, he knew exactly what they were planning.

"Get back!" He yanked Troy away from the window. Not that the impact would harm them this high up. He was just acting on instinct.

The building shook as the bus crashed through the front entrance. The women screamed. The boy peed himself, and Kent could smell it.

The zombies were almost through the door. Several arms flailed and smacked the wall.

"Go!" Kent told the women and the boy. "The bedroom!"

They gawked at him, and he could tell they didn't want to go in there. But it was the only defensible room with a window. The bathroom window was just a vent, too small to climb through.

"Go!" Kent shouted.

They went.

He returned to the window, and Troy came too.

Below, the back end of the bus was buried in the building, littered with pieces of plywood, broken studs, and brick façade, all clouded in dust.

Three men had joined the machine gunner on the roof. They wore trench coats too, and they were firing M16s into the zombies, producing bursts of light. Heads popped into black jelly and jam. Kent had never understood why the brains of the dead were black. He figured it had something to do with the parasite that reanimated them; the Puppeteer, the radio had called it. Whatever the hell *that* was.

"Who are they?" Troy asked. "The military?"

"I don't know," Kent replied. They had been waiting for someone to save them for a long time, hoping for the National Guard or some other rescue team. This group did not look military, but they seemed to know what they were doing.

Downstairs in the lobby, gunshots erupted. More men from the bus, most likely. Kent hoped they hurried.

Wearing a ripped cassock, a zombie priest broke through the door. The side of its head was deflated like a basketball, but not enough to kill it. Kent shot the clergyman, but more zombies barged in.

He and Troy retreated to the bedroom with the guns. They shut and locked the door.

In this room, the temperature dropped noticeably, and the chill whispered. The women and the boy, Payton, sat in the corner farthest from the bloodstain on the carpet. Kent could still see the shape of Josie's head in the discoloration. She'd made a mess in more ways than one, a mess no one could ever totally clean.

The zombies began to break down the final barrier. Fully armed, Kent and Troy waited for the heads to poke through. They never did.

The gunfire of their saviors grew louder and louder, until, right outside the door, weapons discharged and the last zombies slumped to the ground.

One man knocked. "Search and rescue!" he called. "Anyone here?"

Troy opened the door before Kent could say anything. Damn kid.

"Jesus Christ, thank you!" He hugged the man who had knocked, a man with long brown hair and eyes of muddy gold.

Three other men stood behind him. They stared at Kent. One had icy eyes, and they froze the fluids in Kent's spine. Another stepped forward, tall and regal, the faint scent of cloves. He moved almost like water, no sound at all except a quiet ripple. A pentagram necklace glimmered against his breast like a shooting star.

"Good evening," he said, his tone proper and polite. "We have come to save you."

The man's pupils were abnormally large, two telescopes into deep, dark space. Kent could barely look away, could barely think. He couldn't even hear the gunfire outside anymore, though he knew it was there, couldn't smell the meaty, oily stink of the zombies that lay in splats around the room. Someone told him once that certain snakes could hypnotize birds. Was this man a snake?

The women stopped crying as the stranger looked past Kent, but they couldn't stop shuddering.

"Good evening, ladies."

Something about his voice, as if he were speaking inside Kent's head, coiled and hissing.

Move, he thought. *Run*. But if he did, the man with the pentagram would strike, faster than any rattler. Besides, Kent couldn't move. Fear, the greatest Medusa, had turned him to stone.

Smiling with one corner of his mouth, the man with the pentagram turned to his underlings. "Bring them," he said. "I'll gather their supplies."

The soldier with brown hair grabbed Troy's arm.

"Who are you?" the kid asked, his voice hollow and full of echoes. No one answered.

The other two soldiers came forward. One went for the women and the boy, and the second, the man with icy eyes, approached Kent. He grinned, exposing fangs. Then he came down like a blizzard.

Part One
City of Roses

In the darkness of the apartment building, the humans whimpered and huddled in one corner of the room. They were nude. The floor of the apartment above them had been removed, along with the joists. In this upper apartment, hidden in a crisscross of built-in rafters, Shade crouched on a catwalk. Her pupils dilated into discs of jet.

The humans exuded the smell of urine and blood, thick with the taste of ammonia and iron. Strewn across the floor, their quilts emanated the musk of night sweats; their slop buckets stank of feces. Although boards covered the windows, barring sunlight and moonlight alike, although no lantern devils danced upon the plaster, the humans glowed almost infrared.

A child was crying. His mother hushed him and tried to make herself as little as possible.

Shade shut her eyes and moistened her lips, savoring the plum of her lipstick, relishing the prick of her canine teeth. Her onyx hair whispered hexes and incantations. The catwalk groaned beneath her.

Inside her belly, the Beast woke, a hairless mastiff, all muscles and teeth, a collar of spikes and a steel chain, the epitome of her hunger. It grumbled and drooled around molars and tusks. It tensed, snarled, and lunged.

Shade's lashes flittered open. She bared her fangs, and with a whirl of cape, she swooped into the room.

A woman screamed. The Beast tried to attack, but Shade held its chain. Before the zombie outbreak, humans had roamed free, and she had loved to hunt them. Since then, she had spoiled the Beast—had spoiled herself—with convenient blood. Both needed to learn delayed gratification.

Back in the rafters, she perched on a horizontal beam. Her black leather pants tautened; her black boots flexed. A pentagram swung pendulum from her neck.

In their corner, the humans muttered and shuffled, clutching each other. The child sniveled. His mother muffled him with her hand.

Before modifications, the apartment had consisted of four rooms: a living room, a bathroom, a bedroom, and a kitchen. Now the humans were isolated in the living room, what Shade's late father had dubbed the refectory. All the doors had been replaced with redwood studs, plywood, plaster, and three-inch screws. All the windows were shuttered.

Above, the apartment of rafters was likewise sealed, except for a makeshift hatch near the ceiling. It led into the bedroom of a neighboring unit. It was the only entrance, the only exit, the only view.

Again, Shade swooped into the room. The screamer began to shriek, and Shade circled her. Bladder fluid marinated the woman's inner thigh. Unbathed, her bare flesh smelled like patchouli and onions. And her blood, *her blood!*

Shade yearned to pierce the grape in the woman's throat, to revel in the juice as it jettisoned across her face and trickled down her neck, hot and slippery between her breasts.

From a holster on her belt, she withdrew a black whip, no longer than a panther's tail. The leather of her gloves creaked as she tightened her grip.

She lashed out, and the woman fell to her knees, unlucky to hit plywood instead of bedding.

Kneeling, Shade yanked the woman's mane and punctured her trachea with a dagger. She kissed the wound, shutting her eyes to focus on the sweet suction, the tease and tickle of her tongue. She smelled copper. She tasted pinot noir, a red wine.

Shade released the woman's hair, and her head drooped. The bitch heaved, sucking air through her tracheotomy. Urine squirted down her legs and puddled on the floor.

Back in the rafters, Shade became a gargoyle, motionless to silence the boards. Her prey slumped onto her side, one hand working between her legs, whimpering in masturbation. The human sex drive had always responded to the likes of Shade; it was the only way humans could cope with such encounters, gorged with blood and dripping fluids.

The other humans murmured and glanced at the rafters, believing Shade had gone. One even reached out to calm the injured woman, but faltered, ventured a bit farther, and eventually withdrew. The mother removed her hand from the boy's mouth, and he sniffled, wiping snot on the back of his forearm. Around them, the group slowly unstitched.

Yes, Shade thought. *The danger has passed.*

And then, as they stepped out of bounds, she keened like a bat and plunged into the room. The humans jumped back, tightening their weave. The woman on the floor looked up just as Shade's cape enveloped her. She had no time to squeal.

The Beast's teeth locked into her throat and ripped. Blood scalded Shade's face. She caught red raindrops with her tongue, let the fluid soak her hair and spatter the shoulders of her cape. The woman writhed, but Shade pinned the bitch beneath her knee and jammed her forearm beneath her nose.

The blood smelled flat, an iron deficiency. Shade had expected vintage burgundy, but the more the Beast drank, the more its thirst clawed her throat. Soon, the human's struggles stilled; the flow petered into a squirt, a drizzle, a drip.

Shade stood, licking the cheap wine from her lips. Wet hair clung to her cheek, and fresh blood ached between her breasts. Her nipples swelled against the black leather corset top. Her eyes shined timeless obsidian.

In their corner, the humans cowered. Even the child was too terrified to weep. Shade approached them, torturing the floorboards to make them cringe.

The mother grasped her son and shrank into the horde. Although blind without light, the woman stared right at Shade, alert like a cornered deer. An artery throbbed in her neck. Shade could already feel the wine pulsing into her mouth, spilling over and dripping off her chin, Bacchus overjoyed.

She only owned so many humans, the last of their kind. In a room across the hall, human amputees swung from harnesses, now just penises, vaginas, and incubator wounds—*breeders*. Eventually, these torsos would produce new livestock for the refectory, but until then, Shade could not keep killing. She could not let the Beast off its leash.

It growled and pawed at her throat, pawed until she was raw and thirsty. She deserved another swallow. She could muzzle the Beast's killer jaws, just for a taste.

Yes, yes—Shade opened her mouth and lunged.

Someone screeched, ultrasonic, bat sonar.

Through the rafters, a rectangle glowed two shades lighter than the surrounding darkness: the hatch. A man's silhouette blotted its center, and the sound waves vibrated from his mouth.

He had been watching her, had watched her spill blood. Her arms and scalp tingled at the thought. Then the tingles became a shiver: he had witnessed her lose control.

Shade looked at the mother, at her pulsating artery. Then, with a swirl of cape, she disappeared into the rafters. The Beast lay down inside her.

Ω

On the catwalk, Shade strode toward the hatch, clenching her fists and jaws.

Instead of a flimsy lock, three deadbolts enforced the hatch, engaged from the outside. Armed with a .357, a soldier named James constantly guarded the locks. As a Sexton, James maintained Haven security in concert with three other soldiers. He allowed only two people into the refectory: Shade and General Frost, the leader of Shade's Undertakers, executioners of the undead. Usually, James locked Shade in the room until she finished. He also cleaned the messes and sacrificed them to the seer, their resident clairvoyant.

Today, someone besides James held the door, a man with an ice-sculpture jaw and a mourner's veil of hair, scaly unknowns snaking beneath the frozen surface of his eyes.

"General Frost," Shade said, as James shut the door behind her.

The general's eyes fixed her, grim and steady. He ignored her coat of blood, did not even lick his lips at the scent.

"What is it?" she asked.

Frost glanced at James. When he looked back at Shade, secrets lurked beneath the ice. "Walk with me," he said.

Shade nodded.

In this room, a catwalk traversed a pit, where rattlesnakes of barbwire coiled atop segments of column, and orgies of rebar waited to probe flesh. Shade and Frost walked through the rafters side by side. James passed them to unlock the opposite door; he turned his head as if to catch any whispers.

Frost must have suspected the eavesdropper because he fixed his gaze straight ahead and held his tongue. Shade studied him, trying to find hints in the chiseled cheekbone or the pale lips. His face was impassive, his icy eyes unbreakable.

At the other end of the room, she and Frost descended a ladder to a clearing amidst the barbwire. James admitted them into the next room, empty. From there, Shade and Frost stepped into the hallway. Lanterns guttered along the narrow corridor. A cardinal runner—frayed and pocked with cigarette burns—covered the floor, except for the expanse of the refectory. There, a hole dropped to the third level of the building, into more wire-crowned boulders and rebar, a snare to catch escapees.

Frost checked the shadowy doorways for lurkers.

Across the hall, in room 404, what they called the warren, the breeders rocked in their harnesses. Shade could hear their senseless prattling, but little else: she and Frost were alone in the hallway.

"Come," he said, turning right, away from the snare. His cape billowed as he marched. Knives, keys, and other tools clinked on his utility belt. His Glock was lackluster in the murk, like a toy.

Even with long legs, Shade struggled to pace the general. He led her to the stairwell and they went up, skipping five steps at once. Frost peered over the banister and inspected the stairs below. Shade looked down as well.

The staircase spiraled oblong, leaving a central shaft, a freefall from building-top to ground floor. The entire first-floor flight had been axed, in case zombies finally penetrated the barrier and accessed the building. Barbwire, boulders, and toppled vending machines congested the bottom of the stairwell and extended through the doorway into the lobby.

The second floor was reserved for the soldiers' barracks, and the entire third floor was filled with tangles of barbwire and heaps of cement rubble. It was a snare, in case the humans on the fourth floor should try to dig their way out. Only rats inhabited those rooms.

This night, no one followed Shade and Frost upstairs. He seemed satisfied and continued upward. They passed the fifth floor, where the seer lived, then the sixth, which was empty, and finally the seventh, Shade's floor, what the men called the penthouse.

Through a metal door at the top, Frost walked onto the roof, crunching tarred gravel under his engineer boots. Shade followed him past the inert pipes and fans, past the collection of pots and glasses that gathered rainwater for baths. They stopped at the building's edge before a panorama of blackout buildings and gridlock streets, all pallid in the cloud-filtered moonlight. The city reeked of carcasses bloated with gasses and runny with fluids. Its dead bemoaned their graves, forever doomed to wander.

Once, this city had a name. Sapped of all life, that name no longer mattered. Location, community, and culture were mere artifacts, lost in the rubble of day's end. Even the city's alias, the City of Roses, had lost value, though Shade's father Roman had tried to restore it before his death; he had tried to build an empire. Now, Frost's Undertakers called it the City of Corpses, a more accurate moniker, though Shade would never utter it.

"Look," Frost said, pointing down at the barricade over a waist-high parapet.

Made of car husks, concrete mountains, barbwire brambles, and other rubbish, the barrier circled the apartment building, nearly one story high and covering more than half the street. Zombies, ant-sized from this height, constantly bashed, scratched, and clawed the vending machines, burnt trucks, and crumbling Doric columns of the blockage. Some ghouls tangled with the barbwire, flesh nearly raked to the bone from hours of struggle. Others squirmed on rebar or beneath dislodged boulders.

Where Frost was pointing, a cemetery gate surfaced the fortification. It blocked a pipe, which Roman's Bloodhounds had once used to import human refugees. Obsolete now, the Bloodhounds had been a search-and-rescue team dedicated to capturing human survivors. After the population had depleted, the Bloodhounds became the Undertakers, death to the undead.

Since the final delivery, Sextons had sealed the pipe. But the zombies had finally pushed the gate over enough to climb it. One had made it to the top, now impaled and writhing on the gate's cast iron finials. Others clambered upward, sliding down or wedging between the bars, faces snared on the thorny metal vines.

"Soon," Frost said, "they will penetrate the Haven. The barbwire is thin there, easily trampled, and the window shutters will not endure assault."

As the general spoke, a SWAT officer shimmied up the cast-iron bars. His left pant leg was torn, along with much of his calf. He still wore his black ski mask, but had lost his helmet.

"What harm could they do?" Shade asked. "All the lower stairs have been removed. They couldn't reach us."

"True." Frost leaned his elbows against the parapet, staring down at the street. "But in time, they could undermine the structure, cause it to collapse."

"Surely they will rot before then."

Frost did not reply. They both knew the Puppeteer slowed decomposition. The scientists had designed it to maintain tissue and to combat the microorganisms of decay. And with a concerted effort, its puppets might easily bash through walls and supports. Weighted with snares, the apartments would cave. Shade knew nothing of the building's load bearing system to think otherwise.

On the gate, the officer was halfway up. He had slid down, but slowly regained his altitude. More corpses followed suit.

"What do you propose?" Shade asked.

Frost did not hesitate: "Relocation."

"What?"

He stood and finally met her eyes. His gaze could freeze anyone's attention, especially when the secrets of deep skimmed the surface, blurs fishtailing, disappearing into the gloom.

"In the north river, we have found a boat, fully fueled and operational."

"Is that true?"

"Yes. And the Undertakers have secured an uninhabited island off the coast. They have already stocked it with weapons, food, medicine—all the supplies we would need. We could populate it, let the humans roam and multiply. We could build on your father's legacy. We could hunt."

As he spoke, Frost's pupils eclipsed his irises, leaving a blue corona. His fangs began to lengthen. Shade avoided his eyes, those alluring black holes; she looked out at the old brick buildings and the towers with steel frames.

Roman had dreamt of a grand metropolis purged of the undead, gargoyles shepherding humans through crosswalks and roadways, the Haven as their castle. Before his death, before the theater and the assassin in the shadows, he had asked Shade to defend their home. "Rebuild this city, our city, the City of Roses." That night, he left to never return.

"No," she told Frost, still evading his hypnotic eyes. "I will not abandon my father's kingdom."

Frost put a hand on her shoulder. "Had we but world enough, and time, I would say yes, stay. But worms find their way in, Shade. Lust turns to ashes, empires crumble to dust. So let us break these iron gates. Let us fly." A chant hissed between his every word, the forked tongue of the ancients. He was casting a spell, a serpent with an apple and a silver tongue, that old carpe diem. Pick the fruit, Eve. Partake.

Now, as she pictured the island—pursuing a naked man across a beach, catching whiffs of his blood as purple-lined shells gashed his feet—a heat roused in her breast. Moisture livened her loins, decades dry, and something fluttered against her ribs. She tried to smother the flurry in its cage of bone, tried to break its wings because Icarus died in impulsive flight, because they would have at least a year before the puppets destroyed the Haven, her father's castle. But before she could, Frost swept her into a waltz and took the lead.

"Remember what it was like?" he asked, his breath hot and coppery. "The thrill of the chase? Remember how sweet the blood?"

Shade said, "Yes, yes," unable to stop the wings. Her pentagram necklace swayed with her, once more playing the pendulum.

"This," Frost said, licking wine from Shade's neck, teasing her flesh with his fangs, "this is rat's blood, a rodent's disease. We are royalty. We crave vintage!"

He spun her outward, then embraced her, pressing his crotch to her buttocks. Shade gyrated against him, disgusted at her human behavior, yet electrified, Beast awake and purring. Frost placed a hand on her belly, slowing her seduction. He brought his lips to her ear and whispered, the faintest breeze: "Let us hunt, let us be free."

She turned and kissed him, tasting minty lips, flicking and teasing with her tongue. Frost cupped her breast and tested its ripeness while she stroked the swell inside his leather pants. She never questioned how he became potent. He knew spells.

Running his finger over Shade's pentagram, Frost chanted the ancient language. He untied her corset and pried it open like a ribcage, freeing her breasts, letting them bounce and jiggle before tasting each dark cherry.

Shade moaned. Biting her gloves, she pulled them off. She unzipped Frost's pants, freed him, traced vein and underbelly with cool fingertips, surprised at the rigidity and heat of his flesh, surprised to feel his heartbeat. Gripping his girth, she pumped twice, emphatically.

Frost lifted her, and she straddled his waist. He set her on the parapet, with the drop to her back, and he unbuttoned the slit along her crotch. Still suckling her breast, he slid a finger inside her, rolling her vulva with his thumb. Shade bit her lip and let her legs quiver as flames coiled around her spine, as they spit luminous venom into every cell.

With a thrust, Frost penetrated the skin of her plum, stoking the fire, slamming again and again until Shade felt she were falling backward, over the parapet and toward the barricade. The fire climaxed and threw lanterns across her vision. And with Frost's final thrusts, the inferno spurted magma, burning, burning—and then Shade floated on water and ash.

Her hair streamed slowly across her cheeks. It whispered into silence.

Frost pulled away, dripping their sex. He began to sheath himself. Shade sighed and let her head fall back. Twilight stained the sky with livor mortis, in rigor and decaying. She prayed it would seep bodily fluids, to clean the stickiness that plastered her hair and skin, to clear the dew from her brow.

Frost stepped to the parapet and pointed his Glock at the barricade. The shot echoed, a lonely call that would wander, eternally unanswered. The casing tinkled on the gravel at his feet. Below, finally at the top of the cemetery gate, the SWAT officer toppled with a blown-out kneecap. He tumbled past other climbers and halted against a fist of concrete.

Frost holstered his gun and watched the officer drag himself back to the gate. "May I press your decision?" he asked, his fangs withdrawn, his voice a carnal dust that had known the passions of the furnace.

Shade shut her eyes. She saw the kingdom Roman had envisioned, turrets and spires charcoal against midnight blue, a city of shadows, the City of Roses. And even as that stone empire crumbled into sand, even as the clouds eclipsed her shimmering pentagram, a smile won her lips. The words that passed her tongue tasted of ancient wine, long hidden in the world's most dank barrel-vaulted cellar.

"We shall hunt," she said. "We shall be free."

The sky began to weep.

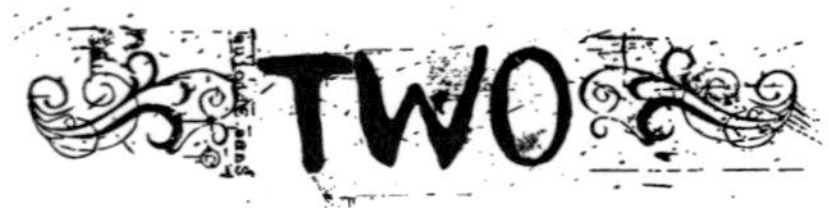

TWO

Humming "Rock-a-by-Baby," Ann pushed Ellie's harness as if it were a cradle. Around them, other harnesses swayed, burdened with amputees, torsos minus limbs, naked Adams and Eves. The slings dangled from hooks implanted into the ceiling joists, which articulated the aches and pains of aged wood.

Near the back of the room, Ann's Mistress mated a man and a woman. She pushed the male as if he were on a swing, simulating his thrusts. The female lay in her harness, oblivious, breasts joggling.

Ignoring the grunts and the slap of flesh against flesh, ignoring her own headache, shakes, and cold sweats, Ann focused on Ellie and hummed louder. She smiled and brushed back what remained of Ellie's bangs. The rest of her sister's hair had been snipped, a fiery mane reduced to a bed of coals.

Cooing, slobbering, Ellie waggled the stubs of her arms and legs. Her green eyes rolled, lazy and aimless and mirroring lantern light. Her skin was freckled and nearly albino.

Ann had the same green eyes. Poppy, their grandfather, had dubbed them Irish Eyes. "It's like I'm looking at me rolling hills," he had explained, voice thickened with brogue, face wrinkled in a toothless smile.

Ann scratched the puncture marks on her neck. How long until the next bite? How long until she could rest from the cramps in her stomach and the nails in her blood?

Naked like the amputees, she rubbed her arms for warmth. She rubbed her hands together and then used her palm like an ultrasound to scan Ellie's belly.

"Yep," she said, nearly whispering. "Definitely a girl, our little Ireland."

Ellie burbled. Ann kept scanning.

She and her husband Michael had discussed parenthood, always in the comfort of their bed, sweat still lingering on their skin. They had chosen the name Dutch for a boy because Michael hailed from the Netherlands. For a girl, they decided to celebrate Ann's heritage and chose the name Ireland. Michael decided Dutch would be an outdoorsmen and would found a commune. Ann believed Ireland would follow in her mother's footsteps and practice medicine, but Michael wanted to raise her as a vegetarian horticulturist. "For the commune," he would say.

They had tried for a baby, but Ann produced too many unviable eggs. Pregnancy was like shooting a thread through the eye of a needle: it required multiple frustrating stabs.

Fighting tired muscles, Ann recovered her smile and beamed at Ellie.

"I'm going to be an aunt," she said. With her hand, she stifled a sob. She glanced back, praying Mistress hadn't heard.

Lab coat parted over cleavage, the dominatrix rubbed her breasts against the male's arm, still coupling him with the woman in the next harness. Mistress' blonde locks splashed against his chest, filigreeing wiry hair with gold. The man hollered. His face sweated, medium rare.

Ann rotated her ring with her thumb, diamond winking in the lantern light. She wiped cold sweat off her brow and tried to stop shaking. "I'm going to be an aunt," she repeated. "And Michael ... oh, Michael—" Another sob disrupted her. She trapped it behind her teeth and hitched silently.

When the convulsions passed, Ann took a shaky breath. She dried her tears and drew strength from her ring. "And Michael," she sighed, "Michael will finally be an uncle." Her hand dropped into her lap, and the ring fell into shadow.

Behind her, the male with the red cheeks quieted. He had planted his seed, consummating another fixed marriage. Mistress buttoned her lab coat. "It's almost time," she called.

Ann looked around and scratched the bite marks. A grin spread across her lips, swelling on endorphins, each a drop of sunshine thickened into honey. Then cold waves crashed over her, and the grin trembled. Soon, she would get her bite.

Ellie whinnied and tossed her head.

"It's okay," Ann told her, brushing back her sister's bangs. "I just have to go away for a while. But I'll be back. I promise. I'm the godmother, remember?" She kissed Ellie's forehead, just a hasty peck. "Love you, sis."

She stood and turned.

In a nearby harness, Frank stared at her. His eyes flamed blue, natural gas alight. With a roan beard and a bushel of hair, he resembled the Unabomber, a Kaczynski that had lost his arms and legs to a surprise parcel gone wrong. His face hung slack and inexpressive, enlivened only by his fierce gaze.

As far as Ann knew, the Kaczynski look-alike did not answer to the name of Frank, but Ellie had dated a Frank in high school, and Ann had always pestered her about it: "Mmm," she would smirk, rubbing her belly, "I'm just craving a weenie, a nice fat *frank*furter." Ann had nicknamed the torso after her sister's old boyfriend.

About four months ago, Frank's harness had hung in front of Ellie's, but Mistress and her nurse moved him after Ellie exhibited morning sickness and a pause in menstruation. They stationed him in front of another woman, this one like a hotdog bun with a wad of soggy bread drooping off her belly.

Frank's eyes lit on Ann's breasts. His penis lifted its head to look at them, too. Ann's cheeks flushed. She crossed her arms.

Frank had stared at her the same way when mating with Ellie, a cold heat searching her body. He seemed inhuman, as if he had shed his skin of emotions and thoughts, reduced to compulsive nerves endings and the ancient reptilian brain. Most of the men here were like that.

Frank met her eyes. She expected a sleazy grin, but his face remained expressionless. His eyes burned blue.

Ann pushed between two harnesses into a different aisle and hurried out of sight. Mistress approached and put an arm around her. Heat blushed behind Ann's breast, and juices simmered between her legs. Her knees weakened and shook; she wanted to run. Her neck ripened for fangs.

"Come on," Mistress said, "I'm expecting company."

They started toward the door. In her apartment, Mistress had converted her bathroom into a prison cell where she locked Ann during the day. Ann usually couldn't sleep. The pangs in her stomach kept her up. She would masturbate and think about the next bite, the sharp prick and greedy suck. And she would cry. She would wish she and Ellie had died with Michael out by the 4-Runner. She never reached orgasm, not until the fangs were in her neck. And she never used the wooden stake, the splinter she had plucked from inside the towel closet. She never killed Mistress as she wanted to.

She thought about asking if Mistress would feed, but Ann wasn't allowed to speak. Mistress would slap her if she tried. Yet a slap was almost worth it. Ann wanted to feel those needles in her skin, that rush of sugar in her veins, that numb haze afterward, the oblivion that made everything okay. She never got the chance, though: someone knocked on the door.

Mistress shoved Ann into the coat closet, into the breeze and caress of clean medical scrubs, into the smell of sunshine and lavender. "Make a sound," she whispered, "and I will brain you." She shut the closet, but its door crept open, providing a perfect view.

Ann scratched her bites and tried not to shake.

Mistress answered the front door.

Three

Frost left Shade on the rooftop with the embers of his spell glowing in her cheeks. His charm waned quickly; she was already mourning the sky. He hastened to the metal door and disappeared inside.

Before descending, he glanced down the staircase. Although the wood settled and clicked, only shadows and sentinels of light inhabited the flights.

Running his hand along the banister, Frost made his way down. The air pressure mounted with each step. It pressed his chest, but he ignored that old anxiety, the old walls closing in.

On the fifth-floor landing, ghost voices and a strange fluctuating hiss sifted from the hallway. They wrapped him in a mist, beckoning him with wispy talons toward some supernatural maw. The seer lived down that hallway, the only occupant on the fifth floor. Not even rats dwelled in the cracks.

Frost hurried to the fourth floor, where the smell of humans thickened. Not the intoxicant of blood either, but a smother of sweat and secreting glands. He entered the hallway, passing through specters of lamplight and imps of shadow, his hair and cape flowing like ink. Frost allowed his boots to clop on the cardinal runner, a sonar to test the distance of the walls. This whole place shrank, contracting like intestines processing food. Every day, the halls grew narrower, the air more stale and compact.

On the apartment doors, brass numbers were still affixed. Earlier, he and Shade had visited apartments 403, 405, and 407, the last being the refectory. On the door for 405, the last digit had been flipped upside-down to indicate the snare within. Apartment 407 had no numbers because its door had been replaced with a wall.

Frost stopped at apartment 404, on the right side of the hallway. He rapped on the door and then tilted his ear to listen. Inside the room, gasps and pants moved in time to the creak of swinging harnesses. The musk of sweat, semen, and pheromones leaked out.

Someone talked quietly. Frost cocked his ear, but the voices morphed into babbling, nonsense, typical sounds of the warren.

After a few seconds, footsteps approached: a light tread, footsteps he recognized. Frost stood erect as the door swung open. He smiled, casting charms and gems of reflected light.

Grace returned Frost's smile, blond hair in a ponytail, bosom subdued by a lab coat. Her eyes glimmered in the lantern light, the blue texture of summer forget-me-nots.

"Are you alone?" Frost asked. Usually, a nurse named Adia helped in the warren.

Grace's smile grew mischievous points. When she spoke, her voice reminisced honeysuckle, sweet, as to seduce bees. "Yes," she said, and she pulled him into the room.

Frost kicked the door shut behind them, glad to be out of the hall, that ever-shrinking hall. Grace pressed against him, kissed him, and then pulled away, humming and licking her lips. "Come with me," she said. She took his hand and led him through the harnesses.

Frost had visited the breeding room twice before, but only for a moment each time. Strapped into harnesses, human torsos hung in rows like beef trunks in a meat locker. In place of arms and legs, they had stumps sealed over with flaps of skin. A few still wore bandages from recent amputations; fresh blood and other seepages reddened the dressings. Adia changed them often, and Grace fed the amputees painkillers and antibiotics.

The females outnumbered the males, so currently there were only three pairs: the females lay on their backs, and the males hung upright, phalluses aligned with vaginas.

The torsos were not just inseminators and incubators; they also supplied the underlings with blood. The soldiers called Adia the Red Cross because she filled the blood bags and distributed them, fresh each night, but never fresh enough.

Still swaying from Grace's coupling pushes, still sporting erections that glistened with musk and lubricant, the men stared at Frost with terrified interest. One man gaped, revealing a stunted tongue and socketed gums, no teeth; Grace removed them to prevent suicides—the tongue could bleed a lot. The man's female, as all the females, stared at the ceiling like a newborn gazing at angels.

A redhead seemed to look up at Frost—clucking, slurring, drooling—but then her eyes roved, and urine dribbled from between her healed-over stumps; it spattered into a white bucket below. The woman's abdomen was bulging slightly, and she no longer had a mate. He had been moved to another bitch.

"Fascinating," Frost said, freeing his hand from Grace.

The woman's hair was cut into bald spots and tufts, and the tip of her ear had scabbed over, as if nicked. Frost passed his hand over her belly. He felt the flutter of a developing heart.

"She's the first," Grace said, stroking his back. "And I think a few more have conceived as well. About a week ago." She reclaimed his hand. "Now come on. I'll show you the maternity ward." Grinning, she said, "I'll show you the birthing position."

The maternity ward, as Frost knew it, was the bedroom annexed to this apartment. A few cots had been erected in this room, furnished with urine-stained mattresses. And the birthing position of which Grace spoke was usually performed with the aid of birthing stirrups, to elevate and spread the woman's legs. Except these cots were not stirrup-equipped, and Grace was not expectant.

That small room, its four walls way too close: Grace tugged Frost's hand, but he freed himself and clinched the redhead's jaw, immobilizing her head. He squinted into the corner of her eye, looking for a scar or a depression, any sign of penetration. "How do you do it again? The procedure?"

"Christ, Frost, I've already told you."

"And you will tell me again." He commanded soldiers with this very voice, and had shot many good men who had resisted its authority; he had left them to char in the dawn.

Grace crossed her arms. The lab coat wrinkled and swished. "We do it with an ice pick," she said, "through the back of the eye socket. Satisfied?"

Frost leaned closer. *Maybe there*, he thought, *the faintest scar.*

Grace dropped her arms. She knelt and unzipped Frost's pants, slowly, so each notch resounded. She reached through the opening, cold fingers creeping like roots that strangle and overtake. She paused, sniffed.

"What's that stench?"

Frost imagined that her nose wrinkled and her lip curled, but he didn't bother to look. The invalid's face held much more interest and novelty. Especially the eyes. The woman's frontal lobe had been scrambled, yet her eyes still feigned intelligence, fragments of gold set in jade.

Grace came closer to Frost's crotch, skimming the black leather with her nose. She sniffed, took a deep whiff, and gagged.

"It's that bitch!" she barked, shooting up to glare at Frost. "You've been with her, haven't you? You've been with that whore!"

Peering down his nose at the redhead's face, Frost spoke with clinical detachment, like a skilled surgeon performing a routine craniotomy: "Such blasphemy would warrant execution, should the wrong ears overhear."

"And who would tell, Frost? These imbeciles?" She gestured to the torsos with a broad sweep of the arm. "These cripples? Half of them have no tongues!"

Frost stroked the pregnant woman's rosy cheek. She did not respond to Grace's diatribe, ignorant with bliss.

"I spoke with her," he mentioned, fingertips grazing the woman's chapped lips.

"You *fucked* her!"

The redhead didn't even a flinch.

"She agreed to the proposal."

"You—!" Grace hesitated. In a voice much quieter: "She did?"

"Yes."

"What did she—?"

"She said, 'We shall be free.'"

"But when? How soon?"

Frost let the invalid suck his fingertip and wondered if she could taste Shade's plum. He still could, even over Grace's lingering honeysuckle kisses, proof that fruit survives the flower.

"She killed another human," he said, recalling the body sprawled on the refectory floor, its cheap arterial wine staining the quilts and the bedding, rivulets dripping between Shade's ripened breasts. He had wanted to join her and drink the blood from her lips. But he had been on a mission. He still was.

"I asked you a question," Grace said.

Frost ignored her. "She will decimate our supply."

"How soon do we go?"

"She simply cannot rein the Beast."

"How soon?"

Smiling, Frost pulled his finger from the woman's kiss. "First," he said, tracing her rounded jaw, "she will seek counsel with the seer."

Grace snorted. "What does that flab know?"

"Much. Her eye sees far."

"But—didn't you charm her? Didn't you charm her Majesty?"

"Yes, of course," Frost said, rimming the invalid's mouth with Shade's feminine gloss. "But charms do fade."

"Then we should just kill her—"

"No."

"It would be easier—"

"It would cause unrest. We need her to convince the others."

"And what if she changes her mind?"

Frost did not meet her eyes, but bolstered his voice with certainty and flickered his tongue to cast the ancient charm. "Then she will burn, and we shall be free."

Grace fell silent as Frost's magic sweetened her blood. She candied much faster than Shade.

The invalid suckled. Joists shifted and creaked, joined by the blathering of a brain-dead torso. Then a sigh of daphne scented the room; Grace had let down her hair, draping her shoulders in garlands of clematis.

"Fuck me," she breathed, exhaling honeysuckle. She parted her lab coat into a V, ending at the snapdragon of her belly button. Her nipples jutted against the white lapels in pink rosebuds. "Fuck me now."

In a short tango, Frost bent her over another invalid, this one brunette. He hiked up Grace's lab coat and widened her stance to expose her flower. She was already hot and dripping, a simple spell. Frost knew it by heart.

Yanking her head back by the tresses, he plunged into her slavering blossom, his veined proboscis parting the pink petals of her orchid. Grace's tongue lolled and melted with the invalid's, their saliva mingling, blending, swimming. With one hand, she stroked between her own legs, shivering. With the other, she tweaked the breeder's tit.

Unable to control her urges, Grace latched her fangs onto the woman's throat. She was not allowed to feed from the torsos directly, but Frost guessed she did it anyway. He would, if in her place. The blood bags could be so cold.

He watched the wine spill as he pollinated Grace's fruitless bloom. But that bloom soon became a flytrap, greedy and trapping; it dissolved him from the inside out, and he had to look away, fixating on a lantern and its pirouettes of flame. The aftertaste of plum brought him back to the rooftop, back to the fire he had kindled with Shade. He could almost feel the heat, could almost hear the needs of the dead as they hungered below.

Up there, higher than any peak in Darien, with new planets in the sky and the golden beach on the horizon, no boundaries contained him. But in here, he was surrounded by walls, always walls—his was a story of walls.

Leaning against the parapet, Shade stared at the barricade. The rain had stopped, but its smell haunted the air. It would return. But it would never wash away the reek of dead bodies.

When her scouts last explored the city, zombies dominated everything: the metropolitan area, the housing developments, even the outlying apple orchards and dairy farms. "They're closing in," the scouts reported. "They're in the billions."

Now, legions clotted the city's arteries and veins, lured to the Haven by the stink of a still beating heart. They lamented, groveling and beseeching entry. They rattled the garage-door armor of the blockade and clobbered its cement keep. They were beggars, the whole world turned homeless and panhandling, the little children showing ribs through bloody shirts, their parents carrying baggage beneath sunken eyes.

Two of the beggars had scaled the cemetery gate: a businessman, his scalp peeled like a hairpiece, and a punk, his right arm merely bones and phalanges. Barbwire had snatched the cuffs of the businessman's Armani suit, and the corporate zombie scuffled with the creepers. The punk had wriggled his way beneath the wire, through crevices and gaps in the concrete slabs, through shattered windshields and busted-out window frames. Spikes of green hair poked up from a gap, then disappeared as the punk stumbled upon a new crawlspace.

Shade sighed and gazed out at the city, at the brownstones and glass, at the white spires of a Catholic church and the air-conditioner-choked windows of other apartment buildings, all dissolving in the darkness. She clutched the pentagram, points digging into her palm.

With Frost's glow faded from her cheeks, she grew frigid. He had charmed her, and in his afterglow, she had watched her father's kingdom crumble. The necklace had grown dim against her chest, and she had smiled.

Some of the Undertakers had despised Roman's decision to enthrone a woman after his death. The soldiers thought females were too weak to lead. Shade was beginning to believe them.

She looked north, toward the river, toward Frost's boat. She closed her eyes and returned to the beach of her fantasy. Waves had worn away her human quarry. She could discern nubs, what remained of the man's legs, but the tide had washed his blood from the purple shells. Hair, like brown seaweed, floated on the surf. And farther down the beach, close yet unreachable, her father's castle still crumbled into the sea. The flying buttresses of its cathedral slowly gave way.

"Rejuvenate the roses," Roman had told her the night he had died. They stood atop the Haven, looking over the buildings. He did not wish to give the city a new name. He wished to revive one of its oldest; he wished to restore its meaning. The City of Roses: it had once been his home.

When he faced Shade, one corner of his mouth frowned, his eyes sad yet steadfast. He had known something then, had known something would go wrong. He had gazed into the seer's eye, no doubt, and had seen the theater, the assassin in the shadows. Had Shade been perceptive, she might have seen his fate reflected on his iris, might have seen his killer, a face, a name. She had not.

"I must go," Roman said, and he embraced her, her father, her family. Together, their blood was strong. Together, they were undying.

"Defend our home," he said, and then he departed.

Yes, he had known, had hidden it in his words, and Shade had not been smart enough to decipher his message, had not been wise enough to save him. And to her, the incompetent, the *woman*, he had entrusted his legacy: "Rejuvenate the roses," his last wish; "Defend our home," his final command.

Someone had killed him.

Shade opened her eyes.

The punk was halfway through the blockade, crawling over the hood of a burnt sedan. His leather jacket squeaked as he moved.

Shade pointed her 9mm. The hollow point lodged somewhere in the punk's skull, and he slid off the car, suspended and twitching in a web of concertina wire until the black widow Death sucked his cursed life.

The businessman had surpassed the barbwire and was stumbling through a maze of parking meters and pedestrian crossing signs. Lengths of barbwire stuck to his sleeves and suit lapel, to the lava-rock-colored legs of his dress pants. Shade began to squeeze the trigger, but he disappeared behind a stack of parking curbs.

"Damn."

She holstered her gun and bounded over the parapet, plunging head-first and shaped like a missile. Her cape flapped against her legs, and her hair moved in torrents where not matted with blood. Pavement, bricks, and marble all rushed up to meet her.

Before splattering against a plane of old sidewalk, Shade spread her cape into bat wings. It caught wind and she rose, soaring to the front of the barricade over heaps of supermarket shelves, park benches, lampposts, and chain link fence.

Lowering her legs, she used her cloak like a parachute to land on a column, one of the many perches that towered over the debris. Most the columns were Doric with plain capitals, taken from the courthouse, but this capital sported the scroll-like volutes of an Ionic.

As Shade landed atop this more ornate capital, dust kicked up beneath her boots; pebbles ticked down into the ruins. The businessman looked up, his cheeks hanging in ribbons, his nose dangling by a thread.

Shade shot him once in the face.

He fell against a pile of stop signs, clanging the red metal. His head slumped on his shoulder, its third eye weeping oily blood, the Puppeteer deceased.

Shade dropped to his side and ripped a piece of barbwire off his suit. Both ends had a clean face, except for burrs at the bottom, as if someone had snipped it so that, with a little torsion, it would break. A second piece reinforced this suspicion.

She tucked a segment into her belt loop and sprang onto the column to crouch.

More zombies crested the gate, headed toward the barbwire.

Shade flipped onto the last pillar, drawing her gun midair and blasting the closest ghouls. One fell over the edge, his teeth shattering as he bit the bullet.

Dropping to the barbwire brambles, Shade clutched a vine and examined it. About every foot, the cable was notched. The segments broke off with a twist.

Before installation, each spool of barbwire had been inspected. Weak and rusty wire had been used for minor snares, whereas the strongest wire had been bundled around the front of the barricade. Had the wire been originally notched, the inspector would have used it elsewhere, most likely in one of the apartment snares. Someone had snipped the wire on purpose.

Groaning, another group of corpses rose from the cemetery gate. Shade leapt onto the column. She clenched her fists and watched.

A dead Latino swiped at the barbwire. He pulled back, and thorns ripped the sleeve of his windbreaker into blue ribbons. The hombre plowed forward, striking. At first, the wire did its job, tearing and springing under pressure. But then scraps busted off, and the zombie tromped a path beneath his Rockports.

Shade cursed.

Jumping from column to column, she visited another patch of barbwire. This one grew farther back in the barricade, congesting a narrow alley between piles of shopping carts. Again, the wire had been scored. Shade twisted a section. It fractured just as easily. She tossed the wire into the carts and returned to the burnt sedan.

Drawing her bone saw, she walked to the pit of razor wire. She slotted the segment of barbwire into the punk's mouth. It grated his molars and caught on his tongue ring. Shade yanked, wresting his cheeks into a joker's grin. She wrapped the barbwire around his head and lifted him halfway onto the car. Her bone saw cut easily through his neck, through the muscles and arteries and spine.

The cadaver fell back into the razor wire, decapitated. Shade held the head on the roof and sawed into the crown, working her way around the cranium. Pulling out a dissection kit, she checked on the invading ghouls.

The zombie in the windbreaker was no longer foremost. Instead, a businesswoman in a pinstriped dress suit led the pack, clambering out of the rubble, following the punk's old path. The left side of her face had been scraped off, an anatomy-book cutaway that revealed muscle and the pearly knob of her cheekbone, the seashell rim of her eye socket, the quartzite rocks of her molars.

A vagrant in a grime-saturated parka and an equally insulating beard trailed close behind. Something had taken his left eye, now just a dark pit. He fixed Shade with his other eye, grinding his teeth like shards of bottle-brown glass.

From the kit, Shade selected a scalpel. As she pried the punk's skullcap with a trowel of scrap metal, she used the blade to slice connective tissues and cerebral meninges. The cap opened with a viscous sigh, like a clam. She tossed it aside.

Inside the cranial cavity, most of the punk's brain stewed a raw pink, a dead gray, and a marbled red: a corned beef boiling in fluids. Shade's bullet had failed to mushroom and had dug a small tunnel, rather than the usual cavern, through the left hemisphere.

Attached to the inside wall of the skull's frontal plate, a black heart pulsed. Its tentacles had suckered onto the brain, probing into the tissue, the tendrils fading into the pink depths toward the brainstem. The heart's oil had permeated the frontal lobe and had started to percolate into the parietal lobes as well. Little black veins meshed all the important centers of the brain, so as to manipulate them, control them.

This blob, this parasite, was the puppet master of the deceased. A castaway of covert Nazi experiments, the Puppeteer was designed to reanimate fallen soldiers; it was initially called Hitler's Heart.

Under private funding, contemporary American scientists had continued the Nazis' development, enhancing the parasite with stem cells. They accidentally bred a mutant strain communicable through the respiratory tract: the parasite shed microscopic eggs through the nasal passage; it also infected the blood and the mucus membranes. The parasite subjugated the host, dead or alive, within twenty-four hours. Only a small population proved immune to the airborne spawn, but no one survived a bite, including Shade.

She had seen it happen to an Undertaker before. In less than ten minutes, the soldier's veins had burst and his skin had sloughed off. He had not reanimated, though. His superior immune system killed him to destroy the germs in his blood.

Dangling from the strings of another Puppeteer, the businesswoman reappeared from the wreckage. Her nylons had gaping runs, and her legs were scratched and cut. The bottom rhinestone button of her dress suit had popped off, exposing her belly, stained green with decomposition. Only a jut of concrete separated her from Shade.

Detaching the Puppeteer's gristly mantle from the punk's frontal plate, Shade nicked one of the parasite's arteries and dodged a spray of black fluid. The parasite lashed out, shooting a tentacle toward Shade's face, octopus suckers groping. She slashed the feeler midair and it thumped to the car's roof, writhing and oozing black.

Three more tentacles suctioned to the car. They constricted and toppled the head, dragging it toward the edge. Tofu giblets of brain matter tumbled from the bullet wound.

Surprised—she had never seen the parasite defend itself before, had never seen it try to escape—Shade cut through the tentacles. She set the head upright, and the Puppeteer cringed; it tried to shrink away.

Using the steel trowel, she extracted it, along with a slice of frontal lobe. She shoveled the diseased tissues into a baggie, where the parasite shuddered and squirted oil across the plastic. It deflated, severed tubes spitting, spluttering, dead.

Floundering over the last jut of concrete, the businesswoman lunged. She reached for Shade with long, cracked nails painted blue. She had slashed her left wrist along the radial artery, and the slash was now a dried incision.

Throwing the steel trowel like a knife, Shade buried the metal deep in the woman's eye. Bone splintered and eye white splattered. The zombie's stirrup pump caught in a fissure and her ankle twisted. With a snap, she collapsed.

Stinking of whiskey-preserved rot, the vagrant crawled over her body, his lone eye seeking and glazed with a cataract, bits of flesh dangling in his whiskers. A new eye, slick and jittery, poked into the empty socket. It was the same sick black as the Puppeteer, only with an opalescent pupil and the nictating membrane of a frog. It blinked and oozed its lubricant. Yet another new ability: never had the Puppeteer generated body parts.

Shade collected her tools and slipped the brain sample into a canister on her belt. She booted the punk's head into the razor wire and leapt onto a leaning column, springing off the fluted sandstone onto the fire escape railing. The bottom portion of the escape had been sawed off. Approximately fifteen feet separated it from the rubble.

Climbing onto the platform, Shade turned to the vagrant. Atop the sedan, he groaned and reached upward. Shade blinded his new eye with a hollow point, glad to see it vaporize, glad to wipe out that bit of twisted magic. The beggar slid off the car and joined the punk in his razor-wire grave. He grew no more eyes.

Along the fire escape, boards covered the windows and entrances, eyelids to block out sunlight and other irritants. Shade climbed to the roof. A rifle barrel met her at the top.

"Your Highness," Edward said, lowering his weapon, a PSG-1. "I apologize."

Edward was a Sexton, specifically a sentry, meant to guard the building from ahigh. He offered a hand, but Shade refused. She did not need a man's assistance.

Edward took a step back as she climbed over.

"You didn't notice me down there?" she asked.

He switched his rifle from one shoulder to the other. He was embarrassed, but his smooth, pale cheeks were unable to flush. "No," he said, "I

just started my watch. Came out the door and
check it out. Sorry."

Shade peered into the puddles of Edw
glimmer. "They have breached the barricade,

His eyes widened; the puddles swelled.

"At the cemetery gate."

He glanced around her toward the drop,
himself and gave her his full attention. His su
lurked beneath the mud swirls and drowning
eyes. Shade's stomach muscles relaxed, but she upheld her posture, never daring to slouch. Not in front of her soldiers. Not in front of the men.

"Keep them at bay," she said. "And call for reinforcements if necessary."

Edward nodded, straightening his own back. "As you wish."

Shade left him. She knew without looking that he had gone to see for himself.

Usually, two sentries manned the rooftop from dusk till dawn, yet when Frost had led Shade here earlier, the roof had been deserted. She hadn't noticed then, but was wise to it now. Had Frost dismissed the Sextons beforehand? Had he vacated the roof so he could moisten long-deadened sexual tissues? And who had snipped the barbwire?

As Shade opened the metal door into the stairwell, she rested her palm atop the canister on her belt: an offering for the seer, a bribe for answers. She looked toward the river, toward Frost's beach, then toward the theater where her father had died.

She went down the stairwell toward the fifth floor. The door clapped shut, and Edward took his first shot, an echoing message, a lonely ode to the nightingale, singing forevermore.

Shivering in the closet, Ann crossed her arms over her breasts and warmed the naked skin. Her wedding ring formed a crescent of ice on her bicep. Her fingers became icicles.

Ajar, the closet door provided a perfect view of the torsos. Through them, Ann could see the Iceman. Frost, Mistress called him, but to Ann he was the Iceman.

Mistress was bent over a harness, her face curtained in golden hair. The Iceman pumped against her buttocks while she necked the torso, suckling like a greedy infant. She lifted her head, her lips rimmed with blood.

Oh, God, Ann thought, leaning forward. *Ellie.*

She focused on the face below Mistress' chin. She thought she saw a hint of carroty hair, but the gloom thwarted her; the harness blocked her view.

Mistress licked her lips. She moaned and returned to the woman's neck. In Ann's chest, a scream clawed toward fresh air, claustrophobic and seeking release.

With a slow dip and twirl, the Iceman whisked Mistress into the maternity ward. She lay down on the edge of a cot, raising and spreading her legs. The Iceman strutted between them.

Ann looked to the woman in the harness and pictured Ellie, her pale cheek splashed with blood, green eyes inert. She could be dying of blood loss. She might need help.

Scratching the puncture wounds on her neck, Ann glanced at the lovers. They were still engaged. The mattress springs still twittered. She went to push open the closet. Her fingertips touched the cool wood, but retreated as she remembered the mouse in the hinge. The Iceman would hear its squeak.

He would pounce and ravage Ann's throat. He would throw her body off the roof, into the arms of the dead, and she would rise. Ireland would be born into Mistress' cold embrace, to never bask in the sunshine of her aunt's love.

Ann shut her eyes and thumbed her wedding ring, circling it around her finger. Michael would fortify her. He had gotten her this far. She would have starved at home had he not suggested the mountains. She and Ellie would have died in their 4-Runner if he had not ordered them to run, Jesus Christ, run! Ann would have died by his side, and death would have done them no part.

Making a fist with her left hand, she peeked out at her sister. She freed one last shuddering breath and then pressed the closet door. It snuck open: silent, silent, a subtle mouse. The hinge bowed and squeezed the pin. Ann pressed harder, harder, and harder still, tightening her chest to stop the palpitations, biting down on a whimper.

She paused and muttered her custom wedding vows: "In sickness and in health, till death reunite." Michael's hand materialized in hers and she clasped it. Their rings clinked, melded, imbuing her fist with strength. Her jitters abated. The walls of her heart flexed.

Ann pushed the door.

She almost screamed when the mouse in the hinge chirped.

She froze.

The only sounds were the rocking of harnesses and the nattering of torsos. Mistress had stopped singing her ecstasy, and the cot springs had stopped tweeting.

At a different angle than before, she could not see her captors. She could sense them, though. Especially the Iceman. He stood right outside the closet. Soon, he would wrench it open and descend with icicle fangs and eyes of hoarfrost. Ann would be caught in his blizzard.

But he never burst in. And now, after the snow had melted from her ears, Ann could hear panting and the quietest smack. The smacking grew louder, and the panting climaxed into loud moans, gasps, and wails.

Ann nudged the closet open a little more and peeked out. She was safe.

Slowly, she slid through the crack, not the first time she'd noticed her weight loss. The outline of her ribs had been the first indication. And her breasts had shrunk—not that they had been big before.

The female leprechaun, that was Ann: stubby legs, stout frame, pointy ears—all the ugly traits, yet she had been robbed of her pot of gold. Ellie had garnered all the gorgeous qualities, the long legs, the round boobs, a slender build. Ann had always been jealous, but now she preferred her small body. Leprechauns are elusive. She would be as well.

To her bare feet, the plywood floor was chilly. The wintry mouths of the air sucked her nipples stiff.

The lamplight shunned this corner, but little tongues of it tested the shadows. Ann avoided the light and crouched along the wall toward the front door, invisible to the maternity ward. Even the torsos took no notice. The women drooled and gibbered while the men stared toward the peep-show, all erect.

Ann's legs trembled, pleading her to run, to throw open the door and bolt.

Mistress usually locked the door from the inside, a dial on the knob and three deadbolts: one at head level, one at chest level, and one near the floor. But in her haste to usher the Iceman away from the closet, she had neglected all four locks. A simple turn of the knob and Ann could escape. She had a basic layout of the hallway, though not the position of the stairs.

What if she did get out? The Iceman would seize her in the hall or the stairwell. Or if she fell into the pits, he would leave her for the rats. Even if she eluded him, there was nothing outside. Mistress had saved Ann and Ellie from the streets, from that zombie with the cleaver dividing his bald spot. She had given Ann shelter, food, company, had even let her keep her wedding ring. The streets had done nothing but take.

Yet Mistress took, too. And every time, Ann felt herself pale, limp in the teeth of addiction. Soon she would not have the vigor to stand, let alone escape. Her eyes and cheeks would hollow; her heart would sag. The bite would be all she could feel.

But Ellie. She couldn't leave Ellie. And she could not abandon her niece.

Ann fixated on her sister's harness and continued to mutter her wedding vows. She made a fist and inched into a phantasmagoria of firelight.

Something lunged behind her.

She froze, a tableau. The silhouette jumped again, just her shadow, projected onto the wall in a silent film. In rows before her, the torsos were her audience, but their heads were turned, focused on the sex show within the theater, not the drama onstage.

Ann scooted into the corner, where the curtains of darkness were drawn. The door was steps away. She could reach out. She could reach out and touch it, open it, run.

No. Forget the door. Help Ellie.

Ann nodded to herself. She stepped away from the wall and tiptoed between the harnesses.

Urine spouted from a nearby torso. The yellow stream drummed into her slop bucket. Ann flinched, kept moving.

In the maternity ward, Mistress' lab coat gaped. The Iceman cupped her breasts. Ann tried not to stare. Mistress would sense it. Ann put one foot forward, then another, and another, until a floorboard complained underfoot.

She halted, eyes darting sideways.

Luckily, the noise had mimicked the complaints of the ceiling joists, which creaked as the torsos swayed. Mistress had heard no misstep.

In a slow, tremulous stream, Ann exhaled. She could see Ellie now, just the top of her head, now the side of her face. She was burbling, happy. No birthmarks of blood.

Ann moved toward her sister.

Someone was watching.

From his harness, Frank's eyes gleamed. His penis pointed at her like an accusing finger from beneath its hood of foreskin. That blank look on his face, the lack of humanity, was somehow colder than the Iceman's stare. Madness flickered in his eyes.

Ann could not move, too afraid to shatter the silence between them. She must have cringed though; Frank began to scream.

The Iceman whipped his head toward the uproar. Mistress stopped crooning, and the male torsos followed her gaze. The females just blabbered on, some new with child, others leaking menstrual blood.

The Iceman tore away from Mistress and streaked through the torsos.

Ann scurried to the door. She yanked it open, jumped through, and tried to slam it, crushing the Iceman's arm. He growled and clawed at her face. His fingernails lengthened into talons.

Ann bolted down the hallway, through clashing armies of light and dark. Axes of shadow swung at her head. Sabers of lamplight jabbed her gut.

Behind her, the door crashed open. She didn't want to look back, didn't want to see Death bearing down, but she *had* to, almost as if hands were twisting her neck.

Amid a dark streak of movement, the Iceman's mouth snarled, an arctic cavern. His eyes became black holes. They stretched and warped the hallway into a vortex.

Over the din, Ann barely heard Mistress' outcry: "Frost, no!"

The Iceman ripped forward, cosmic vacuums hungering for molecules and atoms. There was an insuck of breath, an infernal roar. His talons grazed the nape of Ann's neck.

And then she was falling, the eternal fall, into the eternal abyss. She could not feel the air rush past her skin, but its static consumed everything. The Iceman towered above her at the lip of the chasm, his frosty eyes glowing blue. He shrank as she plummeted.

When Ann hit bottom, pain flared from her temple and flashed red and white. Another blast detonated in her shoulder and hip. Hooks snared the skin on her arms. Her cheek and eyelid, too. The speck of light faded above. The Iceman's eyes were the last things she saw.

As Grace raved in his face, Frost stared down at his prey. The woman had tumbled between two chunks of concrete into a cobweb of barbwire. Blood and ginger hair pooled around her head like a congealing brain splatter. The wound was just a gash above her right eye, not enough to kill her, but enough for a serious concussion, which, if ignored, could be lethal.

The snare consisted of a living room and a hallway. The wall between the rooms had been demolished, and the hallway had been sealed, as had all the doors of the living room. Escape was impossible.

"Get her out of there!" Grace shrieked. "Get her out now!"

Frost met her eyes. The skin had pulled tight against her delicate skull, lines hardened around her eyes and mouth. He could see the same stress in her irises. Had he overlooked the bite on the human's neck, Grace's concern would have puzzled him. But he had seen the wound and had understood instantly.

"She is your pet," Frost said. "You bury her."

Grace searched his face. His visage did not yield to ice picks or pity.

"Fuck you," she said, narrowing her eyes. "Fuck you!"

She swung at him, and Frost grabbed her wrist. He stepped behind her, twisting her arm toward the nape of her neck. She yelped. He kneed the back of her leg and hobbled her, then pushed her to the hole and held her over the edge. Sharp wooden staves waited below.

"You are fortunate," he said, lips to her ear. "I have affairs to attend to. Now," he applied more torque to her arm, inducing another whimper. "Clean your mess discreetly, else I'll execute you for this offense."

Frost pulled her back and released her, let her crumple to the floor. Without looking back, he marched down the hall, shadow minions capering alongside. Grace screamed and threw something, probably her white nurse's shoe; it bounced off the wall far from its mark.

Frost stalked into the shadows, grinning, fangs extended. He could taste blood, though his prey had eluded him. For one second, he had hunted. He had flown beyond the walls.

Shade paused at the fifth-floor entryway, shivering at the drop in mercury. Voices swirled through the hallway in silhouettes and satin wraiths. They streamed past her, clinging to her arms in a reaper's cloak, yawning away as she marched into their haunt. Some swarmed the canister on Shade's belt, sniffing and squiggling like scorched sperm seeking a polluted egg. After they identified their obsession, the sperm wriggled ahead and disappeared into the cloud to report to some furtive master.

An undulating tongue, the cardinal runner tasted the soles of Shade's boots. It drew her deeper into the gullet, toward its simmering bowels. The whispers and laments doubled and the miasma thickened, choking her with the taste of ashes and graveyard soil. Faces pressed against the gaseous pall, some glowering, others the masks of tragedy.

Most of the faces belonged to strangers, previous tenants of the building, but some belonged to Shade's victims, those whose blood had stained the refectory floor. She saw her most recent kill, the bitch with the bland wine, her throat agape. But these countenances were transient: they stirred and dissipated with Shade's mere passage. All except one.

He hovered in the hallway, staring at Shade with charcoal eyes. Fangs extended from his mouth, and a silver pentagram hung from a chain against his doublet.

Shade's hand went to the jewelry around her own neck, gripping the five-pointed star. Just by contour, she knew her necklace matched the ghost's. And his eyes. His eyes were much like hers.

The spirit's misty flesh wavered in the eddies of his brethren, but his stare remained solid. His necklace never dimmed.

Before Shade could react, before she could speak or step forward, a door swung open to the right. The orifice exhaled the smell of incense, and without a sound, the spirit disappeared into the whorls of ectoplasmic fog.

Serpentine and amphibian, a voice slithered and croaked in the room beyond the door. "I smell you," it said, drooling. "Come closer."

Ignoring the welcome, Shade stepped forward and peered into the phantom smoke for the gleam of a pentagram. The ghost had vanished.

Shade frowned and stepped into the apartment.

The door shut behind her.

"Is that blood I smell?" The voice came from a dark corner of the room, beyond the veil of incense breath. Candles—some in candelabra, others dripping black wax onto granite plant stands—filled the space with the flurry of yellow shell moths, quivering on the papyrus wallpaper and swooping, gnawing the mourner's veil of murk that draped the room.

In the left corner, the veil had wadded, thick and impenetrable. There in the darkness, heaped on a khaki futon mattress, the seer chortled. Her jowls wobbled, clustered with moles, and her cadaverous folds shook. In one plump hand, she waved a rod of incense, drawing circles with its red eye. A wattle drooped from her triceps like a scrotum.

"What've you brought me?" the seer asked, her eyes close-set and glossy like olives.

Shade uncapped the canister on her belt. She retrieved the baggie and dangled it, letting it unroll with a slosh, the contents slumping in a cancerous mass.

The seer licked her lips. "What is it? Another menstrual sample?"

"Something much better," Shade said as she stepped into the stench beneath the incense, the stench of excrement and urine and rotting meat. "It's a parasite."

"Yes," the seer moaned, snuffling through phlegm and a deviated septum. "I can smell it. I can smell the brains." She took another deep breath, eyes blacker than the surrounding mourner's veil. "Give it to me. Give it to me now."

Shade went closer. "You shall have it," she said. Then she lowered her arm and retreated a step. "After your eye does its service."

The seer's eye symbolized her ability to gaze into the past, the present, and the future, an innate crystal ball, polished and tinted blue from years and use. It had a ruby iris and a cat's pupil. The ethers folded around it like eyelids.

The seer glared candlelight. "I want it now!"

The candles blinked, nearly snuffed, and then burst into holocausts. All the souls of Hell raged in those blazes, fiends with serrated jaws and crowns of jagged horn. On a gold menorah, the nine jets of fire arced, forming solar-flare gateways into the underworld. The yellow moths huddled into stars at the tip of each votive, anxious to take flight.

"I will have it," the seer said; her eyes had become glaring fireballs, her face spotlighted and scowling. "I will have it now."

Shade took another step back. She began to return the baggie to the container.

The seer screeched and lurched forward. The candles streamed fire into the nucleus of the room, forming one bright sun around Shade's head. Damned souls raked her flesh with flaming pitchforks and nails, blistering and charring her cheeks. She stood fast, not even flinching as the firestorm lit the gasoline trails of her nervous system, not even blinking as Molotov cocktails exploded in her scalp.

Finally, the spouts diminished into phoenix feathers. The scraps of Shade's hair smoldered. Her face sizzled, full of craters, the skin crisped around raw tissue.

The seer sat back in the darkness. "Now," she said, sneering and satisfied, "give it to me."

Shade laughed. Threads of epidermis webbed her face, knitting, crocheting; fresh cells blossomed and shed cinders while her eyes regenerated and her lips re-bloomed. Radiating fluorescent green against her breast, the pentagram had shielded her from the true harm of fire, which would have devoured her if unornamented. Her kind was allergic to light and flame.

Shade finished tucking the baggie into the canister as new hair sprouted and grew toward her shoulders. She pressed the cap until it snapped. "I'm sure the undead will appreciate this morsel." She patted the canister and then went for the door.

"Wait," the seer said. "I—I couldn't help it. I'm just so hungry. Please … help." The plea was automated, trite, and veneered with oncoming tears. The only truth behind it was the grumble of a stomach.

Shade turned her head, smiling. "You will oblige me, then?"

"Yes, yes." The seer nodded, double chins jiggling, moles moving like colonies of worms. "Please."

Shade drew out the silence, let the slob's hunger dull from a rapier's blade into the bludgeoning agony of a bayonet. Finally, she resolved: "Very well." She approached the dark corner and dragged a beige couch cushion from against the wall.

"Wait," the seer said. "I … I want a taste first. Just … a small taste."

Shade searched her face as if in consideration, but really to prolong the suspense. "So be it." She stood over the respiring mound of fat and retrieved the baggie from the canister. She broke the zipper seal. "Tilt your head."

The slob obeyed, and Shade poured the Puppeteer's oil into her awaiting cavity.

Gurgling and slurping, the seer reached for the baggie, as if to milk it. Shade held it higher, but the seer continued to grope with her stubby arms, making greedy glugging sounds. The oil spattered her pasty face as she moved out of the stream, clenching her eyes shut and fumbling overhead. The liquid ran between the slabs of her breasts.

"Enough," Shade said and put away the baggie.

The seer wheezed and licked her lips. She wiped the black fluid off her blue-veined bosom and sucked her slender fingers, shutting her eyes and moaning.

Shade sat on the cushion, puffing dust into the air. "Now," she said, "we commune."

The seer popped her finger out of her mouth, trailing a snail's path of saliva down her double chin. "Give me your hands," she said.

Shade did, and the seer took them in her own chilly palms, fingers still moist as if from fellatio. The dampness conducted the seer's electricity, circuiting with Shade's own currents. Shade's skin cells buzzed, and her bones thrummed. A yellow aura expanded around her.

In the combined energy field, the candle flames darkled, bringing the moths to a hush. The mourner's veil of darkness shredded itself into bats, weaving, arcing, and snatching the yellow moths mid-flight.

As the seer's eyes rolled up in their sockets, she began to chant in the same snake tongue that Frost had muttered on the roof, the tongue of the ancients, the language of spells. Her voice trebled into a chorus: a tenor, a soprano, a bass, all harmonizing and singing as one. Her spaghetti hair crackled blue static as a thunderhead rumbled overhead.

Electron mosquitoes droned in Shade's ears. She closed her eyes. The darkness shuddered, and red lightning throbbed across the night sky of her eyelids. The taste of ozone, of imminent rain, tinged her mouth. Hot, salty droplets pattered her shoulders and hair. She batted her lashes as drops splashed them.

Shade tried to visualize the beach from her fantasy, seashells glistening with the blood of her prey. But the ghost in the hallway materialized from the sand, and the shimmer of his pentagram distracted her.

The red lightning cracked again, web lightning this time. It netted the heavens, and in the nethers of space, an eight-legged shadow waited inside a black hole, watching with its nest of eyes. When the lightning faded to vivid tracers, the shadow scuttled forward on the still-glowing filaments of silk. It sank its fangs into Shade's gray matter, and its scarlet poison liquefied everything inside her skull.

After sucking out the fluids, the arachnid returned to its lair. Shade's consciousness went with it, simmering in the creature's belly, simmering in darkness unrefined.

Still smiling from his clash with Grace, Frost moved downstairs to the barracks on the second floor. He suppressed the grin as he entered the hallway, donning his ice-sculpture persona. He ignored the oppression of the walls.

A few doors down, an Undertaker pressed nurse Adia against the wall. The private sucked her neck, and she tossed her head back, chestnut hair draping her shoulders. As she hooked a leg around him, he pushed her suede skirt toward her hip. She gyrated and rolled her head, digging the heel of her platform boot into the buttocks of his leather pants. When she opened her eyes of alluring turquoise, she saw Frost approaching. Her smile vanished, and she turned to ice in the private's hands.

The soldier looked up at her. "What're you . . ." He trailed off and followed her gaze. "General Frost." The private stood upright and crossed his arms over his claret tunic, forming an X in salute. The olive leaves of his irises wilted.

Without the private's support, Adia slumped against the wall. Her breasts swelled above the buckle of her lace corset top, skin showing between a pattern of leafy blooms.

Frost addressed his underling. "Why are you not with your platoon, Private?"

Nightly, the Undertakers ventured into the city to cleanse the streets of undead puppets, working from the less-populated rim toward the crowded hub, the Haven. Tonight, they prepared the island, one last check for safety.

The private's voice was frail, without steel frame: "I—the colonel held me back. He didn't want me to—I—"

"Come with me," Frost interrupted. "The colonel can speak for himself."

The private turned to Adia. He opened his mouth to stutter, but Frost interjected.

"Leave her."

Frost marched, and the private trailed behind. Though they both wore boots and were of comparable weight, the private's footsteps were not as solid as Frost's, not as sure of their traction. Frost smirked to himself, but reverted to ice as he opened the colonel's door. He gestured for the private to enter first and looked back.

Adia still slumped against the wall. Frost whispered a few arcane words, and red begonias matured in her cheekbones. She moaned and caressed her breast. He stepped over the threshold, leaving the harlot to smolder.

In the colonel's apartment, black candles burned in crystal dishes on end tables. Their flames licked the lingerie of darkness that clung to the room, casting shadow plays and rainbows on the plaster walls. Violet shag carpeted the floor, and a gray leather couch sat in the center.

Slouched on the plush cushions, dressed in a satin cherry sleepshirt with a ruffle neckline and lettuce hem, the colonel's slave did not look around as Frost approached. She stared at the wall as if watching TV, eyes of faded sky sunken into dusky sockets. Her sandy hair was brushed back from her neck, revealing unblemished porcelain.

Aside from Frost and the private, who lingered by the door, the slave was the room's sole occupant.

Frost ordered his private to take a seat, and the soldier chose the leather chair farthest from the woman.

Frost went to the kitchen entryway. "Colonel Bain," he called, leaning through the door.

Neither lamplight nor candlelight illuminated the room's Formica countertops; the imbedded flecks of fool's gold remained burned-out stars. The darkness grew especially dense in the gaps where the refrigerator and cook stove had once stood. As in all the apartments, the appliances had been pulled, used as building blocks for the barricade. All the other kitchen tables had also been removed, but the colonel's kitchen was an anomaly.

Naked, hair frizzled into silver wires, Colonel Bain sat in one of the pinewood chairs circling his table. He had his back to the door and was apparently staring at the pack of cigarettes on the table. He did not acknowledge Frost's presence.

The room vibrated, a sub-audible hum that turned Frost's joints into cartilage-macerating teeth. Dust sifted down from microscopic fault lines in the plaster, and the air tasted of lightning-seared ozone. Barely perceptible, crimson feelers curled from the colonel's aura, undulating like lucent kelp. Red flecks floated in the crimson, and through it, serpents of oil sewed and unraveled Celtic knots.

One of the ethereal feelers stretched to the woman on the couch. It suctioned to her electromagnetic nimbus with a leech's mouth, siphoning, suckling, draining. The colonel drank psychic energy.

"Bain," Frost said, extending a hand into the crimson energy field. He had seen the colonel feed before, but had never disrupted the process, had never plunged his hand into the thrumming mucous beehive of the aura. Red wasps pricked him with electric stingers; honey of blood coursed around his knuckles. Frost touched the colonel's shoulder, unnaturally tepid and statically charged beneath gray body hair.

A swastika was tattooed on the colonel's shoulder blade.

"Bain."

The halo began to wax until undetectable. The colonel stirred. Frost repeated his name, and Bain looked up at him. He blinked, hoary eyebrows moving like caterpillars. His irises softened from ashlar slate into aluminum matte, and his dime-sized pupils concentrated into pinpricks. Their glaze melted and was gone.

Bain turned and reached for his cigarettes with a wolf-like paw. The cellophane crinkled as he fished out a stick, and Frost smelled the raisins of tobacco. The colonel lit the cigarette with a match. He exhaled, flicked ashes on the periwinkle linoleum, and took another drag.

"General Frost," he said, looking at the tabletop. "To what do I owe this pleasure?" His voice was especially gravelly tonight, fragmenting like shale.

"Court-martial," Frost replied.

The colonel blew out a jet stream of smoke. "We've adopted the ranking of the human military," he said. "Let their jargon die there."

Frost fanned away a plume of carcinogens. "This from an officer chained to human vices."

The colonel said nothing, just emitted toxic ring nebulas.

Frost cocked his head toward the door. "Private. Front and center."

The colonel chuffed at the command. Frost grinned.

In the living room, leather creaked as the private stood from his seat. Judging by his footsteps, the soldier was going around the couch, no doubt to avoid the slave, unwilling to pass through the draft of her empty stare. He peeked his head into the kitchen. "Yes, sir?"

The colonel glared over his shoulder. "Don't call him *sir*."

"I—I apologize," the private said, eyes skittering between his superiors.

The colonel turned to the table. "That word is drivel," he said and continued to smoke.

"The private tells me you held him back," Frost said.

"That's right. He's an idiot. He almost got us killed."

"My rifle jammed," the private explained. "It—"

Frost cut him off. "I conferenced with our … Commander in Chief," he said, including the private in the conversation but aiming the speech at Bain's tattoo. "I proposed the island."

Bain turned again, letting his cigarette smolder. He arched one hoary eyebrow.

"I mentioned the boat," Frost continued, reeling in slowly now that he had planted his hook. "Do you remember the boat, Private?"

"Yes, sir."

Bain glowered at the underling. "Do not call him *sir*."

The private cowered, and Frost kept reeling, knowing the line was taut and close to snapping.

"I divulged the plan," he said, sprinkling bait on the water. "I proposed relocation."

Bain puffed on his cigarette. "And what, pray tell, did she say, dear General?" He punctuated his question with a billow of fumes.

Frost, like any crafty fisherman, knew which lure to dibble next. "This is her father's kingdom. She is not eager to abandon his legacy." He regarded the private. "Would you be so eager, if Roman had been your father?"

The private shook his head. "No, sir—I mean …" He shot Bain a wary glance. "No, I would not."

Bain snubbed his cigarette on the tabletop. "Why invoke ghosts, Frost? Why, and to what end?"

Frost did not answer. Instead, he turned to the private. "You are dismissed."

The soldier blinked. He shifted, hesitated.

"As you were," Frost insisted.

All the twitches and creases smoothed from the private's face. He stood straight and saluted, crossing his arms over his chest. "Yes, sir—"

The chair scraped linoleum as Bain spun around. The stake must have been holstered beneath the tabletop, because Frost had not seen it until now. Bain hurled the splinter and it tumbled like a knife, whooping through the air. The private's eyes widened, and the stake plunged into his chest, shattering his ribs and sternum.

As the soldier was thrown rearward, Frost reached out and plucked the stake. The private landed in the living room, swarmed with flesh-eating fireflies. The crackling, popping, and roar of combustion died quickly in a pile of ash.

Bain heaved in his chair, eyes bulging and furrowed. His eyebrows had curled into horns, and the muscles in his neck and face tensed, pulling his mouth into a snarl.

Frost chuckled, more calculation than laughter.

Bain glared at him. "Is that what you wanted?"

"As you observed, he was an idiot. Death was an appropriate sentence." Frost inspected the stake. The top was polished, but the underside was rough and splintery, the tip broken into two points. "Beautiful craftsmanship," he said, turning the stake over. "From the cupboard?" He indicated the gouge along the edge of a cabinet.

Bain turned his chair and fished out another cigarette.

Frost leaned and spoke into his ear: "Tomorrow night, we retrieve armored transport." He reached around the colonel and set the stake on the table. "Brief the troops when they return. We leave at dusk." Then, in a whisper: "We shall be free."

He stepped out of the kitchen, over the private's ashes. On the couch, the slave had not moved. The only change was in her complexion: it had paled; the colonel's psychic drains sapped all emotion.

Frost nodded to her. "Goodnight, madam." He laughed and left the apartment. At the stairwell, he ascended. Not even the walls could dampen him.

Ann shot a glance down the hallway behind her and hurried through the shadows. One struck out, a Nosferatu, but it could conjure only shivers. She tried to slink but the floor snitched; it chirruped, howled, and peeped. The hallway tilted, and Ann dizzied. She heard rasping close by and realized it was her own heavy breath.

She looked forward.

The Iceman clawed at her face.

Ann screamed, too late to realize the Iceman was just another Dracula cast by the lamps. He broke against her like smoke.

A door stood past him.

Ann went through it and down a staircase, spiraling down stairs that grew farther and farther apart, until she was stretching her legs across pitfalls of steel teeth. Bats swooped through the stairwell's central shaft, scratching the nocturnal blackboard with the jagged teeth of their sonar. One tangled in Ann's hair. She smacked it away and slammed through the door at the bottom.

Across the lobby, amber light shined through a glass exit, pooling on the ivory linoleum. On the sidewalk beyond, people passed by, real people in suits and skirts, carrying briefcases and talking on cell phones. A man in a trench coat and a top hat hailed a taxi; he climbed in the back seat and slammed the yellow-and-black door.

Ann cried to the passersby. She flung herself out the door, into a dark alley, deserted except for a few ghosts of litter skating along the pavement. The city and sun had vanished.

At the mouth of the alley, a 4-Runner had crashed into the fluted green cylinder of a lamppost. The lamp had burned out, so only the cloud-filtered moonlight illuminated the vehicle, making it glow a polluted white.

Smoke hissed and billowed from the 4-Runner's buckled hood, the smell of oil and antifreeze. The engine ticked and clacked

On the driver's side, the door stood open. Someone sat at the steering wheel. Through the rear passenger window, Ann could see the back of the person's head.

Holding her breath, she approached the Toyota, leaning forward to see through the open door. The occupant was a man; she could tell by the blockish head and bearish fur. And as she drew parallel, she saw a strong jaw and the shoulder of a gray tuxedo. She gasped, and the person inside whipped his head around. A grin spread his pallid face.

"Hey, Annie."

As snippets of their wedding video flashed across his eyes, Michael climbed out of the 4-Runner. Black tentacles crowned him, writhing from the missing fragments of skull. The flower girl scattered petals down the aisles of his eyes.

Ann faltered back a few steps. Bile scoured the lining of her esophagus and curdled in her throat, colliding with a scream and plugging her airway with wreckage.

Michael reached for her. His wedding ring shined platinum in the moonlight. The tentacles gleamed sickly in his skull.

"Annie," he said, "my little orphan. Come to me."

Despite the dangling carotid artery and gaping trachea of his throat, despite the blood that reddened his tuxedo and the white shirt underneath, his voice sounded normal. He had even used her pet name, little orphan. She wanted to embrace him, kiss him, wanted to hide in those arms that had held her so often, warm and snug during their camping trip in the redwoods, strong and consoling at her mother's funeral.

But beneath his words lurked a sinister chortle, the voice of the tentacles, blackened and distorted with cancer. And now, wedding guests ambled into the moonlight. The men wore carnations on their lapels, and the women wore blue dresses, all dead from various wounds. The ring bearer was missing his lower jaw, and his tongue wagged; the minister's chest had collapsed into his heart.

Wearing a mask of red muscles, Ann's uncle pushed Ellie in a wheelchair. Ellie's head slumped to one side, seeping drool. Her bridesmaid's dress rumpled around the remains of her legs. Ruffled like morning glory, the left shoulder strap had fallen off the stump of her arm, baring her breast. A fetus suckled the nipple.

"Come to me," Michael said. He kept advancing, backed by an armless best man.

The wreckage of scream and vomit exploded from Ann's mouth, splattering the ground with bits of icing, white cake, and plastic shards. One shard was the face, neck, and lapel of a miniature groom. Beside the figurine lay what might have been a plastic bridal veil and the rosy cheek of the bride.

Michael lunged for her and she stumbled back, flailing her arms for balance, twisting away, top-heavy and off kilter. Michael's fingertips chilled the side of her neck, and she blundered forward. He caught her hair and jerked back.

"Come to me," he breathed. One of his tentacles slimed her ear. Another slid around her neck, toward her breast. The wedding guests closed in.

Squealing, Ann bucked and tore away from him. Her hair uprooted with swathes of scalp, and she was free, running deeper into the alley. Hulks lurked and formed arms from the mist. They swiped for her, closing in with the walls. The mist coagulated around Ann's legs, and she trudged on as if running through vanilla icing.

Munching on the strands of red hair, Michael shambled after her. He limped on his right leg, which was crooked from the wreck. His eyes wore milky cataracts.

"Tomorrow, Annie, tomorrow! There's always tomorrow!"

Bawling, Ann dodged a trashcan spilled in the alleyway. Rats scurried from the crumpled paper cups, piles of rice confetti, and popped balloons. Ann tipped more trashcans into the path, spilling crêpe streamers and ripped party horns.

"Annie!" Michael called, clattering and clanking through the cans, wading through the decorations and trash. "In sickness and in health, Annie! In sickness and in health!"

His voice needled her with picture-frame shards. Photo scraps blew past her, echoing with laughter—Michael, smashing cake into his best man's grin while Ann smeared icing into Ellie's tresses; Michael, sliding a diamond ring onto her finger; the 4-Runner, decorated like a cake with whipped cream, balloons, and pop-can rattlers.

Sobbing and spluttering mucus, Ann kept going. Up ahead, a chain-link fence spanned the width of the alley. She smashed into it and began to climb. Michael raced toward her.

The wire dug into her fingers, and she couldn't get a foothold. Her legs scrambled for purchase. The fence clashed and shook.

Entering a shaft of moonlight, Michael slowed to a creep. Instead of his tuxedo, he wore the clothes in which Ann had last seen him, a blue- and gray-checkered flannel, a white t-shirt, blue jeans, and a heavy beard. In his grin, teeth glistened. The wedding guests had disappeared.

"I'm sick, Annie," Michael said in an ailing voice. "I need you."

Ann blubbered and kept climbing. Her fingers were turning arthritic.

"Please." He took a step forward. "Don't leave me again."

Unable to see his death mask, Ann matched Michael's voice to the face she remembered, robust cheeks, a bighearted smile, eyes hazel and sunny and sometimes bloodshot from marijuana. She remembered the way his hair hung and blocked his view (a good sign he needed a haircut), how sometimes when they lay in bed, she persuaded him to pin back his bangs with her hairclip.

Ann shut her eyes and stopped climbing. Her tears turned cold on her cheeks.

Michael moved closer, but she did not turn around. She didn't want the moonlight to overexpose her precious negatives, didn't want the pictures to turn out demented. So she hung, letting the wire cut into her finger joints. She snuggled into the warm bed of her memory, where she could bunch Michael's bangs into a scrunchie.

"Come on, Annie." He skulked closer, into more shadows. "I love you." This was something he only said as pillow talk, her head resting on his breast and her breath stirring his chest hair. He never said it otherwise, though she knew he meant it.

In Ann's arms, the muscles dissolved. Her tears ebbed, and her fingers began to uncurl from the fence. She would just fall into bed, into Michael's embrace. He would kiss her, and she would taste seasoning, the subtle lemon pepper that always laced his lips. The sheets would ripple ice water over her breasts and legs until Michael glided between them on hot-tub swells. He would kiss her again, his tongue as sizzling and eager as the flesh pressing at her inner thigh, and the sheets would melt. They would lay in the puddles afterward, linked by the hand and sharing dreams.

"Michael," Ann murmured, too tired to feel her mind deaden. "I do …"

The sheets shackled her ankle in a cold hand.

"In sickness and in health," Michael said, grinning up at her. "Till death reunite."

He yanked her down.

She started to scream.

Ω

Ann opened one eye. The other was snagged.

Her hair was caked to the side of her head. Otherwise, her swollen brain would have unlocked the plates of her skull, causing continental drift, earthquakes, and volcanoes of cerebral fluid. The other side of her head was not glued together and threatened to erupt. Ann lifted her hand to compress the imminent Mt. St. Helens, but as she moved, her nerves sharpened into steel barbs. They slashed her arms and legs and clawed at her belly and neck.

As her eye adjusted to the darkness, she discerned metal coils and loops of rose vines vibrating around her. Thriving in the absence of light, the creepers grew between Stone Henges and granoliths, forming tiaras and anadems on gravestones and altars. They had ensnared her. They had sunk their fangs into her innumerous vessels, tapping her vast underground streams. Movement only excited a feeding frenzy, a thousand tiny vampires.

Ann moaned, tasting blood in the back of her throat, smelling concrete and musty wood. Her hip and shoulder felt bruised.

"You're awake," someone said from above.

Silhouetted in lamplight, Mistress peeked her head through the hole in the ceiling, just a cutout of black construction paper.

Ann moaned again, shifting. When she spoke, her voice was full of rusty nails; pressure mounted in her head: "Please—help me."

Mistress laughed. "You wish to escape. Let's see how easily you escape this."

"Please," Ann begged. "I—I think I'm stuck."

"Yes," Mistress said, "barbwire can be quite nasty."

At first, Ann didn't understand. What did barbwire have to do with it? But then she grasped it: the rose vines, the thorn in her side, the concrete altars and monoliths—she had fallen into a pit, one of the many traps positioned throughout the building.

Mistress had told her horror stories about the pits. One escapee fell in and tried to climb out. Mistress said that, by the time he died from blood loss, most his skin had been flayed. "In some holes," she added, "we keep a pack of starving zombies."

Ann could not tell if any corpses rambled between the boulders in this particular hole, but every shadow and shape closed around her, grumbling with gluttony and full of teeth. Every creaking board amplified into a footstep, and her every breath clotted with decay.

"Please," Ann said, "get me out of here." She thought of an appeal, a temptation, something Mistress could not refuse. "I ... I need your bite."

"Every time you beg," Mistress said, "I will pull three teeth from one of your armless friends." She paused, then added, "And for every minute you spend in your little hole, I will personally dig the jelly from the idiot's eye and spoon-feed it to her."

"Please," Ann shuddered, thinking of Ellie, "don't."

"That's three teeth gone. And you've wasted a minute already."

"No!"

"Tick-tock, tick-tock," Mistress began to walk away.

"Don't you touch them!"

"Someone hurts with each tick of the clock." A door clicked closed, and Mistress spoke no more.

Ann gave one final protest, vocal cords bursting in her larynx. She thrashed against the barbwire, spikes slicing her biceps and the top of her breast. They slurped at the spilt red fluid, pulling loose skin like meat hooks. The wire turned boa constrictor and coiled tighter around her. Tick-tock, tick-tock: she would never get free.

Shade stood in an Elizabethan theater, looking down at the yard from the highest gallery, the highest tier. The other galleries circled the yard, empty on every level. The benches behind her creaked.

Hoisting a gabled machinery hut over the stage, brown marble columns reflected the moon through the open roof. Their white veins moved in milky spirals. Smaller columns, which supported the upper gallery balcony at the back of the stage, flanked the right and left stage doors, as well as the curtained entrance between.

Tossing back the maroon curtain, a man walked onstage. His boots clopped on the white tile, and the theater's polygonal structure amplified the sound. The man wore a leather trench coat and an expressionless white mask. A pentagram gleamed between trails of raven hair.

Shade's hand went to her own necklace, and though she could feel the cold metal, though she knew her arm was bent, her physical hand stayed latched to the railing. It was wider than usual. And she had never owned a pair of brown gloves.

She was in someone else's body.

Her host leaned forward as the masked performer stopped center stage in a beam of moonlight. He cocked his head toward her and spoke in the musing, noble voice of a soliloquy. His mask held its frozen stare.

"I see him, lurking in the darkness. And I see the shadows that coil around him. Through forked flickers, they whisper and hiss, and I catch only hints of meaning and malice."

As he spoke, dark serpents twisted around Shade's torso, conspiring in her ears and seducing with their tongues. Venom rose in her chest and poisoned her heart and lungs. She had no antidote, so the bane affected her;

the hate of a stranger swam in her veins. She tried to suck it out, but could not.

"Looking into his pitiless eyes, I intuit his intent, and thorns wreath my blood at the thought." The mask, though inert, appeared to frown, now the mask of tragedy expressing deepest despair.

Shade's host reached into the folds of his red-lined cape, retrieving a wooden stake. Made of the hardiest oak, only knots blemished the fine grain.

The actor's mask frowned deeper. "I see him raise his weapon—"

The host's arm cocked back, poising the stake over his shoulder.

"—yet I do not move. I dare not, for the thorns will trench a wound that shall never heal and that shall weep forevermore. So … he strikes—"

The host threw the stake. Its tip parted the air and gored the sound barrier's hymen, shaking the theater with a sonic boom and cracking the beams of English oak.

"—he strikes, and my heart bleeds."

The missile speared the actor's breast and hurled him backward. He disappeared through the curtains, a billow, a thump, and then silence. Ashen motes drifted through the moonlight.

The host hopped over the rail and plummeted three stories to the pit, an area of bare earth in front of the stage where groundlings once watched the dramas unfold. He marched the well-trodden dirt and climbed the white steps at stage right, pushed against the corner of the brick facade. His boots clapped against the stage tile, the only sound in a vacuum-sealed night.

The host threw back the curtains, and moon-glow blanketed the actor's sprawl. He lay face-up. The stake protruded from his chest, and his necklace sparkled like a true star. The host stooped and grasped the actor's white mask.

Imprisoned inside the assailant's mind, Shade leaned forward, clutching her pentagram so tight it stabbed her.

Her host lifted the mask, the face beneath still shrouded in shadow, but with light sneaking in. And when the disguise was off, its secret revealed, Shade thought there might be another mask, because the face—the muscular jaws, the sturdy brow, the staring hazel eyes—this face belonged to the ghost she had seen outside the seer's apartment. It belonged to Roman, the man who had birthed her into eternal night, her blood father, the man who had built the City of Roses from the ruins of mankind.

Once more, Shade sought the pentagram, this time drawing blood along her lifeline.

Her host gripped the stake that jutted from Roman's chest.

No, she thought, defying the act. She thrashed and clawed her cell of gristle and bone. She bellowed, but the walls endured. She concentrated on the vessels in her brain, tried to burst one, tried to cripple her arm. But these muscles were not her own. She could not control them.

With one yank, the assassin plucked the stake from Roman's heart. Fire spread from the wound, and Roman's skin burned like paper, curling from his skull and hands. His clothing burned away, uncloaking his ribcage and his scorched lungs. His eyes shriveled into coals, and as rashes of combustion inflamed his skeleton, his skull shrieked, breathing fireflies and dragons of flame.

The body exploded into cinders, wafting into spiral galaxies, a Milky Way. Moonbeams breathed light into stars of ash, into quasars and white dwarfs, minuscule celestial bodies aligning into solar systems and constellations, all drifting down, down, down, toward the floor where Roman had lain, toward all the cracks to sift through, down, down, down, and as it all settled, the stake clattered to the floor as well.

The last Ursa Major of dust graced the weapon's oak surface, and of Shade's father, only the necklace remained, one star that would never dim, even as Shade's host pocketed it, as he kicked the stake into a corner of the room and exited the stage.

The night closed in.

Curtain.

Gunshots met Frost at the rooftop. Two sentries, Victor and Edward, rested their PSG-1 rifles on bipods atop the parapet and fired into the barricade, sighting through night scopes. The tinkle of ejected brass shells was lost beneath the racket, as were Frost's footsteps.

Edward stopped to reload his twenty-round magazine.

"Cease fire!" Frost shouted, taking advantage of the pause.

Edward caught sight of him and tapped his comrade's shoulder. Both sentries shrugged into the shoulder straps of their rifles. They crossed their arms in salute.

"At ease," Frost said. He walked to the edge and looked down.

Victor stepped beside him. His cheek bulged slightly, retaining a penny; when he spoke, copper clinked against his teeth and tarnished his breath. "They've breached," he said, pointing.

Indeed, half a dozen zombies edged into the barbwire, metal, and cement. Some suffered bullet wounds, arms dangling, skin riddled with bone shrapnel, cheeks crumpled inward, and teeth broken into pea gravel. The others had fallen into crevices. Their limbs twitched like the legs of swatted flies and their skulls leaked black yolk.

At the front of the barricade, more bad eggs crested the cemetery gate, which they had trampled to the incline of a wheelchair ramp. The gate had caught on a steel beam and would probably stay there. For a while.

Frost leaned closer as a gangster accosted the barbwire just past the gate. The thorns snagged his pine-green jersey and his baggy jeans, but the vines snapped. The carcass matted the barbed helixes beneath his Timberlands.

Resisting a smile, Frost stood erect. "Desist," he told the sentries. "Save your bullets."

Edward's eyes swelled with mud. "But, her Liege—"

Frost's face iced over. "Should I remind you the punishment for insubordination?"

"No—"

"Then desist, or die in the sun."

Victor latched his ammunition box, but Edward still gawked. "They'll get in," he said.

"Then let them. They will have nothing to chase but our shadows."

Victor paused, ammo box dangling at his side. "We're leaving?"

"Yes."

Edward glanced at them. "Leaving? To the island?"

The rumor had taken a viral life of its own, spreading, infecting, engendering fevered dreams of beaches, moon-frosted breakers, tide pools, and human quarry. Frost did not wish to alleviate this fever. He would provide no cold washcloth, no ice pack, no healing fluids.

"To the island," he confirmed.

Victor smiled—he looked like a hyena—but Edward's expression had not changed, all smooth cheeks and astonishment.

"This is her Majesty's order," Frost said. "Cease fire."

Victor nodded, still grinning. He worked closely with Frost and had been told this day would come soon. He walked toward the door, and Edward glanced at him.

"Go," Frost said. "The sun impends."

Edward looked down at their invaders. He shook his head and packed up.

Alone, Frost turned to the barricade. A Latino boy, dressed in a red-and-black-checkered flannel, stood atop the white cab of a buried F-150. The parietal plate of his skull had been cracked, and the Puppeteer tested the jags of china with glistening worms. Frost's eyes widened as the tentacles wove a patch of silky flesh over the hole.

El Niño scowled up at him. The boy took a step forward, and Frost put a bullet through the silken graft of skin. The corpse hit the cab, and his tentacles re-stitched the wound. El Niño sat up. Frost shot him again, this time through the forehead. El Niño lay still. Bits of Puppeteer squirmed in puddles on the cab, slowly subduing to quietus.

Several other invaders sported black scar tissue over injuries and sentry-inflicted bullet holes. They also had tentacles thrashing about their heads. One woman's face, which zombies had eaten before her death, was now a reconstruction of organic electrical tape, oozing a gritty lubricant off her chin in strings and loops.

Frost shot her, too. Not in the forehead, but through the right cheek. The Puppeteer restored the exit wound. As the opening fused shut, teeth re-spawned, the color of cavities.

"Interesting," Frost said. He blew her brains all over a canary-colored refrigerator. Giblets streaked down the metal like weak magnets. The woman's body fell.

Frost holstered his gun and scanned the cityscape. Soon, his Undertakers would swoop through the buildings, gargoyle silhouettes, a pack of winged nightmares fleeing the dawn in which all wicked dreams perish, except the rotting dead.

Below, a prostitute with mussed almond hair had reached the building's brick facade; she located a window shutter and began to pound. The Puppeteer had patched several of the prostitute's bullet wounds and bites. Her open mesh chemise remained torn in many places, revealing more skin than the black gossamer intended.

Frost shot her in the arm. The Puppeteer dressed the hole in oily gauze.

A perfect specimen, he thought, catching the wink of the woman's zirconia earrings.

Checking the cityscape once more for Undertakers, Frost boarded the fire escape and descended into the barrier.

Twelve

Bleating, Ann plucked the barbs from her cheek and the back of her hand. Blood stung her eye, making her squint and blink. Every time she freed one limb, the wire sprang back and snagged another. But she kept picking out the thorns, bracing herself with one arm against a boulder, fingers slipping in the pebbles and debris, shoulder throbbing.

In her mind, Mistress was already sliding the scalpel through Ellie's eyeball. Ellie was burbling and brain-dead, and on the wall beyond her, the eyes of a Felix clock ticked back and forth in time with the feline's tail: tick-tock, tick-tock.

Ann's hand came out from beneath her. She fell onto the boulder and skidded down the exposed aggregate on her spine. The iron maiden of barbwire opened up to swallow her.

She twisted at the waist and clawed at the rock. Her nails busted, and the rock abraded her fingertips. She missed handholds and kept sliding until she caught a ledge. Her own weight and momentum nearly ripped the ridge out of her grip, but she held fast.

Whimpering, she pulled herself up. The wire that was latched to her ankles and calves could not hold her back.

Atop the rock, Ann unleashed her legs. She looked up at the hole in the ceiling, her eyes adjusting to the gloom. She saw no ladder or other means of escape, but at least she seemed to be alone in the crypt. If there were any corpses, they lay in their coffins, quiet and at rest.

God, she needed Mistress' bite. Maybe then the shivers would stop; maybe the pain would mix with pleasure. The orgasms had always dulled her depression and her fear, so it might work as an anesthetic as well.

No barbwire topped the boulder across from her, although a pit of brambles lay between. She would have to jump. Ann moved carefully to the edge, favoring her right hip; it felt as if she had lost her leg to a tripwire. She winced as the cement dug into the arches of her feet. Loose gravel slid beneath her, and she backpedaled, kicking pebbles into the steel vines. She steadied herself and quivered with breath.

The landing pad wasn't too far away: more than a step, less than a leap. If she cleared the step-up and its horns of rebar, she would land on a plateau. She had seen Michael perform similar feats at the river. He always played on the rocks while she sunbathed. Now, she wished she had accompanied him. The Irish in her skin had always blanched her tan anyway.

Ann stepped back and steeled herself for the jump. Some helium had inflated her stomach, now a bubble inside her chest. The gap expanded in front of her, from a Columbia Gorge to a Grand Canyon. She would not make it. Her shins would scrape against the edge, and she would fall. The barbwire would spin rose blooms out of her flesh and blood. And another woman would suffer the loss of an eye: tick-tock, tick-tock.

Ann curled her left hand into a fist. Her ring seemed malleable, as if the gold were melting. "Till death reunite," she whispered, shivering as Michael's palm filled her grasp. She dared not close her eyes, else she might see the photo negatives from her nightmare, Michael chuckling through the gouge in his throat, wedding guests moaning for intestines instead of cake. So she tightened her fist and dashed forward. She planted her foot on the edge, ready to spring. But she slid in the rocks and floundered midair, her leap shortened by half a foot. The barbwire bared its fangs.

Ann hit the wall of the step-up, and her hip detonated like a grenade, riddling her nerve endings with shrapnel. She bounced off the wall and tumbled down the slant of the step-up. She fumbled for the rebar horns, but missed and rolled into the chasm.

Tick-tock, tick-tock: another eye went blind.

Shade's eyelids parted like curtains, revealing the seer's apartment. Her hair dripped, but the rain had ceased. The thunderhead evaporated above the seer's head, and the yellow moths of candlelight reflected in the puddles, in the droplets of water drip-drip-dripping onto the plywood floor.

Something dug into Shade's palm: the pentagram. It had punctuated her lifeline and the median crease of each finger. The seer, drooling and unconscious, still held Shade's other hand. Her tongue hung out of her mouth like a dead slug.

Shade let the necklace drop against her breast, which was no longer crusted with blood. The downpour had washed the congealed red, leaving sequins of water on her corset. Shade tried to pull her hand out of the seer's grip, but the claw latched onto her wrist. The seer's eyes snapped open, black and shark-like.

"Give it to me," she said, her voice a pond of water snakes and bull-frogs, of cattails and algae. "Give me the flesh." Her breath reeked of raw meat and mud.

"Let go," Shade said, trying not to vomit.

The seer hung on, searching her eyes. "Will you give it to me?"

"Yes. Now let go."

After one last search, the seer released Shade's wrist. She sneered, and one of her eyelids twitched. Shade stood, woozy and imbalanced.

"I'm hungry," the seer said, black irises flaring as the candles heated up. "Give me the flesh." She held out her hand, jaundiced fingernails long and flaky.

Shade anchored her palm atop the canister, but the whole building slanted like the Titanic. She flipped open the container and extracted the baggie.

"Your reward," she said, and tossed the bag to the seer.

The slob slopped the guts into her maw, splashing oil onto her cheeks. She chewed black gristle and spongy brain.

Shade staggered toward the door as the building rocked on rough waters. She grasped the doorknob and turned it.

"I saw," the seer called through a mouthful of chum.

Shade stopped. She revolved, leaning, tipping, tottering.

A sailor's knot of saliva moored the seer's lip to her breast. The mucus was clear yet veined black, specked with morsels of brain. The ropes jiggled as the seer spoke. One broke loose and dangled off her upper chin.

"I saw the man."

Shade recalled her vision: her host body, the brown gloves, the oaken stake. She swallowed the gorge rising in her throat and stiffened her spine to stabilize herself. "Who did you see?"

The seer chewed slowly, hesitantly. The tissues squelched between her molars. The rope of saliva pasted to her neck.

"Who did you see?"

The fortuneteller grinned, showing black sinew stuck between her teeth. She held up the sandwich bag and shook it, empty except a puddle of oil. "I'm still hungry."

Shade kicked the leg of a nearby end table. The wood snapped into a lance; the table collapsed, spilling candles onto the plywood floor. She swiped up the broken leg and pinned the seer against the wall, pressing her forearm into the blob's neck. She drove the table leg through the seer's belly, through skin and lard and muscle, up beneath her ribcage to the cove between her lungs. The point pricked the bubble wrap of fat on the seer's left ventricle, but stopped short of penetration.

"You tell me," Shade said, so close to the seer she could smell the Puppeteer's grease. "You tell me who you saw."

The seer gurgled and clawed at Shade's face. She grabbed Shade's hair and tried to gouge her eyes, but Shade twisted the table leg, and the seer stopped resisting.

"Tell me."

The seer said something, but her pinched windpipe garbled the words. Shade decreased the pressure against her neck.

"The mask, the mask. I saw the man in the mask."

"Did you see anyone else?"

"You. You killed him. You took his necklace."

Shade wanted to ram the spike home, wanted to watch the seer burn just as Roman had burned. Shade needed her, though. She needed the eye. So she pulled the stake free and threw it into the corner. She backed away, spinning with the moths.

The seer rasped and held her belly. Her wound began to suture itself, skin stitching, the curd of fatty tissue melding. "You took his necklace," she repeated, heaving, out of breath. "The one around your neck."

Shade barged into the hallway. She slammed the door and stooped, retching up nothing.

"You killed him!" the seer yelled through lath, plaster, and insulation. "You killed the man in the mask!"

Shade stumbled down the hallway, leaning against the wall. The wraiths whirled around her, laughing, jeering, accusing. She pushed through them, down the long gullet of the hall and into the stairwell. She went to the railing and leaned over. She shut her eyes and breathed. The world slowed on its axis, and the ocean subsided underfoot.

When she opened her eyes, the pentagram dangled in front of her, sparkling. Roman's face appeared on the silver, but only for an instant. Then Shade's reflection took its place.

She slammed her fist on the banister. She pivoted. Ghosts hovered at the threshold of the seer's corridor, still whispering murder. No pentagram twinkled in their midst.

Shade tightened her fists. With a leap, she was over the railing, plummeting down the central shaft. She lit here and there, bouncing off the balustrade as she descended. And from the second-story platform, she plunged, shaped like a spearhead.

She landed on a vending machine, denting the metal and crouching to absorb the impact. Ten feet away, a soda machine lay dim, its light snuffed long ago. As she came down on it, she smashed the Pepsi-can facade. Blue shards of plastic whizzed past her face, bejeweled with beads of illustrated dew.

Bounding from boulders to ATMs to wooden plinths, Shade moved to the building's main entrance. Snarls of barbwire and blocks of concrete pressed against the doors from outside; rubble piled against it from the inside as well. The glass in the doors had long since shattered, leaving fangs to thirst for intruders.

Kneeling on a boulder in front of the doors, Shade moved aside a slab of oak, which had once topped a lawyer's desk, now stained with the blood and cranial fluid of his suicide.

Somewhere behind her, pebbles ticked into the clutter.

Metal clanged against metal.

Shade thought she spied a fleeing shadow, but it was an illusion. She was alone. Good.

Underneath the lawyer's desktop lay a culvert pipe, an esophagus through the cement. Shade slid down it to the base of the door. Here, the fallen glass had been ground nearly to sand. No incisors spiked the door-frame. Shade ducked outside.

Through labyrinths and catacombs of masonry and steel, through a junkyard of trucks, squad cars, and minivans, Shade sidestepped tripwires and gluttons of broken glass. Beyond the crisscross of rebar and I-beams, beyond nets of fencing and around concrete blocks, the fire hydrant glowed yellow. Shade gravitated toward it, passing by the Bloodhounds' pipe, the one that ended at the cemetery gate.

Stepping beneath a skylight, she checked the moon. The luminary clock no longer shined through the necrotic tissue of the clouds. It had set. An afterglow was all that remained.

Shade moved quicker, to outrun the approaching dawn.

Just past the hydrant, the sidewalk ended. A city bus was parked at the curb, and Shade crawled underneath, snaking through a stash of bricks. On the other side, girders and blue postal drop boxes framed an empty space. Shade stood, and her boots clomped on a manhole cover.

At the front of the blockade, the vagrant undead begged for entry. They clanked and battered and scratched; their bellies groused, pining for handouts.

Shade crooked her arm through a broken bus window and moved aside a few planks, avoiding their sixteen-penny teeth. The crowbar sat in the seat. She pulled it out and wedged it beneath the manhole cover. The lid slid aside with a hollow scrape and clatter.

Exhaling their outhouse breath, the bowels of the city remained silent. Shade tucked the crowbar in her belt and disappeared into the hole. She dragged the cover back over and let it clunk into place. Then she let go of the ladder and fell into darkness. Her pentagram faded, and eventually blinked out.

Ω

Passing a storm gutter inflow, Shade mucked through mud and detritus, crunching cockroaches beneath her boots. Rats squealed and scurried into cracks, retreating to their nests of newspaper shreds, cardboard scraps, and strips of oily cloth. One rat leapt into the wastewater puddled on the floor. It dogpaddled, barely making ripples in the sludge.

Although dank, the sewer was relatively dry, unused since the zombie holocaust had purged the earth above. Luckily, the sewage treatment plant had stopped siphoning from the pipes a while after people had stopped flushing. Shade could step over or walk around most the sewage and rainwater that still polluted the tunnel. But this bog was an entire bayou, belching gas from pustules in its bullfrog hide.

Shade ran in an arc along the wall. Her footsteps echoed brusquely, ending with a clap as she hit the floor. Behind her, the rat kept slogging through the mire. Shade left it to drown.

Skirting a few more puddles, she spotted the orange ribbon, once the collar of a shirt. She had tied it to the ladder of a manhole shaft as a marker, had knotted it around a rung at eye-level. She stepped up to the ladder and climbed to the top. Grime had once sealed the manhole cover, but she had broken the hymen some time ago. Now, the cover opened without resistance. Shade lifted it and peeked out.

While most zombies in the city concentrated around the Haven, a substantial population still wandered the streets. Frost's Undertakers systematically massacred these outsiders, but from the lack of bullet holes, scorch marks, and funeral pyres, Shade knew the troops had yet to purify this block of brick buildings, park benches, and small maple trees. Thirteen ramblers window-shopped at the various stores along the sidewalk.

One shop featured Nerf guns and remote control Broncos behind its shattered display windows. A girl in a tallow nightgown stood beneath the store's rainbow-colored awning, clutching a teddy bear close to her heart. She had no nose, just an exposed nasal cavity.

The zombie closest to the manhole had no lower body. When Shade rose to the street and let the cast iron cover thunk into place, the torso growled and crawled toward her, trailing intestines. He latched onto her ankle and opened his mouth to bite.

Shade shot him in the face.

An instant after the gunshot and the muzzle flash, bone and black matter rained down on the concrete. The corpse's shackling hand went limp, and Shade stepped over him, performing another lead lobotomy on a second ghoul, this one a black woman whose jaw hung on snipped muscles. Her ebony hair billowed in the back as a section of her skull blew out.

Roused by the gunfire and by the smell of cordite, more zombies appeared from alleyways and side streets, one from a stalled Humvee. The little girl dropped her stuffed bear and stumbled off the curb. A balding businessman, wearing a gray suit, shouldered past a crosswalk pole out into the road.

Before they could horde, Shade cut through them toward the alley. Bodies fell, convulsing or lying still. Mists and sprays of blood stippled the sidewalk; squirts and splatters formed action paintings.

Shade ejected an empty magazine. She slammed in a new one before the discard hit the ground.

At the mouth of the alley, a sushi cook in a red-stained apron swung a deba knife. He moved like a windup toy running on dwindling instinct. A group of Japanese waitresses backed him up. The chopsticks in their hair had dislodged, spilling loops and strands of silky hair about their bamboo-patterned kimonos. Past them, a fire escape zigzagged up the building.

The cook slashed at Shade with the knife. She kicked him in the chest, snapping his sternum. He stumbled back, tackling the first two waitresses, and Shade drilled him with a bullet. She trampled his stomach and jumped, launching off the head of a waitress and displacing the woman's spinal disks. Shade caught the rail of the fire escape and boosted herself over. Metal jangled as she climbed the stairs to the rooftop.

Most of the buildings sat side by side, separated by low parapets. Shade hurdled the barriers in succession, and the complaints of the undead diminished behind her.

At the end of the buildings, she glided over a chain-link fence into a park, a cushion of grass. She crossed the lawn. The blades whispered against her boots, shin high.

Streetlamps had once lit the sidewalk of the park. Tonight, as Shade walked it, not even the moon silvered the blacktop or the surrounding copse of oaks. A few carcasses spoiled the aroma of the park's orange and yellow quilt of leaves, but no puppet master manipulated their strings. No infernal hunger inspired their dance.

Like a stream fanning out into a lake, the sidewalk turned into a plaza. In concentric ripples of brick, the plaza circled an island of withered coleus, which had once flaunted green foliage, each leaf bleeding maroon at the heart. Shade scaled the barrier of brick and tromped through the dead plants, knocking back the interspersed stalks of love-lies-bleeding; the stalks were bowed, mourning their long-gone flowers of dripping merlot.

On the other side of the plaza, another lawn stretched to the tree line. Through thinning yellow scotch elm leaves, Shade could see the wood-framed plaster facade and the thatched crown of the Elizabethan theater, her father's final resting place. Her pentagram was still dormant, trapped behind clouds like its celestial counterparts, and she hastened, knowing that

Helios' chariot would soon crest the mountaintops, incinerating the rain clouds and evaporating all lingering puddles of shade.

Ann rolled onto her back and sat up, bumping her head on a rock. She winced and rubbed the swelling, which throbbed in time with her hip.

She had fallen within the barbwire walls of a miniature Auschwitz. Above her, the rock formed an overhang, a crevice no more than two feet high; she would have to crawl. Ann tried to flip onto her belly, but her hip blew up. The blast consumed her pelvis and thigh. She moaned and held her leg. The pain eventually ebbed, and over the dull thud, she heard the deathwatches.

The insects had infested the walls. Their heads tapped, ticking in unison like the Felix clock wired to a bundle of explosives: tick-tock, tick-tock—how long had she been down here? Two minutes? Three minutes? Four?

Tick-tock, tick-tock.

Ann flopped onto her belly, grimaced, and transferred the weight onto her good hip. She crawled into the tunnel, and her elbow chafed rock. She knocked the floor with her knees.

At the end of the crawlspace, Ann felt the roof, crumbling exposed aggregate beneath her fingers. She reached farther, into oblivion. A snake of barbwire bit her and rattled its beware. She kept questing with her hand.

Coursing through a pile of rebar, a narrow path led to another rock. No barbwire sunned atop this boulder, but plenty surrounded its base. Ann stepped over the tangles and climbed up. Aside from the shaft of light that poured through the ceiling, the room was an abyss.

In the hallway above, a door clicked open. Someone approached, and more light flooded the room. Ann slid back down, over the snakes of barbwire. Her heel bumped a coil; it rattled. She huddled behind the rebar and peeked through the gaps, hoping the serpent would not expose her hidey-hole. If Mistress didn't see her, she might think that Ann had escaped. Then Ellie might be safe.

"Tick-tock, tick-tock." Mistress peered down, holding a lantern. "You've just wasted five ticks o' the clock."

Her voice was singsong and merry. Ann could barely resist it. She wanted to stand up and beg, just so she could get out and feel those teeth in her skin, just so she could feel the orgasm ejaculating in every cell, swelling her tongue with honey and filling her skull with champagne. To hell with Ellie.

Ann shut her eyes. She bit her lip and fidgeted with her ring.

With the lantern, Mistress scanned the room. Shadows leapt. Dark bats flew across the walls, and when the light lit on the hideaway of rebar, it filtered through, tattooing Ann's face with ocher snowflakes and kaleidoscopic designs. Ann cowered, certain she had been spotted. But the light continued, highlighting the rock where she had just perched.

Mistress tossed something into the room. Like egg white, the object plopped on the rock. "I can see you," Mistress said. The light of her lantern glistened on the splattered egg, and instead of yolk, Ann saw an iris, not yellow but the feathery blue of a jay's plumage. It stared right at her.

She swallowed vomit, trying not to retch.

"Tick-tock, tick-tock."

Ann stood up. A banshee clawed its way from her throat, shrieking. "Leave them alone!"

Mistress laughed. On a hook over the hole, she docked her lantern and started to walk away. "Tick-tock, tick-tock—"

"I'll kill you!"

"—blind an eye with each tick of the clock."

The warren door shut, and Ann's next banshee shook the door in its frame. She threw a chunk of cement at the hole, but it ricocheted and crashed into the snakes. The image of Ellie with just one eye, an Irish Eye, just a single gem of emerald and clover and shavings of melted leprechaun gold—

Ann climbed back onto the rock, careful not to squish the eye between her toes. She was glad the eye was blue and not emerald, yet she had been so ready to forfeit her sister just for a fix. Tears stung her eyes, but she bit down and shook her head, holding her stomach to stop the pain.

Not now.

Thankfully, Mistress had left the lantern. It lit the entire imbroglio of brimstone and reptiles, which harbored the occasional concentration camp.

Many steppingstones were scattered throughout, placed to facilitate travel. The periphery of the room remained dark, hiding any windows or doors. Ann aimed for these outskirts.

She took a step back and assumed the runner's stance. The ravine between her and the next steppingstone was not the Grand Canyon from before, but her hip and lower back still ached from the fall, and her stomach still knotted from the plunge, not to mention the withdrawals.

She kissed her ring and shut her eyes. Michael was there, in bed, pale and motionless. The deathwatches had documented his time of death and were counting down to livor mortis.

Ann opened her eyes. She took a deep breath and charged. She cleared the pit of barbwire and landed, stumbled, fell. Her knee left a skid mark of skin and blood on the concrete. Her tears spattered the dust.

Bawling, favoring her wound, she stood and limped onward.

The next chasm was too wide to jump, slithering with rattlesnakes. Ann found a two-by-six plank buried in the barbwire. She lay on her belly and reached for it. The rock chafed her breasts and pressed knuckles into her flesh. The barbwire spiraled around the plank and bit in, pulling against her. She gave the board a final yank. The metal fangs grooved the wood and surrendered.

Ten feet long, the board made an excellent bridge. Ann levered it between the steppingstones and tried to cross. It wobbled, but she held out her arms and adjusted.

Halfway across, the board began to bend, braced by a stone pier. Barbwire snaked onto the catwalk and lay motionless, innocent, but as Ann passed, it snagged her Achilles tendon. It pulled tight and jerked back. She fell onto the plank. It tilted, and she began to slide off. She hugged the wood, tossed her weight, and stabilized.

Ann reached back and plucked the barbs from her ankle. Blood welled in the punctures, much like the teeth marks on her neck. She shimmied to the other side.

After moving the board to the next rock, Ann retested her balance. She scampered forward, teetered, and scampered again. Her hip nearly popped from its socket, nearly burst from the muscle and skin. Veering toward the edge, she flung herself forward, knocking the board off its piling. The diamondbacks rattled. Ann hit the boulder and scrabbled up.

She had not kicked the board too far from her platform. She dragged it out and made another bridge, one after the other until she came to the wall.

Standing on a pile of bricks, she ran her hands along the plaster, trying to find the seams of a door or the frame of a window, discovering only cracks and divots and a trail of Braille clues. Tick-tock, tick-tock—Mistress was probably dissecting another woman's eye, maybe Ellie's.

Ann descended the slope of bricks, keeping her hand on the wall. At the bottom, she found a plywood panel screwed in place, the shape and size of a window. She tried to pry it off, but the screws fastened it to the lath and studs, admitting nothing but a murmur of outside air.

She pounded the shutter. She sledged it with a rock, producing dents and too much noise. Bashing, bashing—it would not break. The outside was right there. Ann could smell it, even through frogs of snot. She could smell the autumn seasoning of fallen maple leaves, of acorns and rain. She had to get out. She had to roll in the grass and drink from a stream. She had to breathe.

Sucking at the stream of oxygen, Ann dropped her rock and clawed at the plywood. Slivers burrowed beneath her skin and nested in her fingertips. Her nails chipped, carving ruts in the wood.

She screamed and punched it.

Nothing.

Ann clambered down the brick pile and fell to her knees, ready to weep. But something crumbled beneath her. Through her clogged sinuses, she caught a whiff of moldering lumber.

In a semicircle from the baseboard, the plywood had rotted, as if the window above it leaked. Using another stone-age hammer, Ann battered the floor, nearly cheering as it disintegrated. She would get out after all! She could save Ellie and get her fix at the same time.

Ann pawed away the sawdust, making a manhole-sized opening. Underneath lay a crust of concrete plugging, cracked into tectonic plates.

"No," she pleaded. "No, no, no."

She struck the plugging with her hammer: nothing. She struck it again. The San Andreas Fault broke loose and drifted. Ann dug her fingers into the fissure and picked the tectonic scab. She pitched it into the rubble and busted more plates.

Floorboards creaked overhead. Ann looked up, expecting to see Mistress toting another eye, an *emerald* eye. Or perhaps the Iceman had returned to chill her.

The visitor, if existent, shrouded herself in shadows.

Ann waited, listening: nothing; just the deathwatches.

She returned to her excavation, removing the remaining concrete. She tore out wads of magma-colored insulation from a lava tube, walled with joists and floored with water-damaged lath. Using her crude hammer, she bashed the lath, knocking pieces of wood and plaster into the room below.

Light trickled upward, flickering like flames on her cheeks and brow. She set her rock aside and peered through the breaks, seeing taupe carpeting and the arm of a recliner.

Whoever occupied this apartment did not appear to be home. He could have been crouched behind a chair, waiting to ambush, or he could have been with the Undertakers, performing nightly cremations. Mistress said the troops returned in the cobalt ambiance before dawn. If the tenant were an Undertaker, he would soon come through the door. He would notice the hole in his ceiling and would raise the alarm. He and the others would hunt Ann like a mouse and crunch her bones between their teeth.

But she could see no other escape: no rope ladder, hatch, or slide-aside bookshelf. And the deathwatches persisted.

Ann couldn't leave her sister. She couldn't stay in the pit, either: the pangs, the clock …

She'll stop, Ann thought, thinking of Mistress. *She said she'd stop if I came back.*

Tick-tock, tick-tock.

Ann looked up at the hole.

"I'll come for you, Ellie." Tears began to well in her eyes again. "I swear."

She bent over and continued to mine. Her ring imparted no extra strength, but she worked hard, and the boards gave way.

Frost entered the seventh floor hallway, the penthouse. Only Shade roomed here. Her father had lived here, too.

Frost knocked on Shade's door. Silence greeted him. He did not know of the sewer pipe, but he knew that Shade frequented the Elizabethan theater. She was either there, or still with the seer. Frost assumed the former.

He knocked again, loud and curt.

Nothing.

At Roman's apartment a few doors down, mummified roses rested at the door, wrapped in dusty cellophane. A bottle of Cabernet Sauvignon stood beside the flowers. Frost uncorked the wine and hydrated the petals with a splash of fermented red, concluding the ritual by crossing his arms in salute. Then he extinguished the lanterns throughout the hall and crouched in the darkness, listening to the building's skeleton settle and groan.

The edifice would sleep soon, basking in the orange warmth that radiated from the fireplace of the sky. The rats would stop rummaging in the walls, and the tenants would dream of beaches and blood.

The Haven was a nocturnal creature, a tick. It fed on its inhabitants, sapping their substance and their passions. During the day, it endured nightmares; it suffered sleep apnea, yet it slept. And not long after the sunset dyed the clouds pink and fuchsia, the behemoth woke, hungry and ready to close in, ready to drain. Frost's men wasted away each night, forming wrinkles and stooped backs. It was killing them.

After vacating to the island, Frost yearned to return with plastic explosives, to reduce the structure to bricks and lumber, a pyramid to bury bad memories. But the building would serve as an impenetrable outpost or way station and could not be wasted. It also memorialized Roman, a great leader, though pride and obstinacy had always compromised his rulings.

Before they had moved to the Haven, Frost had warned that it would entomb them all, but Roman had refused to concede. Now he blew with the wind, just a handful of dust, and Frost would free his kin.

At the top of the staircase, the metal door grated open, and many footsteps began to descend. Frost slinked along the wall toward the landing, quicker than the darkness. The first Undertaker came into view: leather trench coat, brown mane, motorcycle boots—Lieutenant Cavanaugh, one of Shade's most trusted and honored soldiers. She was attracted to him.

Frost sidled behind him like mist and locked him in a half nelson, thrusting his left arm under Cavanaugh's armpit and clasping his hand behind the lieutenant's head.

Frost spun Cavanaugh to face his Undertakers and pulled a wooden blade from his belt. He stabbed the lieutenant in the chest, puncturing leather cuirass, skin, and muscle; the shiv slipped between his ribs.

Cavanaugh grunted and squirmed. He tried to bring his M16 around, but Frost drove the knife deeper, threatening to ignite the all-consuming furnace of his heart, threatening to unleash the carnivorous embers. The lieutenant stiffened. His Undertakers stalled on the steps, watching, eyes rapt and glittering. The rifle of one cremator's flamethrower hung limp on its hose. Armalites and Glocks stayed disarmed.

Frost leered and hissed in Cavanaugh's ear: "Your senses have dulled, Lieutenant."

"Fuck you, sir." The lieutenant's voice strained near falsetto, breath shallow and constrained.

Frost's leer widened. "Your tongue stinks of mutiny."

"I have never defied Her Majesty."

"Yet you defy me, he who executes her command."

"I do not. I simply loathe you."

Frost sniggered and wiggled the blade. "Hold a serpent by the tongue, lieutenant. A chafed lion by the mortal paw."

Cavanaugh tensed as the stake grazed a coronary artery. His exhalation trembled, thin as the string of a violin. The Undertakers did nothing, serenaded.

Frost smiled. Blood fermented in his mouth as it had earlier, after he had chased Grace's pet into the mousetrap upstairs. He wanted to kill Cavanaugh, the turncoat, but he could not. Shade would become suspicious and try to prevent the migration. She would mourn.

"Report to the colonel's quarters," he said. "Bring your men, Sextons included." Frost retracted his wooden blade and shoved Cavanaugh forward. The foremost Undertaker dropped his gun to catch him.

Frost dived over the balustrade, into the center of the stairwell. With a billow and a flap of cape, he disappeared into the second-floor hallway, into the subtle reek of reanimated death, of decomposition stilled.

Set into a brick wall at the top of cement steps, the gate hung crooked on its hinges. It was made of wrought-iron leaves and tendrils of ivy, which had crawled up five spires to their spade-shaped finials. Shade pushed open the gate. Its hinges whined. She stepped through, over the chain and padlock rusting on the top step; one of the chain links had been snipped, the work of the Bloodhounds, no doubt. They had raided it the night Roman died. They had found humans.

Ahead, the Elizabethan theater towered, surrounded by a walkway of cobblestones. Forty-five feet high, the theater had been modeled after the Globe, William Shakespeare's workplace and stage in London. The original Globe had burned down during a performance of *Henry VIII* when cannon fire ignited the thatched roof. On the banks of the Thames, it had been reconstructed. This theater, here at the edge of the park, was a triplicate of the Globe.

For the sake of authenticity, it had been thatched with water reed, but had been coated with retardant to appease the city's fire ordinances and to accommodate Shakespeare's more raucous plays. Surfaced with a frame of oak lath, sitting on plinths of Tudor brickwork, and finished in a mixture of lime plaster and goat hair, the building contrasted its backdrop of skyscrapers and apartment blocks, a little bubble of history. It was as dark as Macbeth's castle the night he murdered King Duncan.

Stepping up to a pair of iron-banded doors, Shade unlatched the combination lock from the metal ring handles and hooked the lock to her belt. This entrance, once lit by the arched lamp above it, led to the yard and to the lower gallery, as was written in Times New Roman on the wall above the lamp. Several other doors around the building accessed the upper galleries and the gentlemen's rooms, but padlocks secured them, and Shade lacked keys. A similar padlock once fastened this door, but the Bloodhounds had cut it the night they raided the theater. Shade had replaced the padlock with the combination lock.

She gripped the door handle and paused. She looked up at one of the square windows, slatted vertically and framed in oak lath. In the darkness beyond, she saw the briefest movement, perhaps the flash of a pentagram necklace.

She entered the theater and shut the door. It closed with a heavy clunk.

With a slight whistle and flurry of wings, a flock of rock doves fluttered through the open roof, informants for the dawn.

Shade walked into the pit at the theater's center, smelling timber and earth. In the tiered galleries and gentlemen's rooms that surrounded the yard, darkness sought shelter. When the sun rose, the darkness would hang upside down from the heavens above the stage or retreat into the hell beneath it. The unlucky shadows would turn to soot in the daylight.

Frightened of the light, Roman's assassin had long deserted the uppermost gallery. Now, only sun-sensitive eels threaded through the balusters of riven oak.

Setting a hand atop the stage, Shade hopped up. As she walked between the machinery hut's two marble pillars, the heavens warred on the ceiling above her: the sun shot photons into the night's black-widow underbelly, and the full moon shielded the assault, banishing lemony shuriken into the clouds that padded the sky.

A balcony jutted over the curtain to the inner stage. On its pillars, granite maidens stood watch. The sculptures were crowned in ionic capitals of gold, and their robes puddled around their hips, exposing plump, alabaster breasts and toned bellies. While their unblemished cheeks and dove-gray skin feigned innocence and virginity, their eyes were bloodshot and jaded. They tracked Shade's progress across the stage.

Walking between the balcony's small marble columns, she drew aside the maroon curtain. Beyond, the inner stage was the urn of dead shadows, a last stand against the dawn. It smelled of desiccated cinnamon and thyme. Inseparable from the dust, Roman's ashes had dispersed, blown around by secrets of the breeze.

A single rose, disrobed of its wrapping, lay withered on the hardwood floor.

Frost had been present the night Roman was slain. The human refugees had holed up in the theater's attic, huddled among racks of jerkins, cartidge-pleated skirts, and bodices of brocade. The attic appeared to be their hideaway in case of invasion; they had barricaded the entrance with trunks. They had also converted the stage balcony into a dining room, complete with table and chairs, once props in a play. Deeper in the balcony, the humans had laid sleeping bags, all covered with a grouse- and partridge-patterned quilt.

After helping another Bloodhound box up the canned corn, minestrone, and bottled water stored in one corner of the balcony, Roman had gone to inspect the space beneath the stage. The other Bloodhounds returned to the bus with the refugees. According to Frost, Roman had been alone: "He was the last one in the building," the general claimed. "He … and one other."

Fingering her necklace, Shade stepped up to the rose on the floor. The seer's eye, ruby and catlike, opened in the folds of her brain. In the tics and twitches of 8mm film, Shade's revelation replayed on its iris.

The rose moistened, flourished, and blushed carmine. It began to pulse, and serum engorged its netting of arteries and veins. Around the flower, dust stirred and swirled, conglomerating into a brain, two lungs, and a trachea. The esophagus developed, a mouth and tongue at the top, leading into the stomach and then down and around into the intestines.

From the rose, two trunks, the aorta and vena cava, branched toward the brain, rooting in the legs. Vessels twined through muscles and wrapped around bone. Capillaries enmeshed liver, spleen, and head. The spine calcified, as did the ribs. And as the dermal layers stretched from the anus and lips, as hazel eyes filled empty sockets and raven hair sprouted from the scalp, a guise of skin hid the skull's chuckle, spread from ear to ear. The skin rippled down the neck, down the torso, to finally overlap the other surge of flesh, to button up at the navel. A pit remained in the chest, exposing the rose.

Two punctures bruised the side of Roman's throat. Shade leaned forward, peering through the grainy lens of the vision. Before she could identify the wounds as a bite, splinters peeled from the floorboard, warding her off.

Around Roman's cadaver, the wooden needles stitched the seams of darkness, clothing him in a leather trench coat, coal-colored boots, and leather pants. Roman's collar hid the marks on his neck, and the slivers united over his torso, forging an oaken stake. The weapon revolved, poised for a nosedive.

On the breast of his smoky doublet, moon dust sprinkled a pentagram and a silver chain. He stared up at the ceiling, unmasked, eyes glazed.

Shade swiped for the stake.

Too late.

It plunged, headed for the wound in Roman's chest.

Shade kicked, missed.

The stake bored into her father's heart.

Squalling, Shade dropped to her knees. She could not remove the Excalibur of oak. It was transparent; her hands passed right through it.

Behind her, the curtain opened. The assassin entered, red-lined cloak swishing about his boots. A hood concealed his face. Brown gloves covered his hands.

Snarling, Shade pounced.

He sieved through her pores, leaving a chill of rime on her skin, a cold snap in her veins. She landed on the other side and tangled with the curtain.

The assassin hunkered beside Roman and reached for the stake. Shade pounced again.

The murderer's pinky finger curled around the hilt, followed by his ring finger and middle finger, his index and thumb.

Shade came down—a roman candle went off in her face. Nebulae of azure and vermilion blinded her, spinning and spinning, and geysers of magenta forced her back. Meteors blazed past.

The assassin, obscured in pyrotechnics, took Roman's necklace and stood.

Shade stalked forward. The room had turned into a snow globe, precipitating ashes. She fanned at the flakes, but they did not whorl, except around the assassin as he emerged.

Shade's snarl escalated into a roar. She hacked at his face, but no flesh lodged beneath her fingernails. The assassin leached through her and disappeared beyond the curtain.

Casting the maroon fabric aside, Shade stomped across the stage, firing her gun into the yard. She jumped into the pit, firing, firing. The gunshots thundered in the galleries. The bullets splintered beams and balusters, emancipating oak aromas.

Click-click-click: empty.

Her target had vanished. No mist or wisp of smoke remained.

Shade wailed and threw her gun. It jounced off a balustrade and landed in the dirt. Rain began to fall and crater the ground around it, creating a lunar topography. The droplets tapped the theater's roof, slow and erratic at first, then accelerating as if to douse some cannon-inspired blaze. Shade let the rain streak down her face. It smelled like freshwater. It tasted like tears.

Weightless and disemboweled, she drifted back to the inner stage, followed by the rain's applause. The rose lay on the floor, bloodless, leathered. The dust had resettled; the snow globe had stilled. The only sign of disturbance was a set of footprints. Just one set: Shade's.

She made new tracks.

The stake hid in the corner, under a cobweb. She was surprised she had not seen it before. Then again she never had a reason to search the room; she had trusted Frost—or had *wanted* to trust him.

Shade retrieved the weapon, exposing a clean patch of floor underneath. She blew off its dusty gown. The oak grain had but one defect: an engraving, "Sturm, Swung, Wucht."

Shade ran her finger across the sans-serif grooves, hoping for a sliver, the prick of understanding. Unable to translate, she holstered the stake on her belt.

She picked up the rose. It rustled.

Returning to the edge of the stage, Shade baptized the flower in rain, let it quench its eternal thirst, let the water pollinate and revive while tears of runoff coursed down her cheeks.

Beyond the gangrene-blackened gauze of the night, the sky had paled from midnight to indigo, preparing for the sun. Shadows squirmed. Bats had long since fled to their roosts.

Shade stepped back inside. The rose wept on the floor, leaving splashes in the dust. She kissed a petal and reinstated the bloom. Though nourished, the flower did not inflame or circulate blood. It lay in its puddle, without pulse.

Shade saluted and ducked through the curtain, gone to reclaim her firearm.

As she walked beneath the heavens of the stage, her pentagram aligned with the painted celestial bodies, completing the constellation. The necklace flared silver with a flashback. She and Frost stood in a hallway, buttered in lantern light. Frost was uttering condolences; Shade was staring at his hand.

In the cradle of his palm, a five-pointed star effulged like a garnet.

Gloved hands folded behind his back, Frost stood sentinel outside Colonel Bain's apartment. The wall across from him breathed, expanding like flesh. The whole building focused on him, bent its mind against him. He thought of being buried alive. He thought of a coffin, and his brow broke out in cold sweat, the ice sculpture melting.

Frost tightened his jaw.

In the stairwell, footfalls rumbled. Cavanaugh entered the hallway, Undertakers and Sextons following suit. The soldiers did not speak, yet they quieted as they noticed Frost; their trench coats seemed to hush. Some repositioned M16s and flamethrowers, bearing them with more care, while others straightened their posture.

Cavanaugh bulled onward. His eyes roiled with sea foam and iron. His leather cuirass remained punctured, yet his skin had mended.

Frost fixed his gaze on the wall and willed his face to freeze. He opened Bain's apartment, letting the door swing inward. Cavanaugh pushed past. Undertakers and Sextons filed in after him.

Frost could feel their eyes, tracing the ice melt down his cheek. Could they see the tremble in his lip? Could they find a spot in his armor soft enough to pierce? He thought, yes, they could. If they looked close enough.

The last soldier entered, but Frost lingered outside. He wiped away the sweat and took a deep breath. Then he stepped inside and shut the door behind him.

Already, a few men muttered about the stench as they settled around the room, some in pinewood chairs from the kitchen, others on the couch. Cavanaugh took the leather chair, and the remaining troops leaned against the walls or crouched on the violet carpet.

Seven soldiers total. Three Sextons—Graves, Edward, and James (Victor would be there soon, making a quartet)—and four Undertakers: Thomas, Liam, Fry, and Cavanaugh. And then there was Bain.

Dressed in leather pants, boots, and a cape, all black, the colonel paced behind his couch. He had slicked back his silver hair, and around it, smoke flowed like a mane; a cigarette burned between the gray fingers of his gloves. He scowled at Frost. "Bastard," he said, eyes metallic and bloodshot.

The chatter stopped, and the soldiers gawked at Bain. They turned to Frost for his reaction. He laughed, trying to sound nonchalant, and he stepped between two Undertakers into the middle of the room. "I assure you, good colonel, I was sired in wedlock."

Bain stopped pacing and pointed at the kitchen entryway. "I want that stench out!"

Frost breathed deep, as if savoring a woman's strawberry shampoo. His lungs clotted with the stench of a gas-expulsing corpse. "I rather enjoy the smell."

"I want it out, now!"

All the false humor bled from Frost's face. "Mind your rank, Colonel."

Bain shook his head and snubbed his cigarette in a glass ashtray on an end table. He lit another and continued to pace, mumbling and dropping ashes onto the floor.

"What is that smell, anyway?" Liam asked. He was a cremator, his flamethrower still mounted on his back.

Frost stared at him, and Liam shied away.

"Victor!" Frost shouted. "It is time!"

In the kitchen, a chair leg cheeped against linoleum. Two sets of footsteps progressed across the tile, one shuffling, the other solid. Dressed in an open mesh chemise and a pleather miniskirt, a woman appeared in the entryway. Victor stood at her rear, nudging her forward. Greasy tears of mascara streaked the woman's cheeks. A white cloth gagged her, and wire bound her hands behind her back.

When the Undertakers registered the woman's pasty complexion and the strange black growths on her arms and legs, they tensed. Colonel Bain stopped pacing and stood at the other end of his couch, near the ashtray.

Victor untied the woman and removed her gag, then pushed her into the room. She chortled through a veil of almond hair and lunged at Fry, a nearby Undertaker.

"Puppet!" Cavanaugh blurted, springing out of his chair and leveling his M16. The Undertakers nearest the zombie stepped back, drawing Glocks, Berettas, and Magnums.

"Halt!" Frost commanded. "Hold your fire!"

Fingers eased off triggers, but eyes glanced askew. Muzzles held their aims.

"Victor," Frost said. The sentry looked up, and Frost made a cutthroat gesture, drawing a finger over his Adam's apple. Victor nodded and stepped behind the woman. He pressed a knife against her neck and carved a toothless, gray-lipped smile.

Because their hearts no longer pumped, zombies did not bleed. All their serums had pooled. But when Victor's blade severed carotid and jugular, blobs and rivulets of oil gushed out. Fry dodged the fluid, which soiled the rug.

After a few more spurts, the zombie's blood coagulated into a black, fibrous scab. The woman kept coming, undaunted by the many firearms that targeted her skull.

"Cut her again," Frost said.

Victor leered, truly a hyena. He amputated the woman's ear. The shell of cartilage thumped onto the violet carpet, zirconia earring twinkling. A few strands of hair drifted down to garnish the auricle, and a new ear unfurled from the woman's head. It was the color of licorice slippery with spit.

Eyewitnesses prattled and cursed.

"Shoot her," Frost instructed Victor.

The sentry pressed his Glock above the woman's cloned ear. The blast jolted her sideways, and a maw opened in the side of her skull, disgorging brain confetti and black gelatinous globs. Hairy abscesses bedecked the plaster, wriggling and drizzling down. Smoke from gun and cigarette peppered the liverwurst stink of cerebrum.

The Undertakers moved as the zombie lumbered sideways. Her shoulder rammed the wall, and she hinged like a door, back hitting plaster. Her knees quaked and started to collapse. But she stood. And the grave in her cranium sucked in fill dirt; seeds germinated and grew black hair.

The woman pushed away from the wall, still animated and still hungry. Many of the Undertakers gasped.

Frost seized the zombie by her neck. She grumbled and groped for his face. He ignored her, addressing his audience.

"As you can see, the puppets have developed regenerative abilities. A general headshot will no longer dispatch." Pausing, Frost pulled the slide back on his Glock and pressed the barrel to the woman's brow. "Only a direct hit to the subject's forehead will suffice."

Lightning struck, powerful, thunderous. A brass shell glimmered in the light, and the woman slumped to the floor. She did not get up, she did not regenerate.

Pushing back his cape, Frost slipped his gun into the nylon holster on his belt. He laced his hands behind his back and paced, chin lifted. "Our adversary strengthens each day. Sentries inform me that a brigade has penetrated our keep, and that it will soon storm the Haven."

Cavanaugh chuffed and lowered his gun. "Zombies, infiltrating Roman's fortress? That's absurd." He returned to the leather chair and crossed his arms.

Frost revolved on his heels, looking down his nose at the lieutenant. "Mere zombies do not renew brain tissue and bone."

Cavanaugh said nothing, furrowing his brow.

Frost continued to pace. "They grow stronger, and we must protect our flock."

Without pausing, he lifted something from one of the end tables. He lifted it up and it sloshed, liquid ruby in the lamplight.

"Blood," he said. "Hot from the vein, cold in the bag. But how many of you long to bite flesh instead of plastic? How many of you miss the hunt, the pounding of your heart, the smell of prey and fear?"

Frost's fangs had extended, and his eyes had gone black. The lanterns brightened until the light itself caught fire, setting everyone in the room ablaze. The fever heated each and every soldier, provoking their canines, and in that singular moment of light, Frost saw them for what they really were. He saw the beasts beneath, ancient beings, gray skin withered against indestructible bones, bald except for liver spots and straggles of dead hair, eyes pure black, mouths all snarls, their hearts nothing but prunes shriveled around pits of stone.

"The puppets are an omen, a sign! We must abandon this City of Corpses. We must journey to a place where we can raise and hunt our drove, where we can bathe in the moonlight, a place where we can be free!"

"The island," someone rumored, and the word rose, a Van Gogh moon, coloring the firelight cerulean and azure, highlighted in aquamarine. It lured the cold fire into currents and waves, and the soldiers swayed, eyes glazing with mother-of-pearl dreams.

Cavanaugh's eyes remained iron, though his teeth were as sharp as anyone's, his breathing just as heightened. "The puppets are everywhere," he said, panting, visibly clenching the excitement from his chest, visibly denying the tide. "How would we transport our slaves?"

And then the moon began to wane, calming the waters, Van Gogh's night receding. Reds and yellows crept back into the light.

Some soldiers nodded and quietly agreed with Cavanaugh, naysayers such as Edward, just coming off their high.

Frost sighed, now only ash. "Not long ago," he said, wondering if this strange weight and emptiness in his chest would allow him to breathe and continue, "Roman's Bloodhounds retrieved and transported slaves using a bus retrofitted with steel and equipped with a plow."

"The Redhound," Victor contributed, leaning against the kitchen doorframe, arms crossed.

Cavanaugh laughed. "The Redhound? It's inoperable. It's junk."

"Wrong," Frost said. "After its last run, I secured the Redhound in an automotive shop. Its alternator was faulty, but Victor," Frost pointed at the sentry, who raised his hand and smirked at his peers, "Victor has the gift of a mechanic. He has assured me the Redhound is fully operational and capable of this mission."

"It's got one mean son-of-a-bitch machinegun, too," Victor said.

Cavanaugh finally stood up. "So you plan to pile our sole food source into a bus and drive through thousands—no, millions of starving corpses? Tell me, General: have you forgotten what happened to the Redhound? Has it slipped your mind?"

Frost stared him down. "It served us well until that night," he said. The zombies had found a way into the bus and had killed two Bloodhounds. "The puppets were lucky to find the chink in its armor. But this time, there will be no chink. Victor has seen to that."

"We're just going to forsake our home, then, is that it? A home that Roman sacrificed his life to create?"

"We will migrate to the island, yes. We will be free."

"And what would Roman think of this, General? Roman, our founder."

Frost looked at Bain from the corner of his eye, but the colonel just puffed on his cigarette and arched a bushy eyebrow, as if to reiterate the question with a sarcastic slant.

Frost donned his mask of ice. He thought of the rose. He thought of the plum. "Roman is dead," he stated. "And her Highness has already consented to my proposition. These are her commands."

Cavanaugh narrowed his eyes. He opened his mouth to retort, but the words rotted in his throat.

Frost suppressed a grin and turned to assess his audience. "Tomorrow night," he said, voice booming and magnetic, "at twilight, we prepare for our pilgrimage to freedom." He crossed his arms over his chest, over his heart: "Sleep well."

Cavanaugh threw open the door, burying the crystal knob in the wall. His boots rapped the floor as he marched away.

Gradually, Undertakers and Sextons filtered out too, trench coats soughing, the only whispers. All along the hall, doors opened and shut as the soldiers retired to their quarters. Victor was the last one in line, dragging the woman's corpse by the wrists. He had tucked her severed ear between her cleavage and had heaped her brain matter in the basin of her stomach.

"Well done," Frost remarked. He stepped to the door as Victor passed into the hall.

Behind the couch, Bain sparked yet another cigarette. "So," he said, "Roman's empire finally crumbles."

"No," Frost replied: the rose, the plum. "This kingdom never crumbles. It prospers." With a tug, he extracted the crystal knob from the wall. He stepped outside and shut the door.

Only Victor and his burden occupied the hallway. No commotion sounded from behind the many closed doors: sleep took the soldiers quickly.

"Victor," Frost called. "Wait."

The Sexton stopped, still holding the woman's wrists.

"Allow me." Frost lifted the body into his arms, so that its legs hung over his biceps, as did its head. "Go," he told Victor. "Sleep."

The Sexton complied, and Frost continued down the hall with the corpse. He walked through the clouds and vapors of his soldiers' dreams, where oceans sighed, where seashells of amethyst dotted the sand. Cavanaugh's apartment leaked red tide and oil spills, poisoning the beach reveries. Frost traipsed through and cleared the waters, so the rest of his disciples would not be disenchanted, so that by tomorrow they would all be his advocates.

The bedroom door was cold against Ann's ear. She held her breath, listening for the quietest noise, any signs of life, like a doctor with a stethoscope.

When she first lowered herself into the apartment, two candles had burned on a coffee table, spilling lakes of wax in varying layers of liquid and solid. Blueberry and apple-cinnamon, they barely masked the humidity of automobile fluids. Next to one of the candles sat a stack of pennies, polished and reflective, as if shined with spit.

No one crouched in the unlit kitchen or behind the recliner. No one sprang from the many closed doors.

Wiping away tears and blood, Ann had parted the front door. In the hallway, sprites of lantern light cavorted, somersaulting wall to wall. Chimeras picked them off from the shadows. No Draculas, no footsteps: desolate. But as she began to open the door, a silhouette entered from the stairwell. It wore a cape and had frosted eyes.

Ann's breath turned cold. She couldn't shut the door. The Iceman would hear. He would thrust it open, and the mere force would pulverize her bones.

He stopped a few apartments down. He was standing guard.

Not soon after, an army in black leather uniforms trooped into the hallway. The Iceman opened the door for them.

Ann eased her door shut, releasing the knob slowly so that it would not click. She pressed her ear against the wood. Silence, just silence. Then muffled voices, twin gunshots. She should have escaped then. She should have returned to Ellie's side. But if she had opened the door, the Iceman might have seen her. And by the time she had convinced herself he wasn't out there, a parade of footsteps re-entered the hall. Doors opened and shut, and Ann retreated to the bedroom.

Now, beneath her heartbeat, two voices rose in the hall.

"Victor, wait." That was the Iceman. He and another male exchanged words, but walls muffled them. Ann pressed her ear harder against the door.

Footsteps, she heard footsteps, a clink and a swoosh as the front door opened.

Ann gasped. She shrank into the darkness and butted her knee on the bed frame. Hobbling, she fumbled along the wall for the closet, the closet—this room had to have a closet!

Mr. Anonymous shut the front door. His footsteps stopped, no doubt at the mound of dandruff and lath that littered the carpet. His gaze would naturally go to the ceiling, where Ann had dug a hole just wide enough for her shoulders and hips.

She found the closet. The knob rattled as she opened the door.

Inside, motor oil and grease stifled her. Something tickled the back of her leg. She almost screamed. But she stood in the jaws of a mousetrap, a device triggered by sound instead of pressure: just one sound, one peep, and the jaw would swing down.

Ann scooted farther back, pushing aside the pile of cloths that had startled her. Her head bumped a shelf. Her shoulder brushed the wall. Underfoot, the carpet felt grimy.

The bedroom door opened, and Mr. Anonymous walked in, probably following the trail of Ann's blood. He stopped outside the closet. Ann could sense his hand reaching for the door. Leather chafed leather. A floorboard nagged.

Silence.

A scream matured and bloated her neck like a fetus.

Mr. Anonymous shifted. His breath magnified into a heavy rale and fumed through the rifts of the door: fish slime, mucus, vomit. Something scraped across the closet door, a talon, long and yellowed.

An urge to scream, to abort her baby, tormented Ann's lungs. Her husband was dead, her sister was a vegetable, and her niece—oh, God, her niece. She needed to rest. She needed to lie down with Michael and fall asleep in his arms, eternal slumber, eternal night.

Scream, scream, scream!

Mr. Anonymous stepped away from the closet.

Ann's scream died stillborn.

The man lit a candle, and light gilded the doorframe. Sliding open dresser drawers, he jangled something together. Tools maybe: wrenches, ratchets, a screwdriver. He undid a zipper, perhaps on a bag. The tools chorused like silverware as he dumped them in and zipped the bag shut.

Footsteps again. Mr. Anonymous left the room. He had to notice Ann's hatch, the crumbs beneath it, had to notice the trail of blood. Perhaps he was preparing for a hunt. But why the tools?

Ann realized she had to urinate.

From all the camping trips she and Michael had shared—Crater Lake, Hellsgate Canyon, an island in Puget Sound—Ann was accustomed to peeing outdoors and to substituting maple leaves for toilet paper. Once, denied a public restroom, she had even relieved herself in the corner of a parking garage. But since waddling nude through her Aunt Hildy's red two-story Victorian, decrying diapers, Ann had not discolored a carpet. She could still remember the smell, like butane and salt, rising from Aunt Hildy's Persian rug. Aunt Hildy had heard her piddling from the other room and had yanked her up by the arm. She swatted her until it no longer hurt, until the tears bled from the dull ache inside.

No doubt Mr. Anonymous had keener ears than Aunt Hildy, and he would devise ways to prolong the pain.

Clenching her teeth, Ann tried to ignore the twinges of her bladder, tried to focus on her cuts and bruises, on the perpetual explosions in her hip, the itch and need of Mistress' bite. She thumbed her ring. But her bladder throbbed as if with infection, as if her urine had fermented into tequila.

Mr. Anonymous re-entered the room, and Ann's jaws tightened into fists. Urine sizzled into her urethra.

Mr. Anonymous approached the closet. He jostled the doorknob. A squirt of yellow trickled down Ann's thigh, and salty ammonia tinged the cloy of oil.

Something scuffed and slumped against the door, just below the knob. Tools clattered. This was it. He was going to open the door. He would smile. His fangs would glint.

He took a step forward—and blew out the candle. The doorframe floated briefly, a dissolving ghost of light. Then springs creaked as Mr. Anonymous settled into bed.

Ann counted off seconds, minutes. She stiffened her legs, bit her cheek, and thumbed her ring. Another squirt seared her leg, burning the cuts, the claw marks and bites of feral wire.

Mr. Anonymous shifted on his bed. Springs squeaked. Ann shut her eyes. Silence, except for the deathwatches, ticking quietly above.

Mr. Anonymous began to snore, his nose a flute, his deviated septum its reed. Would he smell her? Would he smell her piss if not her blood?

Unable to hold it any longer, Ann sighed and let the broth stream down her leg, let it pitter-patter briefly on the carpet. The smell was worse than that day at Aunt Hildy's. It was like gasoline, heady and flammable, but Mr. Anonymous did not stir. He continued to play his tuneless flute, leaving Ann to simmer in her juices.

Through the static and mineral scent of rain, Shade crossed the park. She tracked mud onto the brick square and left footprints in the grass. Her hair drooped, strung with liquid beads. When the beads dripped off, they pattered the shoulders and breast of her leather jacket.

The sun was coming. A somber gray had already crept over the horizon, heralding the dawn. Soon the clouds would part, and cherubs of sunlight would surpass the mountaintops, trumpeting golden horns. Warriors in platinum breastplates would descend in heat waves, hurling mercury lances and slashing through the darkness with fiery swords. The shadows would scream, spilling smoky entrails. Their bodies would burst into cinders and ash.

At the row of buildings, Shade climbed another fire escape. She dashed along the rooftops, over the dividing walls. Rain crackled; gravel crunched.

On the third roof over, just outside the open stairwell door, a man was hunched over several containers: glasses, cups, bowls, an aluminum coffee can stripped of its label. He was collecting rain, probably for drinking water.

Shade stopped behind the gunmetal cube of the cooling unit. Drops tapped her eyelashes, but she did not blink. The man was already foggy, a holograph, illusory. If she blinked, he would dissipate. His rain slicker and jeans would deflate, topped with a dark tarp of hair.

The inhabitants of the Haven had long thought the human race to be extinct outside their home. Roman and his Bloodhounds had combed the entire city. They had pressed their eyes to every rathole, had searched every nest and building. But perhaps Roman had died before this building was scheduled. Perhaps his murder had prevented it.

Careful to remain unseen, Shade glided around the cooling unit. Rainman's head sprang up. He whipped out a flashlight. Shade did not dodge the beam. She stood still and let it glare red in her eyes.

Raindrops drummed the hood of the cooling unit. They plinked and plunked into the coffee can. Rainman twitched. He began to turn into mist, as Shade had feared, just a hallucination. Then he dove into the stairwell.

Although the sun was cresting the distant mountains, although Frost was plotting the collapse of her father's kingdom every second of her absence, Shade rocketed forward. The Beast woke in her belly. It clawed through the mediator of reason, leaving its corpse in a heap of steamy bowels. It drove Shade forward, possessing her blood, growing in her stomach. Her eyes became its eyes, black and voracious. Her fangs lengthened into points, and she could taste wine.

Before Rainman could lock the stairwell door, Shade wrenched it from his grip. He tumbled down the stairs, thumping and flailing and sprawling onto the landing. He scrambled to his feet and kept going, limping now, favoring his right leg. Shade leapt down to his level.

The air had died here, slimy and bloated with putrefaction. Moans drifted up from the lower stairwell: zombies. Rainman was either oblivious to the threat, or somehow protected from it, wriggling deeper into the rot like a maggot. His beam darted across the ghouls. They crowded the staircase, unable to ascend because someone had chopped out several steps. The puppets had grown leech-colored tentacles, which struck at the light. Eyes gleamed. Mouths chewed imaginary flesh.

Just at the sight of them, Shade felt sick. They had mutated. She wondered what else they were capable of.

Below, Rainman disappeared into a hallway. Shade kicked through the door, splintering the frame and bending the hinges.

At an apartment down the corridor, Rainman fumbled with a set of keys. His flashlight bobbled underarm, lighting up the blue carpet. Shade advanced, stomping, making each footfall resonate. The flashlight shined once in her face. Rainman whimpered, leaking adrenalin: flammable, pungent, high octane—the very gas that fueled the engines of the Beast.

With a jingle, Rainman found the right key and threw open the door. Shade pushed him across the threshold. She shut the door and bent Rainman's arm behind his back, pinning him against a blue spackled wall.

"Please," he said, panting. "Don't kill me." His voice sounded like a rusty hinge.

In the apartment, the air was undergoing a different stage of decay. A cheesy stink overpowered the onions of Rainman's body odor. Mold had grown on the oxygen, lying over everything in a suffocating rug.

Even after his tumble down the stairs, Rainman still held his flashlight, black metal the length of a baton. Shade snatched it and played it across the room.

Separated by a small table, a brown couch and suede recliner faced an entertainment center. The center's glass doors reflected the flashlight, as did the TV behind them. Heavy comforters veiled the windows, repressing what little light remained in the world, hiding the hell that lay beyond them. Landscapes hung in frames, a beach here, a waterfall there, the passions of grass, orchids, and sky diluted in watercolor. The paintings only sapped the already bloodless walls.

The room harbored no corpse, zombie or otherwise, but the stink could have come from any of several doors, all closed.

"Please," Rainman repeated. He had wet his pants, and the chicken stock stained the fawn-colored carpet.

Something crashed in another room. Something shattered and clanked. Shade highlighted the door just to the right of the recliner. The noise had come from in there.

"Please—"

Shade put more torsion on his arm. "Who's in there?"

Rainman stopped squirming. "Oh God," he said, and his voice trembled. "Mother."

"Show me," she said, pushing him toward the door. She shined the flashlight over his shoulder and pressed her gun to the back of his head.

"Wait," he said, throwing up his hands. "Wait. She—she might've gotten loose."

Shade jabbed the muzzle into the back of his neck. "I said show me."

"But—she's my mother. You'd shoot her. You'd—"

The boom of Shade's gun silenced him. He jumped, squealed, and squirted more urine. White dust floated down from the bullet hole in the ceiling.

Shade put the gun against his head. "Open the door."

"Fine. Just—please. She's my mother."

With a trembling hand, Rainman reached for the doorknob. He flinched as something else broke behind the door. Judging by the echoey acoustics, the room beyond was a kitchen. The decay had taken on mass and color here, the runny green-black of putrid lettuce.

"Open it," Shade said.

Rainman swung the door outward, and an inkblot moth unfurled from the darkness. Shade skewered it with the flashlight, illuminating a white counter, a chrome faucet bent over a chrome sink. “Go inside.”

Rainman hesitated. “I don’t—I don’t think—” He didn’t have time to finish. The tentacle yanked him in by the neck.

Twenty

Cradling the woman's corpse, Frost entered the fourth floor hallway. Grace was crouched at the lip of the pitfall, holding a lantern overhead and peering down. Frost's shadow rippled up her back, over the folds of her lab coat. It whispered murder in her ear and traced a talon across her throat. She turned, shining the lantern in Frost's eyes. His shadow leapt behind him, flickering on the wall.

He smiled. "A bouquet for you," he said, offering the corpse.

Grace stood and raised an eyebrow. "One of your sluts?"

Frost maintained his grin, though his shadow bared its fangs. It would be so easy to push her over the edge, just a simple nudge. It would be just as easy to slide his wooden knife between her ribs and dance in her fireworks. But the torsos required a midwife. They needed her, so Frost kept his shadow behind him and kept smiling.

He nodded toward the pitfall. "I trust you resolved—"

"Yes," Grace interrupted. "She was dead. Zombie food." Her eyes narrowed and pierced. Frost almost looked away, but Grace did first. His shadow grinned.

"Bring her," Grace said. She scooted around him toward the warren.

"She's contaminated."

Grace opened the door and looked back. "She won't bite, Frost. She's dead."

"And the eggs?"

Grace arched her eyebrows. "You really think the torsos would've lasted this long if they weren't immune?"

Frost did not answer. His shadow seethed behind him, yearning to shove her into the room, where it could grow and claw out her windpipe.

She turned away, as if stung by his eyes. "Just follow me."

In their harnesses, many torsos snored, some whirring like the ebb and flow of the ocean, others gurgling agates in stone throats. Emaciated silhouettes fed off the sleeping amputees. The lantern light cast burning hieroglyphs, chanting ward-off spells. The silhouettes hissed, dissipated, but quickly reassembled after the light had passed.

Entering the kitchen, Grace motioned to a table that stood in the back, similar in position to Colonel Bain's table, only rectangular. On the counter, she had arrayed surgeon tools and other medical utensils. The linoleum beneath the table had a rusty stain to it.

Frost unloaded the corpse onto the stainless steel tabletop, and Grace stepped to the counter. From her surgeon's tray, she selected a bone saw, a straight razor, a scalpel, and a crowbar. She approached the corpse. Frost stepped aside.

"So," he said as Grace used the razor to shave the woman's hair into a mohawk, "your pet: how did you remove her from the snare?"

She paused, letting ribbons of almond hair float to the floor. "What's this?" she asked, indicating the patch of black hair and regenerated scalp above the woman's ear.

"A change in subject."

Grace glared at him and continued to cut. "Rope," she said, finally answering. "I used rope."

Frost crossed his arms. "And how did you dispose of her body?"

"I told you. Zombie food."

"She was dead then?"

"I told you that already."

"What killed her?"

"The fall."

Frost smiled. "Do you miss her?"

Grace lifted the woman's head by the mohawk and began to shave the hair in back. "She was a slave, Frost. Nothing more."

"But didn't you love having a warm throat to suck? Much better than those blood bags, already half cold."

"Damn it, Frost!" Grace slammed the razor onto the tabletop. "Let me work, or get the hell out of my warren!" Her hands trembled, even when she clenched them.

Frost's grin sharpened. "Zombie food, indeed."

Grace looked away and continued to work. "I should be able to have my own slave. For Christ's sake, Bain has one. Who cares that he's different?" She picked up the bone saw and began to cut into the woman's forehead.

"Where did you find her, anyway?"

"Does it matter?"

"Yes."

"On the streets, okay? I saved her. She's mine."

"You mean she *was* yours."

Grace traded the saw for the crowbar. She wedged it into a notch in the corpse's forehead and began to pry. "Whatever, Frost. Just shut up and let me do my work."

He had caught her, and if she ever rebelled, he would use the information against her. His shadow chuckled, spying from behind his shoulder and scheming, its eyes wicked and keen.

Opening the skull, Grace sliced the connective tissues with the scalpel. The crown fell onto the table, releasing a meaty stink. She cut through a few more layers and leaned in for a better look. "Jesus. This thing's got tentacles."

Frost nodded. "It has evolved. It can heal itself."

"This brain's, like, thirty percent rebuilt." She did not exaggerate. A black jelly had remolded the section that Victor's gun had obliterated, though the substance had not patched Frost's final bullet.

"I want to know how it regenerates," he said.

Grace parted the tissues with her scalpel. "Let me take a sample."

A microscope sat next to the surgeon's tray. Grace prepared a cross section of brain on a glass slide, which she clipped to the microscope's stage. She clicked the power button, and a battery-powered light went nova underneath. Pressing her face to the eyepieces, Grace worked the zoom knobs, slowing down to perfect the view.

"Some of these cells haven't even specialized yet. They're like … cancer cells."

"Or stem cells," Frost said.

Grace stood up and looked at him. "Of course. *That's* how they regenerate tissue. But where does it get them?" Grace stooped to the microscope and shifted the slide.

"I want to know how to stop it," Frost said. "I want to know how to kill it."

She ignored him and muttered to herself: "It must be using some kind of enzyme to speed it up, or …" She stood suddenly, her eyes alight. "From brains and bone marrow," she said. "And skin."

"Excuse me?"

"That's where it gets the cells. From the people it eats. Or even from its own tissues, like we do."

The virus that had created Frost's kind used stem cells in existing tissues to rapidly heal wounds. It made them nearly invincible. "Can it be stopped?" he asked.

"Well, if you cut off its supply; if you keep it from eating embryos. And if it's feeding on adult stem cells, I think it can only restore so much."

"How much?"

She crossed her arms. "You're asking me how this thing can do in minutes what scientists couldn't perfect in years, and—you're asking me to figure that out tonight? Don't be an idiot, Frost. I'm not—"

"Yes," he said, "you *will* figure it out. But before you do, you will prepare a gurney. For the torsos."

Her eyes widened. "We're leaving, then? We're finally leaving this ratshole?"

Frost didn't answer. "We'll need something to wheel them to the transport." Without another word, he turned and started toward the door.

Grace grabbed his arm and pulled him into an embrace, into a kiss. Her mouth no longer tasted sweet, rather bitter and tingly, like chewed iris petals, and when she looked up at him, her face was withered, a dying annual. Her grin tried to seduce but managed desperation.

"Take me with you," she said, and at first, Frost thought she meant to the island. But when she said it again, he knew. He scooped her into his arms and carried her toward her quarters, much the way he had carried the dead woman minutes after shooting her in the head.

He would keep her happy. She had a purpose to fulfill. For now.

Twenty-One

It was daybreak. Ann could feel it, even though she lived in the dark. The fluids in her brain and spine had changed tide. Her every cell thirsted for sunlight, and her ears craved the woodwinds of the early birds, the flutes and the ocarinas. But this place, this prison—its walls muted everything. It gobbled the light with stone molars and barbwire fangs.

"Listen," Michael said, his breath cold against her back. Less than an hour ago, he had developed from the darkness, barely a ghost, a nearly invisible blur. Initially, Ann had dismissed him as a draft. Then she felt his breath and tensed, fearing that Mr. Anonymous had somehow snuck behind her. But then Michael's scent drifted by, an evanescence of pepper and sage, and She knew it was him, except a new smell had corrupted his natural cologne. It reminded Ann of spoiled pork, of the corpses that prowled dark alleyways.

"He's asleep," Michael said.

Indeed, Mr. Anonymous snored on his mattress. He had neither tossed nor turned, deep in the abyss. He was in a place that Ann wanted to go. Her feet hurt. Her whole body stung, ached, and throbbed. She just wanted to float, eyes closed against a squirt of citrus sun.

"You should go," Michael urged. "Go now."

During their marriage, Michael had never lied to Ann. Oh, there had been omissions, times she could smell pot smoke in his flannel; he never told her when he got high, but if she asked, he would confess. He would tell if he disliked the pocket watch she gave him for Christmas. He would tell if the pasta was too sticky. He would not lie, especially about something big, like when his ex-wife had kissed him: he had pushed her away and had told Ann everything. She had no reason to distrust him, and yet this Michael spoke with a snake's tongue, forked and slippery.

"You need to get back to our little Ireland," he said.

Ann thumbed her wedding ring. She knew it wasn't really Michael. Her mind was impersonating him, the imitation distorted now with some new impression, something she could not place, something from a dream. It was that smell, that rot. That's what it was: her Michael had died, and so the only realistic figment was his zombie.

"You have to get back," he said.

Pure poison. He was right, though. Ellie needed her. Ireland needed her, because the deathwatches had never stopped their countdown. Mistress had not abandoned her scalpel. But rats hid everywhere. In hinges, in floorboards, ready to snitch. And Ann, the blind mouse, was prone to bump into something: a bedpost, a dresser, a wall. Mr. Anonymous would hear. He would lunge from the depths, eyes black, rows of teeth ready to shred.

And if Ann did get past him, Sextons patrolled the hallways. "Escape is impossible," Mistress had once warned. "Even during the daylight." Returning to the warren might be just as impossible. The Sextons would use her for themselves, too. She was illegitimate. Whoever caught her would use her, kill her, and probably feed her to the zombies, all without a word to his superiors. She could only guess how they would use Ellie and the baby.

Michael reached out and took Ann's hand. His knuckles were cold, the joints of a skeletal branch. His ring clinked against hers, but the metals refused to meld. "You have to go," he said, lifting her hand toward the doorknob. "Now."

I can't.

Suddenly, she had to urinate again. Urinate, or scream.

He'll hear me.

Michael tightened his hand over hers, making her clutch the knob. "You have to," he said. "She'll die. Our daughter will die."

Ann knew he meant *niece*, not *daughter*, but she didn't correct him. Somehow, it sounded right: their daughter, their beautiful Ireland.

She shut her eyes, muttered a short prayer, and said, "Okay." Together, she and Michael grabbed the knob.

Gun and flashlight aligned, Shade jumped into the kitchen. Dressed in an off-white nightgown, a woman stood in a pile of plate shards and pans, hanging Rainman with one of her tentacles. The hollows of her cheeks and eyes were bruises in the congealed milk of her face. No doubt this was Rainman's mother.

Behind her, against the back wall, knotted ropes spooled on a wooden chair. She must have chewed through them.

Gargling, unable to scream, Rainman clawed at the python around his neck. His fingernails could not gouge the tentacle's hide.

From the tangles and rats of the woman's hair, a thinner tentacle uncurled and wormed into Rainman's ear. Its muscles contracted and expanded, pumping out lumps of cerebral gelatin. Rainman's legs twitched. His arms went limp. Mother's feeder kept sucking, and a third tentacle uncoiled. It excreted gray and red slop, which plopped onto the plate shards in wads of ground beef, leftovers from Rainman's brain.

Never had Shade seen a Puppeteer feed in such a manner. Usually, its marionettes gnawed flesh from bone, then sucked out the marrow. Usually, they cracked the skull and scooped out brains with their hands. She had seen many zombies bloated from gluttony, their throats backed up and spewing carrion, and she had always suspected that the Puppeteer absorbed nourishment from the stomach or the intestines. But this? It was an abomination.

Shade shot Mother through the eye.

The zombie only faltered. A new eye, black and alien, pushed out the egg white.

The tentacles tossed Rainman against the refrigerator. He slid down it, head slumped, eyes glazed. Mother stepped forward, crunching plate shards and scowling into the flashlight.

Shade's next bullet punched through her forehead. It tapped oil, a gusher.

Mother stumbled and slipped in Rainman's brains. She fell onto a bed of broken china, spasmed, and lay still.

Shade stepped up to the bodies: Mother, Medusa slain; Rainman, a wine bottle clouded with inky death. She could almost taste the spoiled grapes, the mold and decay. What a waste. She clenched her jaws and shot Mother in the face. The body jerked, crunching more shards, leaking more oil.

Loading a new clip, Shade left the bodies to rot. No time to search the apartment. She discarded the flashlight and went to the front door. She opened it. Tentacles rushed in.

Somehow, zombies had traversed the hole in the staircase and were now swarming the hallway. Shade tried to shut the door, but tentacles lashed at her, using the puppets as battering rams. The door shook, and she could only close it partway.

A man stuck his head through the gap, snarling, eyes rolling, long brown hair mimicking his feelers. His mouth frothed maggots and the reek of excrement. Shade put him down with a bullet to the head. She booted his face, breaking his nose and driving him into the hallway.

Holding the door with one hand, Shade fired into the mob. A few heads jolted, spraying black juice, and a few bodies crumpled to the floor. Resistance waned. The door began to close. But a tentacle suctioned to the back of Shade's gun hand and tried to disarm her. She squeezed off a final round, performing a tracheotomy on an inmate in an orange jumpsuit, his bald head lackluster in the gloom. She twisted her arm and tossed the pistol, kicking it deeper into the apartment, away from the questing feelers.

Ignoring the jagged fingernails that pawed for her face, ignoring the bloody finger bones, Shade bulled her shoulder into the door. Hinges screeched. Wood groaned.

A tentacle latched onto her cheek. Armed with baby teeth, it nibbled, trying to break skin. Shade bit back, gnashing. Warm oil gushed into her mouth, tasting of olive juice and clots of vomit. She spit it out, along with a chunk of meat. The tentacle shriveled and shied away.

Shade pushed harder against the door, pinching arms and tentacles between it and the jamb. She wedged her boot beneath it and braced the wood with her knee. She drew her bone saw. Its metal teeth chewed through flesh and grated bone. Arms hit the carpet, convulsing. Tentacles snaked away, sneezing ink.

With the crunch of gristle, Shade finally shut the door. She locked it. The zombies kept pounding, throwing their bodies against the barrier. The doorjamb began to crack.

Shade picked up her gun and went to the windows. She tore off a blanket, snagging the blinds underneath.

Smoldering behind rain clouds and atmospheric ash, the red coal of sunrise seared her face. Her skin reddened. She screamed, flashblind, seeing only the photo negative of the skyline, white buildings against a black sunrise, raindrops forming an assault of silver arrows.

Shade fell away, pulling the blinds and splitting one of their wall brackets. She bent the slats and dawn speared through, a chaos schematic of infrared lasers. She stumbled through the security grid, and her skin sizzled, trailing smoke. The room's fire alarm blared. Shade shot at it, one well-placed slug, one sonic boom. Plastic shattered and sprinkled the carpet: silence, except for the insistent pounding of the marauders.

The blinds crashed to the floor, filling the room with sunrise.

Shade found the wall and fumbled along the spackling for a door or any other escape. She found a knob, tinny, hollow, and rattling in its socket. She threw open the door. Sensing the folds of darkness and the musty smell of coats, she plunged inside.

The light narrowed as she shut the lid to her upright coffin. It disappeared except for a line at her feet. Shade yanked a coat from its hanger and stuffed it along the bottom of the door. She sank back into the flannels and jackets, back to the rear wall. Nylon and wool whispered and consoled her. A rain slicker placed a cold compress against her fevered cheek.

Finally, the marauders penetrated the shadows' keep. They admitted the warriors of daylight, armed with solar flare swords. The zombies would find her in the closet, she had no doubt, and maybe it was time. Maybe she wanted to face the sun. She would envision Frost's stone face, his frozen eyes, and she would take out as many zombies as possible, shooting even as the swords blazed through her guts, even as the inferno ate her from the inside out. She would cackle fire, and she would die.

Shade aimed her gun, waiting for the first ghoul to poke in its head. They passed the closet without so much as a sniff. Their shoes fell on linoleum: they had entered the kitchen, obviously attracted to Rainman's corpse. They ground plate shards beneath their feet, and after that, the sound of ripping meat, cracking bone, and slurping tentacles echoed flatly in the room.

Shade gritted her teeth. Not only had the Puppeteer used Rainman's mother to defile him, it had raided his sanctuary to reap his flesh. She would have spared him. He would have spent his life in a harness, breeding and donating blood. But the zombies had won.

She wished she could shoot them, just run through and blast, watching heads explode, feeling the warm sleet of blood and brain matter. She would hack off a fat tentacle and wrap it around her neck like a trophy. She would paint her face with their blood.

No, she thought, and she grasped the pentagram. She shut her eyes and meditated, trying to concentrate on Frost's face, screaming and ablaze. The skyline negative was still burnt into her vision. Roman's castle was there. Frost's beach, too. Both disintegrated into the ocean, into the stomach acids of the earth. The granules diffused, and two dreams dissolved in the sea.

Beneath blankets the color and scent of bluebells, Grace dozed beside Frost. She nestled into the crook of his shoulder, hand resting on his chest, hair splashed against his neck. Her breasts pressed into his ribs, and her leg crossed over his. She still smelled salty from their sex.

The bedroom was crowded with dressers, armoires, and dressing tables with oval mirrors and rosewood drawers. Vases of fake marigolds, dahlias, and other plastic flowers covered every surface, scented with perfume. Candles of cherry and watermelon glowed atop an oak chest. The combined fragrance reminded Frost of a funeral home. It reminded him of something buried deep in the ravines of his past: his mother, wilted in her coffin, painted to look alive.

She died when he was seven. Aneurysm. Open casket. He had dreamt about that sleek ebony box, trapped inside, thrashing to get out, thumping his elbows, knees, and forehead, scratching until his nails cracked and splinters delved beneath them. He would wake, soaked in sweat and stinking of urine.

And now the room was closing in on him. It had started during sex. Frost had been on the bottom, and Grace had straddled him, hunching over to smother him with her bosom. His breath stagnated in her cleavage and in the pocket between their bellies, thick and unbearable. Grace wouldn't stop, so Frost gnashed her breast and rolled her over, pinning her to the bed. She moaned, shuddered, and held him against her, pulling him deep inside, clenching her muscles to trap him. Then it was over and he could breathe again.

But now, in the cold aftermath, in the smell of plastic flowers, the ceiling lowered inch by inch, waiting to suffocate him. The candles sucked all the oxygen from the room, turning the atmosphere anaerobic and burning.

Grace's hand and leg gained weight, trapping him, pinning him against the bed, and that familiar angst tightened around his chest.

Frost threw back the covers. He slid out from beneath Grace and dressed quickly.

She stretched and looked up at him. Blankets whispered around her. "Where are you going?"

"Out."

"What?" She propped herself up on her elbow. "You're not going anywhere. You're staying."

Frost buckled his belt and bent to tie his boots.

Grace grabbed his arm. "You're staying," she said, eyes set and hard.

Frost pulled away and finished knotting his laces. He swiped up his shirt and cape and headed for the door.

"Frost. *Frost!*"

In the hallway, he pulled on his shirt and donned his cape. Timbers groaned around him. The walls undulated like a throat swallowing food.

He climbed the stairs toward the exit, climbing, climbing, the staircase contracting and growing longer, a whole house of stairs. The seer's gaseous minions clawed for him on the fifth floor. They dragged him toward the passageway, disorienting him in their thunderclouds, in the flicker and twitch of lightning, images from the seer's nightmares, screams disjointing and disfiguring jaws, eyes frying opaque like eggs.

Frost's mother materialized, rippling like a reflection on water. She reached out to hug him, and the vapors became her burial dress, ethereal black. Her eyes stayed shut in the prune of her face, cheeks blushing a clownish red to match her coffin's lining.

She opened her mouth, those gaudy lips, teeth looking white and false. She tried to pull him in, tried to trap him.

Growling, Frost slashed her. The ghost did not disperse. She groped at his clothes, mouthing endearments, inviting him in. He tore away and sprinted up the stairs, gasping for breath. At the top, he gripped the doorknob. He almost turned it, just to get outside, just to breathe air and rain instead of digestive gasses and stale wood, instead of fake flowers and dust. Then he saw daylight trickling like ancient sand through the door's seal.

He almost opened it anyway. This building was his coffin, and he knew he would be there forever. The dry rot of boredom would eat at his soul, and his muscles would atrophy as the walls constrained him.

Frost shut his eyes and clenched his teeth. He dreamt of the island. The spray of surf, the swoop of bats. A glacier moon shedding ice crystals. And human blood, midnight drippings puddled in seashells.

He sighed with the retreating sea. He released the door handle and opened his eyes. Still the coffin, still the dust. He would escape it soon. He would punch through the wood and claw through the soil, claw until he rose from the ground, up into the air.

Frost sighed again. He set his jaw, straightened his cape, and then left the stairwell. His own room seemed spacious compared to Grace's, his bed less constricting. Less like a coffin, less like a death.

Twenty-Four

Ann and Michael turned the doorknob. A mouse scuttled in the mechanisms, making noise, but not enough to rouse Mr. Anonymous.

Ann opened the door, forgetting about the bag slung on the knob. Metal tinkled inside it. Michael's hand slipped away, just a draft along her forearm. Ann wanted to hole up again, but he nudged her forward and withdrew. The door swung open, and the tools chimed.

The room was dark, a beast's lair, the beast himself purring on the bed. Ann held out one hand like a walking stick. She wobbled, treading through the darkness, through purgatory, an emptiness; the floor was the only boundary, the rest just pitch black, stretching toward the door—where was the door? Ann could sense the bed to her left, something looming and breathing down her neck; the breath was hot and slick and gritty. She waded through it, still reaching, trying to be quiet. She touched the wall. And the darkness rippled behind her.

She scrabbled for the doorknob.

The darkness solidified and gained gravity behind her. It breathed against her neck, something like antifreeze that coagulated into axle grease on her tongue.

She found the door handle.

A fingernail grazed her throat. She stiffened, fossilized.

"Your blood," Mr. Anonymous said, rumbling like an engine. His fingernail divined the pulse of her artery. "Like melted pennies."

A callused vise-grip clamped her windpipe. Ann squealed, and Mr. Anonymous pulled her from the door, back into the darkness, into the abyss.

Twenty-five

Beneath the moon's skeletal grin, Shade stood on a strip of beach, staring at the silhouette of her father's castle. Instead of sand, the bones and ashes of the Holocaust covered the shore, unexplored and void of footprints. Cold waves lapped at her feet. They swept the ash into the sea, rippling black and silver into oblivion. No vessels, no boats, no beacons.

The breakers had already worn away a section of the castle, its cathedral. A turret was caving in as well, undermined by the sea and crashing into the ocean.

Shade ran, hoping to buttress the structure and to block the waves. She had no tools or columns. She would hold it up with her bare hands. If it crushed her, so be it. She would not watch it fall.

Somehow, the beach elongated. Shade kicked through water and foam, feet gashed open on rocks and seashells and splinters of bone. The castle grew farther away, dragged by the moon.

Around her, dust devils stirred the ash. The particles replicated brains, hearts, and lungs. Adopting a human disguise, each skull hid beneath gray skin, beneath a wreath of seaweed tendrils.

Handling cudgels of driftwood and seashell spades, the golems chased Shade down the beach. Seaweed reached for her and slimed the back of her neck. She turned and fired. One of her aggressors atomized, a puff of sand, but in a cyclone, it restructured. It grinned, showing pebbles of quartz. Shade kept running, her gun utterly useless.

Ahead of her, something crawled out of the sea. Something black with numerous tentacles. Something like a squid. Droves of them, flopping forward, glistening in the moonlight, pulsating with alien breath. They assembled skeletons of driftwood and shaped bodies of wet sand around them. Like puppeteers, they attached their tentacles to the wooden bones and pulled the bodies to their feet.

The closest puppet whipped its tentacle at Shade. She caught it and yanked. The squid pulled free, and its host crumbled, disgorging a jellyfish heart. The sea monster wrapped around and suctioned to Shade's arm. At the base of its tentacles, flesh unfolded around a serrated beak. The jaws gnashed Shade's leather sleeve and gashed her flesh. Its disease polluted her blood.

Shade pressed her gun against the squid's forehead and fired. The monster exploded, leaving a quivering mass of black and red, splintered with the white fragments of its internal shell. Shade tossed the squid into the waves, where it floated like an empty bag. She shivered and held her arm. Infected with Puppeteer spawn, the wound festered and bled. It would not heal. And soon, her flesh would melt from her bones.

She had less than ten minutes.

The puppets and golems surrounded her, moaning.

She shot two more squids and cackled as they burst into inky entrails. Then the tentacles chained her. They jerked her arm, and she dropped her gun. She flexed, trying to free herself, but the contamination weakened her like anemia. Her knees trembled.

The puppets reached out to bite her, mouths stinking, full of disease. She shut her eyes.

The wave hurled them against rocks. Shade's ribs cracked against an outcropping, and mussel shells shredded her leather coat and skin. When the water receded, she lay atop a heap of sand and driftwood bones, the squids buried underneath, except for a few limp tentacles.

She stood, dizzy, side full of scrap metal and broken glass.

In new cyclones, more golems began to form. Shade staggered down the beach. Her faced sagged. Her arm blistered and popped. The poison worked fast.

Eventually, she reached the drawbridge of the castle. She lumbered beneath the spiky portcullis, through double doors, and up a spiral of black stone, passing a gargoyle that resembled her father. In every sconce, torches had blinked out, leaving only slats of moon through lancet windows and stained-glass panes leeched of color. No golems followed.

Through a window, Shade glimpsed them chipping away at the castle's foundation with scallop shells and hands. Waves crashed around them, black with white spray, dragging the loose sand into the mouth of the sea.

Shade collapsed on the stairs. The squid's poison sizzled in her veins. Black muck and crimson streaks dripped from the cuff of her sleeve, and scraps of skin floated in the mess, melting black around the edges.

She dragged herself to her feet and continued up the stairwell. She came to the throne room, tapestries flat against stone walls, once cardinal, now gray. From the roof, pebbles and debris showered the floor. Rusty suits of armor rattled and fell apart.

In the throne, her father's skeleton sat erect, his crown tarnished, its jewels fallen out.

Shade tried to go to him, tried to call his name, but she had no voice, and her legs could no longer support her. She collapsed and splattered the floor with her skin.

Roman's jaw unhinged. His bones shifted, slumped, and crumbled away.

Shade reached for him. From the highest armament to the lowest dungeon, her siren carried. It rang in empty wine glasses set on long dining tables draped with cloth. It echoed in bedchambers, behind the tapestries, and in the stomach of a rusty iron maiden. It rang, loud and clear, forever unanswered, forever unheard.

Roman's ashes whirled, and then settled on his throne.

On a dwindling foundation, the castle began to shift and slide. Ceiling stones fell, smashing canopied beds and racks of torture. Rock powdered, became ash, and dissolved into the sea, which rushed back in, washing the bones from the prison. The golems invaded those lower cells and chipped away at the limestone.

Shade's stomach ruptured, vomiting partially liquefied innards. She dropped to her knees, cradling her guts. Her intestines folded on the floor in a single rose. It was the castle's only color. The bloom furled and wilted to gray.

Shade closed her eyes and clutched her pentagram. The sea roared, the wind howled. Her face slid off her skull and wadded around her neck like double chins. Stone came down around her, then darkness, like waterfalls, like being drowned.

Part Two
City of Corpses

Flames flapped around Shade in red tanager wings, and Frost embraced her, lifted from the Haven's rooftop in a yin yang of fire and ice. They rose from the tomb of bricks and wood to blaze over the city. Frost began to melt and cast a mist of ice crystals and stars. He dripped flurries of rain, snow, slush, and hail. He held tighter, twining his limbs with hers, weightless now, here in the darkness beyond the Haven. And on the horizon, he could see the ocean. He could hear the waves, bringing an eternal note of sadness in.

Shade flapped her wings of flame and carried them ever closer.

But Frost dissolved, a trickle, a droplet, now steam. Shade's comet faded toward the horizon, and that eternal note of sorrow called, an old prayer from ocean to rain. It filled Frost's head with waves against naked shingles, a withdrawing roar that woke him up with his name.

"General Frost!"

Footsteps. Loud, hurried—someone in his apartment.

"General!"

He recognized the voice, like the rustle of dead leaves. It belonged to Graves, the day watchman. The footsteps stopped at his bedroom.

Without riling his bedsprings, Frost moved to the door. He had left it open, always open, but his appearance was sudden enough. Graves took a step back, startled. His cheeks resembled old burial plots of settled earth. The plots grew shallower as Graves eyed Frost's bare chest and erection.

"What?" Frost asked, struggling the urge to run a hand over his face and smooth out the wrinkles. "What is it?"

Graves avoided his eyes.

Coward.

Aside from Edward, the Sextons hailed Frost. He offered them freedom, a world outside the smothering walls of the Haven, which they so dutifully protected. Graves conformed to whoever held power. He was two-faced, solemn and obedient on the surface, sneering and traitorous beneath the dirt.

"It's the puppets," Graves said. "They've breached."

"Let me dress."

Graves left the apartment, and Frost contemplated in the darkness. The percussion of semiautomatic gunfire found him, even through the walls, pipes, and insulation. He had not planned for the contamination so soon. He had wanted to control the infection, to force Shade into the exodus in case she changed her mind. Perhaps now she would not get the chance.

Frost donned his uniform and checked his 9mm: full magazine, ten rounds. He had several backups. He holstered the firearm and left.

In the hallway, the gunfire amplified. Graves had snuffed the lanterns, but he carried a flashlight, spilling an artificial sunbeam onto the floor and walls, casting huge shadows that jumped and guttered. The building shifted its bones and complained, angry that the men had disturbed its slumber, feverish from the zombie epidemic.

At the staircase, Graves started to ascend. Frost glanced down at the snare, where he had expected the disease to begin. The night hid in the Haven's bowels. It had nothing to conceal.

On the fourth-floor landing, two Sextons, Edward and James, were firing upward. Daylight, faded to nothing at this depth, had leaked into the shaft. Zombie viruses poured forth, endowed with tentacles to latch onto healthy cells. Edward and James dispensed immunities, punching bullets into torsos and limbs.

"They got in from the roof!" Graves yelled over the fusillade. "We think they might've climbed the fire escape!"

It seemed plausible, but how had the puppets reached the escape? They weren't intelligent enough to boost each other, nor to construct a makeshift ladder, unless brainpower had accompanied regenerative abilities. It didn't matter at this point. They were in, and Frost had to manage them.

No gunshots echoed down from the penthouse. Shade was either hiding, absent, or dead. No way to tell; sunlight would incinerate anyone beyond the fifth-floor landing. But even under the cloak of night, Frost doubted he would attempt her rescue: the infection was forcing its way toward the humans—he knew his priorities.

"Come with me," he told Graves.

Down the hallway, they stepped inside apartment 403, the empty room before the snare and the refectory. Here, with the door closed, the gunshots were not as deafening.

"Bring barbwire," Frost said. "We must give the staircase thorns."

Graves refused to meet his eyes, looking instead at the wall behind him.

"Do you understand?" Frost asked.

"Yes, General."

"Good. Wake the others. Except Victor and Cavanaugh—and Bain. They've earned their rest."

"Yes, Sir."

Graves followed orders too well; he did not even question. No matter. Frost had told the truth: Victor had earned his rest. The other two would just impede, Cavanaugh with his defiance, Bain with his insanity.

At the stairwell, Graves descended. Frost watched as the building swallowed him, then drew his gun and joined Edward and James. His shots added a strange misstep to the rhythm and bursts of their M16s, but his 9mm complemented the rifles perfectly: the automatics held back puppets, and the pistol dispatched them. Only a rifle would have worked better.

Frost grinned. He waited for Edward to chop into a zombie and then stole the kill with a headshot. He kept mental score, not surprised that the Sexton was losing. Frost could even take James' scores, not missing a beat while reloading.

Bodily gasses and the smell of Puppeteer blood began to permeate the shaft. Corpses piled on the stairs, trampled beneath the survivors. Soon, carcasses tumbled over the banister, some alive and thrashing as they crashed into the first-floor snare.

When the troops arrived with a bundle of barbwire, Frost stationed a firing squad several steps up from the landing. Edward and James kept their M16s, and Undertakers Liam and Fry were equipped with Glocks. All four soldiers were expendable.

As the firing squad held off zombies, Graves and an Undertaker named Thomas formed a construction crew. They nailed barbwire to the balusters and then wrapped it around a two-by-four, which they nailed to the wall to create a fence.

"Make a snare!" Frost instructed, and the Sextons begin to spin more barbwire down toward the landing, weaving it between the balusters, imitating the spastic web of a black widow.

On the stairs above, James cried out. A skinhead in a sleeveless jean jacket coiled tentacles around the Sexton's neck and forearm. The zombie throttled him, crunching ulna and radius. It snatched his M16 and aimed it at the firing squad.

Frost almost laughed.

The first burst of lead hornets stung Edward in the chest, driving him back against the balustrade. Many hornets went astray, drilling the walls and the underside of the staircase like carpenter bees. A few hit Liam and pushed him into the fence. Fry hit the barbwire too, cheeks potholed, teeth shattered. A baluster busted, and the fence began to sag.

The skinhead unleashed another hive, this one directed at the construction crew.

"Get down!" Frost yelled, diving into the hallway.

Only Thomas failed to dodge the swarm. It knocked his head back, popping his eye and perforating his skull diagonally.

While the skinhead provided cover, more zombies attacked the firing squad. Edward managed to scramble beneath the fence, but Liam and Fry were caught up in tentacles. The feelers stretched Liam, rending his arm in a spray of blood. The puppet that entangled Fry gored him with a broken baluster. Whether out of luck or knowledge, it stabbed his heart, and a brief flurry of fireflies flushed the walls.

Still wearing his hardhat, a construction worker picked up Edward's M16, which looked small in his jackhammer arms. The Puppeteer had reconstructed Hardhat's lower jaw, black and gristly compared to his sunburned face. His bottom teeth had grown into tusks, like twisted rebar, curling over his upper lip. He wielded the weapon like a nail gun, crucifying Edward facedown on the stairs.

Two more puppets filched pistols from Liam and Fry. They pressed forward, flattening the fence and executing Graves. Thomas tried to retaliate, his face and brain still mending, his eye wilted like a jellyfish, dead on the dune of his cheekbone. He shot the closest zombie in the chest, just above the turtle logo on the breast of its shirt. Unfazed, the zombie splattered James' head all over the stairs. The unfinished web of barbwire snagged bloody bugs of scalp and brain.

Minus flamethrowers, the puppets were copying the Undertakers' purging strategy: slaughter the mob with an automatic rifle and then kill the individual with a handgun. How had they learned the tactic? From observation? Frost could think of no other way.

The skinhead depleted his magazine, and Frost pivoted onto the landing, shielding half his body behind the wall. One shot and the zombie dropped. It released James, and he plunged over the railing, neck broken and flopping. The M16 fell too, useless without ammo.

Hardhat swiveled his rifle. Frost ducked away as lead nails bit plaster next to his face. He pressed his back to the wall, and two zombies confronted him.

They had fallen into the snare and had climbed out, their clothes in tatters. The barrage had camouflaged their footsteps. They had snuck up. He didn't have time to shoot. The first one was on him, a confusion of dishwater hair, anaconda tentacles, and nicotine-yellowed teeth. The other zombie went past, headed for the warren, for the smell of red meat.

A feeler arrested Frost's biceps. One went for his throat. He punctured it with his fangs, but it curled around anyway. It tightened and crumpled his windpipe. The zombie snapped at his face, belching gasses and spittle from a road-kill gut.

Blackness plagued Frost's sight. Oil congested his sinuses and skull. His jaw muscles loosened, his body relaxed, and in his stupor, true darkness spawned, the eternal night. It opened its wings to envelop him, silky, flowing, liquid, and he drifted out, hushed in the waves, in the folds of a gothic rose. No smothering walls. No puppets. Just coffin velvet caressing anesthetized flesh: calm, quiet, and everlasting.

Frost's eyelids fluttered and closed. His gun began to slip from his hand. This was his island.

Boom!—the zombie's head erupted, an explosion of bone, brain, and ratty hair, misted black. The zombie lurched sideways, carried by the blast. Disembodied tentacles slid away from Frost's neck, and blood flooded his skull. He staggered along the wall, pustules of gore draining down his cheek. He caught himself and squinted into the stairwell.

Cavanaugh sprinted across the landing, shotgun blasts lighting up his face. "Come on, you fuckers!" He discharged his last shell and rolled into the hallway just as M16 rounds pocked the floor.

Suppressing his vertigo, Frost whirled toward the other zombie, gun extended. He saw double: the zombie and its doppelganger had made it halfway to their destination, each in a different hallway. Frost shot one and both toppled.

He faced his lieutenant, proud that his aim had not disclosed his dizziness. The two halls finally converged, bringing Cavanaugh into strong focus.

Leaning against the wall, the lieutenant jammed red shells into the shotgun's breech. Across his chest, more shells lined a bandolier. "Why didn't you wake me?"

When Frost spoke, he made sure not to wheeze. "You have a history of disobeying orders, Lieutenant. I cannot trust you."

"I saved your life."

Frost's face iced over, perfectly solemn, perfectly cool. "I spared yours."

The puppet with the turtle shirt peeked into the hallway. It pointed its stolen pistol and—*boom!*—its neck vaporized, along with its lower jaw. The body dropped, and Cavanaugh lowered his shotgun.

"Well, General, what's your command?"

Frost slammed in a new magazine and jacked back the slide. "We reclaim our staircase. And then we wait for nightfall."

Cavanaugh nodded. "Yes, sir."

He led the way, shotgun roaring.

Twenty-seven

Mr. Anonymous had gagged her with a rag soaked in motor oil. He had strapped the rag down with a belt and had bound her to a wooden chair, wrists knotted to the armrests, ankles shackled to the legs, rope yellow and coarse.

Pushed into the closet, Ann could not tip the chair backward or sideways. If she tried to go forward, Mr. Anonymous would only right her.

He was studying her now, holding a candle over her head. "Very beautiful," he declared, running a fingernail along her jaw.

Mr. Anonymous was nude. His chest was a battleground of scars and cicatrices, old burns and lacerations. The flaws had been shaped into symbols, a meandering cobra, a flesh-tone crow, worms, leeches, and fleas. He had made them himself, Ann realized, some terrible illustrated man. And as he leaned in to examine her throat, the self-inflicted images came alive. A scraggly tree shook leafless branches. A skull moved its jaws.

He pressed upward on Ann's chin, tilting her head to one side. "Hmm. Looks like someone has already had a taste. But I don't mind leftovers."

He scraped his nail over the bite mark on Ann's neck, and she recoiled, shocked with sparks of pain, fear, and pleasure. Maybe he would bite her. Maybe he would stop the ache.

Mr. Anonymous pulled his hand back and grinned, the same grin that reminded her of a jackal.

"Jumpy," he said.

Then his hand shot out.

Ann winced, waiting for the smack. But his palm halted inches from her face, casting a heavy shadow. Mr. Anonymous laughed.

"It's because I'm a stranger, isn't it? That's why you're so afraid."

Ann could list a few other reasons.

"Well, let me introduce myself then. I am Victor. And you are?"

Ann said nothing. She just shivered and wished that she were clothed, wished she were with Ellie—wished he would just bite her and take out the pins of withdrawal that pricked her stomach, make her orgasm swell into an earthquake.

Victor smiled. "Well, I guess your name really doesn't matter, does it? After all, if a farmer names his sheep, he might never butcher them." He lifted a lock of her hair. "Delicious color," he said, playing it between his fingers like the world's smallest violin. "It matches your wounds."

Even when she had first lowered herself into Victor's front room, where candles had burned, Ann had not gotten a good look at the many scrapes, gashes, and bruises marring her body. She could only feel them. But now, as Victor lowered his head toward her stomach, the injuries demanded attention.

When Ann was little, she had tried to pick up a feral calico. The cat had hissed and had tagged the back of her hand, leaving three red trenches garnished with peels of skin. She had cried, not because of the pain, but because the kitty hated her. Now, similar trenches scribbled her entire body. Like so many vaginas, several menstruated. Others had begun to crust.

Victor flicked his tongue along a still-weeping cut on her side, in the soft spot between pelvis and ribs. Ann shuddered. Michael had always tickled her stomach that way, but Victor's tongue was so chilly, the tongue of a morgue corpse. It stung the lesion.

He pressed his lips to the cut and began to suck. Ann moaned into her gag, breathing heavier now, feeling wet between her legs. Her skin tautened, trying to break the suction of his frigid kiss, but it only managed to split developing scabs.

After circling her navel, Victor moved slowly up her belly. Ann shut her eyes, and suddenly it was Michael kissing her, his lips dead and bereft of sensuality, wanting only to feed and to taste. She concentrated on Ellie, on her red hair and freckles. But every time Ellie's eyelids opened, they revealed empty sockets. And Ellie's stomach had deflated. A C-section incision smirked along her lower abdomen.

Victor cupped one of her breasts. "Petite," he said, and although his smile frightened and aroused her, Ann would have kneed him in the crotch had her legs not been secured.

He tongued her nipple, which was erect. From the terror. From the cold. From the pleasure. He closed his mouth around it and suckled. That part of her tit had always been extremely sensitive, so much so that she could barely endure stimulation, even during sex. It had always felt like rubbing raw nerve endings, and she wondered how mothers could stand it, nursing their young.

Victor was so gentle, though, tongue tiptoeing around her aureole, gliding quickly over the tip of her nipple, smoother than lotion. Energy lit up her nerves, conducted through the lightning rod of her spine, tingling to her fingertips and toes and setting blazes in her breast and belly. But the voltage had an edge to it, a fringe of static electricity, gritty, crackling, and unpleasant.

Ann retreated into her imagination, where once again Victor became Michael. Better that her husband pleased her, even pale and flesh hungry. Michael looked up at her as he nursed. A smile arched his upper lip and bushy eyebrow, an expression very close to his foreplay face, the one he would assume before sucking her toes, or something else that made her squeal and laugh.

Then the smile turned greedy.

He bit down.

Like the silver needle of a piercing gun, Victor's fang lanced the brown bump of tissue. Ann yelped. She bucked and tried to knock him away, but as with a leech, only a flame could remove him.

He withdrew his tooth and continued to suck, drawing out red milk. Ann fainted into the pain. Not completely, but enough to blear the edges. Tears ran hot against her cheek. And still she felt wet, muscles aching around the emptiness of her vagina.

With a pop, Victor pulled away from her teat and licked off his bloody lipstick. "They say it tastes like wine," he said, leering, "but I say it tastes like pennies." He dabbed at Ann's trickling nipple and cleaned his finger in his mouth.

Holding it high in the closet, Victor tipped the candle. Wax bubbled at the lip of the crater and fattened, fattened, suspended for a moment before it fell. The droplet plopped onto Ann's bosom, and more globules followed. They dribbled down her cleavage in scalding gobs.

Behind her eyelids, Michael gloated over her, holding his dripping penis with his left hand. The wax was his semen. Each sperm wriggled its tail and tried to burrow into Ann's skin, tried to inseminate her pores. The ooze congealed, and the sperm slowed, cooled, and died. It began to itch.

Michael chuckled. His wedding ring was not on his finger. In fact, his skin had paled so much the ring's tan line had disappeared.

Ann sobbed quietly into her gag, even as she gyrated against the chair. Her husband had never degraded her like this, had never used her like some kind of rag. It made her feel small and dirty. Especially with Ellie watching them from the bed, her one eye cognizant, her expression blank. Above the headboard, the Felix clock swished his tail. The constant tick-tock had deranged him. It made his eyes go haywire: back and forth, back and forth, tick-tock, tick-tock, tick.

Prancing naked, Michael went to the dresser and grabbed a scalpel off the top.

He was going to cut Ellie. He was going to gouge out her other Irish eye.

Ann flexed her jaws and fists. Was this why Michael had coaxed her out of the closet? So he could humiliate her and blind her sister? So he could take the baby for himself? If so, she wouldn't let him. She would kill him. Ireland was hers.

New tears steamed from her eyes, and when she returned to Victor's room, it was he who held the scalpel, only it was a knife, seven inches long and notched into shark's teeth near the hilt. And he was approaching her, not Ellie.

Victor stopped halfway across the room and cocked his head.

In the hallway, someone yelled and banged on doors. Other men shouted back, and several pairs of footsteps clamored through the hall. No one came for Victor. No one pounded on his door, and after a while of silence, he came back to Ann.

"Whatever it is," he said, "it must not be important."

He held the knife tip over the candle, and the flame searched the blade's underside, curling around, curious to explore the top. The metal began to blacken.

Victor leered at Ann over his miniature forge. "Instead of a name," he said, "I'll give you a brand. A 'V,' for Victor."

She should have guessed his intentions well before he stated them. Her trek through the barbwire had exhausted her though, and her brain had turned into a useless lump, shocked to death in a bath of cerebral fluids and neuron lightning. Watching the knife heat up stirred those neurons back into motion. Her brain began to cook, eyes bugling from the pressure.

Once the tip of the knife glowed, Victor set down the candle and lowered the blade toward Ann's bust. She squirmed, reared, tried to shred her gag with a shriek, but the knife kept coming. Its aura of heat touched her, grew hotter and hotter until it reconstituted Michael's semen. Again, the sperm embarked on their journey, tunneling to the follicles of micro-fine hair, some migrating through the valley of her sternum to solidify just before the fine white sand of her midriff.

Victor stamped his initial into the upper mound of her breast.

Ann's scream grew razor blades, hacking trachea and vocal chords. Victor's blade grew cold, numbing, and a blizzard took her, wrapped her in its deadening embrace.

Transient, the whiteout thawed, and Ann could feel again. The V smoldered, one diagonal curved like the blade. The burn was second degree.

"Mmm," Victor said. "Smells like barbeque."

Ann could smell nothing. She could barely breathe through all the snot, struggling for just enough oxygen to fuel her consciousness. She had to stay awake. She had to get loose and stop Michael before he took her baby.

Too late, little orphan. He was so close that his words chilled her ear. *Too late.*

He was lying. He had broken the trust, his ring had disintegrated, and he was lying.

Ann ignored him.

The rope. There had to be some way through the rope. She had to concentrate on that. She had to get free. If only she could stay conscious. If only she could resist her addiction, her need.

Victor holstered the knife and set the candle atop the dresser. He came back holding something in his fist: a penny. He brought it toward Ann's brand. She shied away, but he pressed the penny against her. The metal was a glacier disc rimmed with magma.

"Feel good?" Victor asked.

Ann exhaled heavily through her nose, blowing bubbles and strings of mucus. Michael had left, leaving only the forensic evidence of his semen. It was dried now, but still traceable.

His absence did not relieve her. If he wasn't here, he was elsewhere, anywhere. Hunting Ellie, hunting Ireland.

Victor placed the penny in his mouth and savored it. "I've got a treat for you," he said. He grabbed the bag from the closet door and set it in front of the chair. He unzipped it. All sorts of tools poked out: small clamps, zip ties, scissors, a horseshoe band of aluminum spiked with thumbscrews—a hammer.

Victor chose a pair of vise grips.

"Are you ready?" he asked, bending over her. "'Cause now it's time to have some real fun." Smiling, he opened the vise grips. And then he clamped them shut.

Twenty-eight

Done with Rainman and his wife, the zombies evacuated the apartment, all except one. It ransacked the other parts of the dwelling, breaking things, beating on doors, harmless.

The day waned, and the sun advanced its army over the western mountains, searching out other quarry. If not for the rain clouds, the solar star would have bloodied the horizon.

Shade sailed on a thin current of sleep, not truly resting. This deep in the building, the rain made only a murmur, a lullaby, a melancholy warmth. It grieved the night. It grieved Roman. On the evening of her father's death, Frost had pulled Shade aside, into the privacy and lamplight of the hallway. He held out Roman's pentagram.

"We thought we had confined the refugees," he said. "But one remained. He had a stake. I'm sorry." Frost closed her hand over the necklace.

She had missed his cryptogram, his subtext, the sanguine glint in his eye. But Shade did not need to see who had killed her father. She knew, and she knew why.

And she would wreak her revenge.

Ω

Thump—something hit the closet door. Shade woke, listening, wondering if the noise had been an illusion. It came again, louder, real: *thump.*

Shade modeled the green stink like clay, fashioning a corpse, its eye dangling, its cheeks chewed into ribbons from the inside out. Its lungs remained slurry, each breath gurgling phlegm. The zombie clobbered the door with its fist. Its knuckles did not mush, as would clay. The zombie struck again.

Shade could have shot it; the door was hollow. But the bullet would have left a peephole for the daylight. Too late, anyway. The light knew where she was, and its force incarnate was bashing into her final hideaway.

A tentacle pushed the coat from under the door, letting in sunshine, grayed by clouds and weakened by sunset. It tested the ground for Shade's boot, stringing slime. She drew her knife. It sheared easily through the feeler and carved a line on the floor. The tentacle pulled out, spitting like a broken pen.

Shade stuffed the coat into place and wiped her blade on its sleeve. She shrouded herself in the other jackets and waited.

The puppet had stopped breathing.

Dead?

Not likely.

Thump: a tentacle whapped the door. It moved slowly against it, scuffing, like a snake winding on a wooden surface. It gripped the knob. It pulled, it turned—the door began to open. An ax of sunlight cleaved Shade's recess, colorless and dead.

She wrenched the door shut. She held her side of the handle, using her strength as a lock. The tentacle was muscular, the metal polished. She had to use both hands to stop it.

Never had she thought the zombies capable of opening a door. Bashing through it, yes. But opening it?

The tentacle released the knob. Shade held it, and the zombie continued to hammer. Wood began to give. More puppets gathered around the noise, the battering ram reassembled.

The door would only hold for so long. It would fracture and fail, and the Puppets would pull her into the light. Her only hope: nightfall.

More feelers pushed beneath the door. They wrapped around Shade's boot, tasting leather and dirt. Unsheathing her knife, she knelt, slashed, missed one. It cuffed her wrist and yanked. Her fingers buckled against the wood, and she dropped the knife. Sunlight burned her knuckles as three other tentacles braided up her arm.

She screeched and pulled her hand out of the light. The tentacles tugged against her, and her shoulder began to part from its socket. They would dismember her.

Her knife lay in a cleaver blade of light. She grabbed its hilt with her free hand, but a tentacle slapped around her forearm. She gnawed through it and severed the feelers on her arm and boot. Freed, she stepped back.

Without the coat, the gap below the door allowed a right triangle of light. Shade searched for something solid to block the opening.

Above the clothes bar, a shelf held an array of items: a baseball cap, a furled umbrella, a Frisbee, and few other objects she could not identify by touch. Screwed into the closet walls, two blocks of wood supported the shelf, which remained unfastened and removable. Shade tipped the contents onto the floor and swiped the board.

The doorknob turned again.

Shade dropped the shelf and reengaged her hand lock. The knob slipped in her fist and the door jerked. The light hewed at her sleeve, but only for an instant before she shut it out. Her opponent resigned.

Shade stooped quickly and covered the gap with the shelf. She jammed her foot against it, grabbed the doorknob, and leaned back, securing the lid of her coffin.

Then a piece of beveled steel chopped through the door.

The puppets had found an ax.

Under the watchful muzzle of Hardhat's M16, three puppets had occupied the landing. Brandishing broken balusters, more came down the stairs.

Graves and Edward had crawled into the spools of barbwire. They played dead, trying to heal. Liam and Thomas did not have to pretend. Bitten, both had hemorrhaged to death. Skin and organs steamed around their skeletons in a grisly soup. Some tendons still attached muscle to bone, but the muscles were sloughing off, runny with fat.

Using the shotgun, Cavanaugh annihilated the nearest zombie on the landing. The ghoul's head evaporated. Frost destroyed the other two.

Out of thirty rounds, Hardhat's M16 still contained twelve. Cavanaugh took two to the biceps, but the third in the burst missed him. Letting the shotgun dangle in his ruined arm, he decapitated the gorgons with his machete, pushing them back from the landing, away from Edward and Graves.

Frost shot Hardhat's helmet. He dented it, knocked it askew.

With a second burst, Hardhat erased most of Cavanaugh's other limb, which hung now by a piece of leather and skin. The lieutenant's machete clanked to the landing, rendering him unarmed. He kicked at the puppets, and tentacles detained his leg.

Rotating, Hardhat tried to tack Frost to the wall. Frost darted. He sheltered himself in the hallway as holes appeared in the lath.

"Get them off me!" Cavanaugh yelled.

A sash of tentacles attempted to crush him around the waist. Another tentacle stabbed at his chest with a piece of wood, but Cavanaugh crossed his arms. The wood bit into them, stubbing bone.

Frost had always imagined killing the lieutenant himself, in a duel. Shade would have asked too many questions though, markedly more than when Roman had died. She knew Frost loathed Cavanaugh. He didn't conceal that razor of contempt. He was too suspect.

This puppet, however—it proved the perfect murder weapon. Frost would kill with sheer neglect. No fingerprints, no evidence, no questions. Just two witnesses, Graves and Edward. Frost would have to still their tongues. He needed them though. He and Victor could not emigrate alone. Not even with the help of Grace, Bain, and Shade.

He reloaded casually, letting Cavanaugh suffer and growl. Frost had a spare magazine, but insisted on refilling his spent one.

"Shoot them!"

Frost sighted Cavanaugh's forehead. *He had been bitten*, Frost thought. *As had Liam. I ended his misery.* He had lied to Shade before. About who had killed her father. He could do it again.

He shot the zombie instead.

Cavanaugh hit the floor and scooted away from oncoming adversaries. So pathetic.

Frost ducked onto the landing, avoiding Hardhat's last storm of nails. He tossed his 9mm to Edward, who had completely repaired beneath the wire. Graves had not; his head was still misshapen from bullet wounds, eyes unfocused, coordination poor.

Cavanaugh's shotgun lay under a corpse. Frost plucked it up and—*boom!*—he was staring through the guts of a zombie. Part of its colon slouched into the hollow, but black cords and membranes enmeshed it, hoisted it up. In less than a second, intestines redeveloped, growing like a Fourth of July snake.

Frost thrust the butt of the gun into the zombie's forehead twice, hard, driving bone splinters into the dark heart of the Puppeteer. Intestinal restoration ceased. The puppet collapsed.

The *blam! blam! blam!* of Frost's pistol joined the fight. From the safety of his briars, Edward weeded out the puppets crowding the stairs. Tentacles jabbed at him with stakes. He shot the Puppeteers, and the spikes clonked like wind chimes on the steps.

Hardhat discarded the M16 and raked aside barbwire, digging for Edward.

Frost booted the machete toward Cavanaugh. The lieutenant's arm had recovered enough. He and Frost tackled the next surge of marauders, beheading bodies, demolishing brains, succeeding. Cavanaugh shed his bandolier and gave it to Frost. He handed over the shells in his pocket as well, thirty rounds in all.

Hardhat moved the last spiral of wire. Edward shot. The zombie's helmet jumped off. Rippling with biceps, triceps, and other muscles, three tentacles disentangled, coming from fleshy black ports in Hardhat's glossy scalp. The smallest member snapped off a baluster for a stake.

Edward's next shot struck an empty chamber: clack. Hardhat assailed him with a wooden fang. But a bullet put a period through his eye. Graves held the smoking gun.

As Cavanaugh helped Graves to his feet, Frost covered him. Edward took Graves' magazines and joined Frost. Together, they decimated the invaders.

"Finish the snare!" Frost commanded, reloading.

Seven shells and going fast.

Behind him, Cavanaugh picked up the hammer and pulled out the nails of the original fence. Graves looped a strand of barbwire around the handrail, and Cavanaugh nailed it down. Unlike the balusters, the rail would withstand weight and aggression. It would have to.

"Faster!" Frost said, looking over his shoulder. He flattened a gas pump attendant in a navy-blue uniform. Four shells now.

After braining an old lady wearing a green robe, white socks, and hair curlers, Edward stopped to refill his 9mm: his last magazine.

Three shells and counting.

Graves added a second wire beneath the first. Cavanaugh fixed it to the railing and then started the web, working around the skeletons of Liam and Thomas. He tracked through their stew, stamping gory footprints and smears.

Two shells.

"I'm out!" Edward said.

With half her scalp peeled away, a blonde waitress hurled a knife of baluster. Edward stepped aside, but the baluster pierced his shoulder. He yapped, clutched his arm, tottered. A trio of tentacles tried to rope him but he retreated, running along the wall over the wire. He made it to the landing, where Graves was constructing another fence to corral the snare.

One shell: Frost scattered it into the belly of the masses. The charge did not repel them for long. Tentacles reached out.

"Done!" Cavanaugh announced, ducking under Graves' fence and finishing the last snarl of web.

Frost launched into a side somersault over the fencing, cape flapping, legs extended and opening like a Japanese fan. Octopi feelers chased him.

His arm arced, pointed with a silver blade, and he cut the octopi legs. They swam away in a smokescreen of ink.

On touchdown, Frost's legs closed to a shoulder-width stance. He made no more noise than a wasp settling on a woman's skin. He gave Cavanaugh the shotgun and took his pistol from Edward. Installing a full magazine, he turned to the snare.

Zombies rushed it: two black men and a clown, stripped of his wig and shoes but not of his sherbet suit or the cherry of his nose. A whole circus of puppets rioted behind them. The handrail groaned, bowed. The fence held.

Frost did brain surgery on the rabid clown, and the zombie did a pratfall from which he would never recuperate.

Too soon, the zombies would learn to crawl through the wire.

Frost holstered his gun. "Lieutenant. You and Edward hold them back. Add more wire and keep shooting."

Cavanaugh stared at him.

"Do you understand?"

"You were going to let me die."

Frost gave him a cold, blank expression. "Hold them back. Protect your home." He motioned to Graves and said, "Come with me."

They started down the steps, but Cavanaugh stopped them. "Where are you going?"

Frost stopped. He spoke over his shoulder: "We leave tonight." He let his words hang in the air for a moment. Then he and Graves continued downstairs.

It was time to wake Victor.

Like a pair of molars, the vise grips chomped Ann's nipple. The pain grew its own teeth and chewed through her. She tried to howl and bit her gag, bit until her incisors hurt.

Victor smirked. After a few seconds, he unlocked the steel jaws. A hot breath of pain radiated from her nipple.

"Pain and pleasure," he told her.

Lubing his finger with saliva, he probed between her legs, *Michael* probed between her legs, adding a tongue of ecstasy to the teeth of torture. His grin did not turn perverse, no sexual excitement. He seemed to get more enjoyment out of tampering with her wiring, mixing the signals, caressing, tormenting. Nor did Michael have an erection. He was naked, but no erection.

Victor closed his other hand over Ann's throat. Blood accumulated in her head and she grew drunk on it, faint yet heavy with pressure. Unconsciousness corroded her vision, sweet, sweet oblivion. No one waited for her there. Not Ellie, not Ireland, not even Michael. Just darkness.

Victor slipped a finger inside her, and she rode that one high note of bliss into the void. Then Victor let go of her throat, and consciousness rushed in. She clambered from the darkness, suddenly afraid of the eyes that watched her there, afraid of the things that slithered past. Victor scared her, but those prowlers were worse. Even guided by candlelight, she could not completely escape them, trapped in the blackout, in the numbing craw of misery.

"That gag looks uncomfortable," Victor said; Michael echoed him, their voices overlapping. "Let me adjust it."

Undoing the belt, Victor crammed the rag all the way into Ann's mouth. A corner of it covered her airway, threatening to choke her and make her retch. Victor trussed her jaw with the belt, circling it under her chin and over her head. He cinched it so tight the gag squashed her tongue.

Victor rummaged through his bag of tools. "Now where's my—ah hah!" He held a small tackle box filled with fishhooks. He selected a hook gussied with red and black feathers, an insect gifted with a barbed stinger. Victor made her wear it like an earring on her left lobe.

"Pretty," he commented. "Beautiful." With his index finger, he sorted through the other hooks. "You know, I used to love to fish. My grandfather taught me, used to take me out on his boat. He'd get drunk, and I'd get all the bass."

In the light, he examined a hook that must have been used to catch shark. He put it back and continued to search.

"I killed my grandfather when I was twenty-seven."

The next hook was small, like some kind of germ specialized to impale and overrun healthy cells.

"I cut out his eyes and put him in a room full of broken glass. There was one path through the room. He never found it. So I shot him."

He put the metal germ back into the case.

"I loved my grandpa," he said, unsmiling. "But my parents ... let's just say I didn't show them any mercy."

Victor decided on a hook of medium size. He deposited one in the skin over each knuckle of Ann's right hand, starting with her pinky, excluding her thumb. He planted more up the length of her forearm, stopping level with her abdomen.

Out of his bag, he pulled a needle, tied to a reel of fishing line. Victor ran the needle through the eye of each hook, threading them together.

"I could patch your wounds," he said. "Would you like that?"

He licked one of the deeper vaginas on Ann's stomach, hydrating the crusted blood. With his thumb, he wiped away the moisture and then began to suture the wound. Ann felt no more than pinpricks.

When the sharp metal passed through her punctured nipple, it bit like a stinging nettle. The cord tickled slightly as he pulled it through and roped it to her earring. He unrolled extra line and severed it from the reel, then tied the end to the hook in Ann's pinky knuckle.

"By the time I'm finished," he said, "you'll unbutton yourself if you even drop your arm." He touched her lips and inspected her face. "Hmm, I'll need a bigger hook here." He brought the needle to her mouth. "Time to zip it shut."

Ann turned her head and bared her teeth. Victor pinched her lips shut, but she managed to pry them open, shaking her head to thwart him.

Victor needled her brand. She mewled, rolled her eyes, and cried.

"Are you going to behave?"

Ann nodded: Yes, yes—oh God, please stop!

"Good." He grabbed her by the chin and aligned her head. "Now hold still."

He poised the needle, ready to penetrate. Someone knocked on the front door and called his name. It was the Iceman.

Victor set down the needle and thread. "Don't make a sound."

He left and closed the door.

Ann tested the rope that tied her hands to the armrest: unbreakable, as was the piece that fettered her feet.

From the living room, where Victor and the Iceman were conversing, winter encroached the bedroom. On the carpet, rime crystallized. Ann's breaths haunted the closet.

He would apprehend her this time. No pitfall would save her. No Mistress. Ann was chained. Ann was vulnerable. And if the Iceman didn't come, Victor would. Who knew what other devices he had in store?

The rope. She had to shuck the rope.

"It's pointless," Michael said. "I've won."

He was behind her, though that was impossible. Her chair was backed against the wall. No person, no matter how thin, could fit. Brawny, Michael was no skeleton.

"I've got Ireland in a safe place," he continued, "a special place. You'll never see her, you'll never know her. She's gone. Give in."

A tear formed against Ann's eyelid. *I hate you*, she thought. The tear swelled, trembled. *I hate you*. She blinked, and Hell's mercury coursed down her cheek.

Using her thumb, Ann divorced the ring from her finger. Her hand was very small without it, feeble. She let the ring drop anyway.

Victor had told her to be quiet, but the ring clunked on the floor, as if solid gold and heavy with regret. No one entered. In the living room, the conversation did not stop. And Michael was gone.

Ann worried about him, about what he would do for vengeance. He would trip her up. She knew he would. Her heart was much lighter though, an abscess drained. She had been summoning strength from the ring, and it had robbed her of her own. Her muscles had atrophied. But no longer. She flexed them and worked at the rope.

The armrest. It was pulling loose. The balusters were uprooting from their moorings, old glue breaking. She could dislodge it, use one hand to untie the other.

In the living room, the front door shut. Victor opened the bedroom. Beside him, the Iceman stood with eyes of cryogenic charm.

The ax put another hole in the coffin lid. Dusk slanted in. Shade had to elude it or be seared; a sunburn, superficial, but nasty nonetheless. She scooted closer to the knob, still using her foot to wedge the shelf against the bottom of the door.

A zombie pulled the ax from the cleft, and the steel squeaked against wood. The zombie chopped again, broadening the rift, and two tentacles came through. They suckered onto opposing sides of the hole and started to crack it open.

Shade buried herself in the coats. Two magazines: one in the gun, one in the belt. The sun's remains could not reach her so deep in the closet. If she dealt with the puppets, she could live until dark.

The tentacles cleared a window's worth of wood. Gaunt, wrinkled, and pale, the puppets beyond had been fashioned after corpses. One wore a disguise of crisped flesh: black, blistered, and cratered red. Its left eye had ruptured. Its hair was singed. Its true self, its skull, grimaced beneath the burn.

A group of feelers browsed the jackets for flesh. They leafed through the flannels and undressed a few hangers. A clammy sensor slicked Shade's neck. She lopped it off, knelt, trimmed another. Six more tentacles smacked the floor.

Shade let four bullets take wing: two scarabs to delve into brain matter, two flies to sow maggots. Each insect found its meal, but slowed nothing down.

Reduced to a flimsy outline, the door wobbled open.

A three-tipped tentacle connected to the spine of each puppet. The tentacles met at the rear of the room, where a lone zombie stood by the TV cabinet. He was black, and he wore a National Guard uniform. The top of his head had been cut off. The tentacles plugged into an apparatus of spongy black meat and tubules, grafted to the Guard's brain. They convulsed, and the other puppets came to disinter her. The Guard was their puppet master. He was controlling them.

Shade implanted a fly into the barbequed zombie's forehead. The maggots had no effect. Even a second fly proved ineffectual; a scarab, inept.

Shoulder to shoulder, only two grave eaters could share space in the closet. The barbequed zombie and a skinny girl shrugged their way in, teeth nipping rapidly. Shade's gun disfigured them, deformed the structure of their skulls, yet they persevered. She kept them at bay with her foot, but a third zombie—this one female, Asian, and dressed in a jumpsuit—began to climb over them. No amount of lead could deter her, no amount of lead.

Tentacles hogtied Shade and picked her up. She cut a few. They sprained her wrist and made her drop the knife. She pressed the gun to her side. The feelers did not notice it, did not bother it.

Twilight dusted her boots, and the National Guard came into view. Impulses agitated his tentacles; each time, the linked puppets reacted.

Shade repositioned her gun, targeting the organism on the Guard's brain. Sunset bleached her pant legs, her pelvis, her belly. It swathed her hand like melting plastic.

She had a single bullet: one shot, one chance. Her spare magazine was out of reach.

She thought of Frost and pulled the trigger.

The bullet plowed through the puppet master's brain cap, its ventriloquist's gift, and a pall of watercolor swashed the entertainment center glass.

The zombies took a final bow to the carpet. Their bones clattered. Their orifices expelled pent-up gas, a collective burp of fecal stink and rot. Shade landed on one of the bodies. A massacre covered the floor, a mass suicide: one stone, fifty dead. How it killed them all, she did not know. But it had, and that counted.

She picked up her knife and stepped into the closet.

The final strokes of daylight grayed. From the corpses, charcoal grew in patches of chiaroscuro shading. It mushroomed, and its spores obscured the room.

Darkfall.

Shade rose like the dead.

Thirty-Two

Frost sent Graves to restock the weaponry and went alone to Victor's apartment. The mechanic answered the door in the nude. His apartment was rich with the salt of urine and the tang of blood. Frost's eyes dilated.

"What are you hiding?" he asked.

Darkened, the room behind Victor censored the mystery from prying eyes. Before, it had been well lit, a trusted space, one out of an entire complex of devious chambers and vampiric halls. Frost would fumigate if necessary.

"I don't know where she came from," Victor said, breath coppery with coins. "She came to me." His confession brightened the room, but did not eradicate all the shadows.

"Show me," Frost said.

As Victor led him through the living room, Frost wondered what other enigmas hid in the pockets of the Sexton's apartment, under the couch cushions and behind the bookshelf full of vehicle manuals. Would Victor show him so willingly if he asked to see?

The bedroom was the darkest lair, hazy with candle smoke and the smell of wax, the briny scent of tears laden with motor oil.

In the closet, Victor had concealed a female. She had pissed the chair to which she was tied, shivering and frozen. The barbwire had carved a red surgery plan into the woman's skin—augment breasts, enlarge thighs, insert silicon here—and Victor, no doubt, had placed bizarre piercings along the woman's hand and arm.

Instead of a surgeon's tray, the good doctor worked from a physician's bag, which sat at the foot of the chair. Most of the instruments were rusted.

"She broke through my roof," Victor said, a hyena without humor. He was going to say something else, most likely an excuse. Frost did not give him the chance.

"I know where she comes from," he said, staring at her, transfixing her. Her blood still flavored his tongue, though he had never tasted her. He had only sampled the thrill of pursuit, the sulfuric aftertaste of fear. "And I know who marked her throat."

"What should I do with her?" Victor asked. Half his body was cloaked in gloom, the other slathered in candlelight, as if he were too terrified to reveal himself entirely.

To see Victor's dark side, Frost would have to appeal to it. "Keep her," he said. "You deserve her more than her former warden."

Victor turned his head, face still guised. "You're serious?"

"Yes."

"Mine," he said.

"Yes."

"I can do whatever I want?"

"Within reason, yes."

Victor turned to him then, fully illuminated, carnivorous humor restored. "Mine." That single word perverted his face with repressed thirsts. This was why Victor yearned for the island: this independence, this freedom for his demons.

"We have work," Frost said, leaving the bedroom. "Get dressed and wait for me."

"What's our mission?"

Frost serenaded him as any pied piper. "Tonight," he said, "we migrate."

ʿΩ

To bypass Cavanaugh and the skirmish on the stairwell, Frost traveled via the hole that the redhead had made in Victor's ceiling. In the snare, he bounded from boulder to boulder, pausing to admire the corollas of blood that dripped from the barbwire, tokens of the woman's passage.

"Zombie food," Grace had told him. He had smelled the lie then and had evidence now.

Frost boosted himself into the fourth-floor hallway. On the landing, Cavanaugh was still shooting zombies while Edward stacked wire. The soldiers were shouting, but they appeared to be in control.

Frost let himself into Grace's room. There was no light. *Still asleep*, he thought.

A gun prodded his temple.

"Jesus," Grace said, stepping out from behind the door and lowering the pistol. Her hair was frayed, windblown, dandelion fluff. "What the hell's going on?"

"Armageddon." He shut the door, and Grace followed him into the room.

"Zombies?"

Frost lit a candle and highlighted Grace's face. Her eyes were sunken.

"Do you remember your task?" he asked.

"They're out there, aren't they? They've gotten in. They've—"

"Do you remember?"

"Yes, the gurney. Now goddamn it, Frost, what the hell's happening?"

He set the candle on Grace's writing desk. "Your fear informs you well."

"Zombies. Fucking zombies. What—"

"We must vacate. Tonight. Prepare the gurney."

He moved to the exit, but Grace clung to him, trying to hinder him with her arms, vines that enclose and stifle neighboring plants. "Don't leave me." Beneath her usual flowery bouquet, she reeked of pillows, bed sweat, and sour need, an odor that left a pickled aftertaste. "Don't leave."

Frost pushed her away, struggling against the tightness in his chest, those walls that constantly closed in. "Prepare the gurney."

He retraced the redhead's escape route to Victor's apartment. Grace would not risk desertion. She would do as he said. And once she had served her purpose, Frost would kill her, in favor of Shade.

Ann had pissed herself in the Iceman's artic gale. She had expected him to take her in his snowstorm, but he had done something worse: he had given her to Victor.

Now the jackal watched her as he dressed in leathers.

"Don't worry," he said, pulling up his pants. "I'll come back. And when I do," he slipped a shirt over his scar-tissue tattoos, "we'll finish our little game."

Donning his jacket, Victor came to her. He spit the penny into his palm and laid it on her thigh, still moist.

"A souvenir," he said.

From the duffel bag, he removed a cordless drill and a box of screws. He shut her in the closet. A plank, or some other timber, clunked against the doorframe. With a few quick zips of the drill, Victor had sealed her in.

"Stay very quiet," he said through the wall. "Stay very still."

He exited with a laugh. The front door clapped shut, and Ann pitched her leg, sending Victor's penny to the floor. Where the copper had touched, her skin seemed to prickle with worms, ants, and centipedes. She could not wipe them off, *needed* to wipe them off, more urgent than an unreachable itch. And even more critical: she inhaled the corner of her gag.

Raising her arm, Ann cracked the armrest where it doweled into the seatback. With a little more exertion, she busted off the whole length of wood.

Wearing the armrest like a splint, Ann pawed at the belt. Victor had strapped it so tight that the buckle pin had lodged in the eyelet. She needed both hands to unhook it. But to her fingertips—chafed, deadened, and deprived of circulation—Victor's knots were Gordian; each convolution tensed when another relaxed. Her hand was stuck.

Ann pulled on the belt, and the eyelet stretched. It bulged against the pin, which began to slide out. Free. She threw the belt and did magic: voila, the rag, an endless pull of filthy cloth. She hunched over and dry heaved. Bile, caustic and clear. She blinked away tears and choked back acids. She swallowed, gasped—she could breathe.

Tick-tock, tick-tock.

Ann solved Victor's knots, emancipating both hands and feet. Across her knuckles and up her arm, the fishhooks throbbed. The gentlest touch elicited new stings. She tried not to irritate them.

Through her nipple and through the labia on her stomach, the fishing line tingled like a yeast infection. Ann unstrung her ear hook and her breast, but she left the suture alone. She'd had stitches before, in her knee. Extracting them had not been fun.

She stood from the chair, but had to re-sit, dizzy and hurt. Her injuries had combined into a single agony. She wasn't sure if she could walk without hurting her hip, but she had to try. For Ellie. For Ireland.

She stood again, woozy but stable. She put a little weight on her battered leg. Her hip protested. She could hobble, but running was out of the question. Her muscles were too stiff.

Boarded shut, the door would not budge. Ann butted it with her shoulder. She kicked it. It was sturdier than her bones.

Victor had left his bag inside the closet. Ann rifled through it, careful to use her good hand. A pair of scissors pricked her. She used them to snip the fishing line on either side of her stitches. She also discovered a hammer.

After a few clouts, she knocked a hole in the wood. It would be hours before she could escape. No guarantee that Victor would be gone long enough. No promise that Ellie would survive.

Ann whacked the door closer to its frame. The screws began to grate and rip up their threads, pulling from the jamb. Ann bashed until the impact resounded up her arm and settled like a toothache in her jaw.

She rested on the edge of the chair. Her breath was still hard to catch.

Get up, she told herself.

The hammer weighed like an anvil. Her arm was too lazy to lift it.

Get off your ass.

She had almost convinced her muscles to do so when the ceiling creaked. In the apartment above, rocks shifted, rocks clunked.

Someone dropped into Victor's living room. The bedroom door opened, and once again, the air went sub-zero. Ann could not move, icebound. Someone had heard her working. Now he would come. He would come, and he would shatter her.

Shade marched onto the roof and punted Rainman's panhandler bowls, scattering dimes of water. The sky held clouds, stratum of unrefined coal. Its dust had suffocated the world, had draped throw covers over cars and sleeping buildings. Not even precipitation could cleanse it. Only daylight could do that.

Out of pixels of darkling rain, puppets materialized and loped toward her. The foremost zombie wore a tuxedo ornamented with a carnation. Tattered, his left sleeve hung short, and a black arm grew forth, riddled with melanomas, carcinomas, and other malignant tumors. The next zombie had tried to clone a second head, fetal, its beady eyes warped out of alignment, its frown baring crooked baby teeth.

Shade inserted her last magazine, and—one, two, three—her gun became a stroboscope. The groom and the mutant went down in a break dance. The others boogied onward, exhibiting more perversions: an extra lung, external and slouching like a skinned tit; a third arm, dwarfed and boneless.

Shade backpedaled. She shot two more and fled.

The puppets kept up with unusual speed. Normally they plodded, hampered by dead muscles. But they had changed. So she raced, and the puppets lagged behind.

More clogged the fire escape.

Blond and eerily lifelike, an undead vixen lunged up the ladder. Tears of mascara streaked her face. Her viridian lipstick had smeared.

Sidestepping, Shade kicked her, a roundhouse. The vixen spiraled. Her breast flopped out of her halter-top, and she tripped over the parapet, clashing with the trashcans below. The Japanese waitresses took her place on the rooftop, still dressed in their kimonos.

Shade shoved the zombies back and dashed to the front of the building. Dozens of puppets loitered on the street, too many to shoot. They had seen her enter the sewer before, too stupid to pursue, but their intelligence had increased. They could wield axes, they could open doors. A manhole cover would not challenge them. Not for long.

Waitresses and abominations surrounded her. The only noise was the silent-film susurration of rain. A waitress pounced. Muzzle fire painted her face with sunrise. A Hindu dot appeared on her forehead. She dropped, and more tentacles lashed out.

In a flitter and flap of cape, Shade leapt from the building. She soared over the street, over the maple trees and zombies. In the farthest lane, a Humvee was parked. Shade had seen it on her way to the theater. A puppet had crawled out and had left the driver's-side door ajar. Shade landed on the vehicle's roof and jumped down.

Zombies pursued.

The interior of the Hummer was well kempt, the faux-grille floor mats pristine, the leather upholstery unscathed. Even after several months of neglect, the pine-shaped air freshener dispersed aromatic needles throughout the cab. Its fragrance was so potent that, in contrast, it heightened the city's decomposition, a stench to which Shade had acclimated, a stench that would ultimately saturate everything.

From the steering column, a set of keys still hung. The key ring featured an aluminum Darwin fish. Shade hopped behind the wheel and slammed the door. The engine turned over on the first try.

Zombie carjackers pummeled the passenger-side windows. A vagrant offered to wash her windshield with his spittle and fist. Shade reversed, bowling over a few muggers. Something popped, and the Hummer's back end sank. The rear tire slap-slap-slapped against the blacktop.

With a swerve and the squeal of brakes, Shade parked the vehicle over the manhole. She stepped out and spent three bullets on the carjackers. Then she snaked beneath the Hummer's belly.

The manhole was situated under the gearbox of the rear differential. Shade opened it with the crowbar from the bus and then slipped inside. She replaced the cover and waited halfway down the ladder, waited for the zombies to peek.

Water rushed below her.

The Humvee sat silent above.

After four minutes, no zombies appeared. She put away her gun and descended.

Ankle-deep and rising, runoff had gathered into a small creek along the sewer floor. French fry cartons, paper shreds, and other litter swept past, accompanied by stems and gravel, dirt and dead leaves. Shade splashed through it, fighting the currents, fighting the urge to drift away from the Haven, away from the barbwire, away from the stone. The sluice would carry her to an isle, and she would lie on the sand. She would let the waves baptize her, let the sun purify her soul. She would let the City of Roses become the City of Corpses.

Clutching her pentagram, Shade pushed harder against the torrent.

In her other hand, she gripped the oaken murder weapon. She would show it to Frost, and he would either confess or lie. Honest or not, he would feel the rage of his own design, the sturm, swung, wucht of the wood.

Honest or not, Frost would die.

Victor's front room was empty, his bedroom humid. Frost could feel the redhead's aura behind the closet door, her blood so rich, her artery mature. Only a frail piece of wood protected her. But she bore Grace's mark, her taint, and Frost would not drink after a weed, despite the vintage.

He shut the bedroom door and entered the hall. Victor and Graves were in the munitions store, an apartment stocked with M16s, Glocks, crates of various grenades, extra flamethrowers, a few shotguns, ammunition, and much more, including melee weapons such as machetes. They had pilfered many of the weapons from the federal armory. Others had come from the police department and gun shops. The Glocks, for instance.

In one corner sat four gas cans. The red one contained fuel for the Redhound, which was already full, with an extra can of gas onboard. The yellow jugs held petrol for the boat, also fully fueled. For this trip, Frost would not need gas. He would come back for it before the evacuation.

Victor and Graves filled magazines for their M16s. Victor had affixed a grenade launcher to his rifle and had fastened a belt of M406 high-explosive grenades across his chest. Graves' rifle was standard, but he wore MK3A2 concussion grenades. A machete hung against his hip.

"Reload your handguns," Frost said.

Victor tossed Frost his Glock. "Way ahead of you."

Frost holstered his gun and tucked spare magazines into his belt. He considered an M16, but decided on a submachine gun, a mini-Uzi. Crowd control. They would need it.

One month ago, the Undertakers had neutralized the area surrounding the automotive shop, but like scar tissue, the zombies had reclaimed it. To retrieve the Redhound, Frost's squad would have to open old wounds.

Out of a gray box, Frost got a cordless drill and a Phillips head bit, his key to the outside world. Fully outfitted, they left the munitions store with Frost in the lead.

Colonel Bain waited for them in the hall. He was leaning against his door, smoking and armed with a flamethrower. On his breast, he wore his swastika, carried in a wreath by a German eagle. "Going somewhere, General?"

"You need your rest," Frost said. "Return to your chambers."

"I'd rather go with you, if it's all the same." A grin touched the corner of the colonel's mouth. He took a drag from his smoke, and his eyes glistered with amusement.

Arguing with Bain was futile. He would do as he pleased and would enjoy diminishing Frost's authority in front of an audience. He had played a similar game with Roman, except back then Bain had been subtler.

"Very well," Frost said. "Fall into rank."

After a long pull from his cigarette, Bain stomped the smoke beneath his boot. Frost expected him to assume the head of the line, but the colonel moved behind him, ahead of Victor and Graves. Bain's eyes burned against Frost's back, but Frost carried on.

In the stairway, they ran into Edward. He was carrying a disarray of barbwire up to the fourth floor. He had a flashlight.

"Follow us," Frost told him. "Drop the wire."

Edward began to object, but Frost started walking.

On the third floor, they entered an apartment with an upturned door number. Overgrown with steel briar, crumbled statues cluttered the living room.

At the window, Frost handed the drill to Edward. "Unscrew the shutter," he said. "When we're through, remount it and return to your task."

Since this window accessed the fire escape and was meant to be a hatch, no board had been bolted to the Haven's brick facade. Only a square of tarp and an interior panel blocked out the sun. When Edward removed the panel, the building inhaled decay. Tentacles shot in.

Frost drew his Glock and cleared the window in one blast. He stepped up and leaned out. Zombies had overtaken the fire escape. A police officer stood amidst the barricade, using his tentacles to crane the other puppets to the landing. Plugged into each puppet's spine, the tentacles detached with a slimy pop. More zombies waited to be lifted.

Aside from Frost's kill, no other zombies occupied this section of the fire escape, but a whole gang of them was almost to the top. Six had turned back, alerted by Frost's gunshot.

"To the zipline," he said. "Graves first, Victor second." Frost went next. He didn't like the colonel at his back, but he wanted the flamethrower to spew opposite their travel: better to run from the fire than into it.

Once the squad was through, Edward sealed the window. The buzz of the drill hardly transmitted through the brick. The moans of the dead were louder. Rain effervesced.

The zombies trotted down the stairs, constrained to single file.

"Conserve your bullets!" Frost shouted.

With his machete, Graves lopped off the tentacles of the leading attacker, a meth addict with a wife-beater and chipped teeth. Graves swung again and the dope fiend's head tumbled into the barricade. As he cut down the next zombie (a deadhead in a tie-dyed shirt), Victor dispatched the one behind it. Together, they hacked a path through the jungle of zombies, steadily gaining ground; the puppets beneath them moved quicker.

Bain rotated, sousing the mob in flames, each ghoul a sentient fireball rushing to engulf them. Frost cursed. With three headshots, he demoted the firebugs to ordinary pyres, which the rainstorm would eventually douse.

"You should have brought a gun!" he shouted.

Bain smirked and torched the next group of ambushers. Again, Frost had to inhibit their blaze. He shot the cop in the barricade before it could send up reinforcements. Hopefully, another zombie would take its place after they had left the fire escape: Frost wanted to keep Cavanaugh busy.

At the penthouse landing, Graves and Victor held back zombies while Frost unlocked a safe welded to the fire escape grate. Inside, they had stowed thirteen handlebars fitted with pulleys.

To facilitate the ventures of the Undertakers, two cables, two ziplines had been suspended between the Haven and a building across the street. One angled down from the Haven. The other angled up. The handlebars were meant to trundle along these cables, providing transport from one building to the other. At one time, all thirteen handlebars had been necessary.

Frost distributed a set to each squad member. Bain went down the zipline first, then Victor and Graves. Frost hitched his handlebar to the cable. He shot one more zombie and pushed off, zipping down over the barricade, through the rain, closer and closer to the island.

Ann no longer felt the frostbite. The Iceman had passed through, had even entered the bedroom, but he had left quickly. She was alone. She had to get free.

Recharged with adrenalin, she hammered the door, vaguely aware of the jolts that wracked her arm. The screws shrieked from the jamb, and the closet opened. Ann stepped forward, onto something cold: her wedding ring.

She lifted her foot off it and took another step.

Then she stopped.

She turned, stooped, and picked up the ring. It weighed down her finger, but it felt safe, familiar, slotted into its old indentation in her skin. Ann left the closet, feeling heavier on weary legs.

Victor's bedroom was blacker than any unlit torture chamber. Behind the bed and in the corners, inquisitors skulked. Ann scuttled across the room, and the tormentors harassed her with cat's paws and branding irons, aggravating her injuries. One terrorizer resorted to mallet blows, sledging Ann's hip every other step.

At the front door, Ann pressed her ear to the wood. She had wished the hallway to be quiet, but gunfire echoed through it. Otherwise, it was empty.

Ann scampered down the corridor and slowed near the stairwell, sliding along the wall until the end. The barrage was deafening here, the deathwatches magnified. Three or four stories up, muzzle fire pulsed; a man cursed between shots.

Ann did not remember which floor she had come from. The third or fourth, high enough to bump into the shooters, close enough for Michael to rat out her position. The gunman would probably kill her, shoot her. Or he would apprehend her and vent his demons on her flesh, just as Victor had.

Tick-tock, tick-tock: the sound of irretrievable time.

Keeping her hand on the wall, Ann crept up the stairs. The gripes of old wood were lost beneath the volley, concentrating in her hip with every heartbeat. She rested after a few steps, relying on the handrail for balance.

Something moved below her, a near inaudible shift in the staircase. Then footsteps, only perceptible during the breaks in firearm tempo. Footsteps and groans: Michael.

Like a long sinewy creeper, his tongue greased Ann's arm. He wanted her out of his way. He wanted to snuff her so he could slurp Ireland out of Ellie's womb.

Ann hurried up the stairs. Michael was right behind her, groping for her with his tongue. She couldn't scream, she couldn't scream. She couldn't sound the alarm.

On the landing, Ann looked up. The muzzle fire highlighted the gunman's profile with each flare. The man's target hid around the angle of the stairs.

Michael groaned again.

A flashlight turned on in the hallway to Ann's right. "Hey!" the light bearer yelled.

Michael's tongue seized Ann's throat and yanked her off her feet. The flashlight briefly revealed him, a businessman in a suit chewed through with bullet holes. He opened his mouth, and tentacles came out to bite her.

Coming up from the lobby, Shade saw the flashlight shining out of the hall. A zombie stood on the stairs, and the redhead was trapped in its clutches.

Shade reached for her gun, but the Beast roused, hungering for gore. The puppet opened its mouth to consume.

Just let it, Shade thought. *Let it take her. Let it rip off her face.* And she would have, except the woman was a stranger. Not from the warren and not from the refectory. She had been whipped and lashed. A mystery. Perhaps she had answers.

Shade shot the puppet in the back of the head. It puked on the woman, tomato sauce and meatballs.

Screaming, clawing at the mess on her face, the redhead dropped to her knees. Shade lifted her by the armpits as Edward emerged from the hall, bearing the flashlight.

"What's happening?" Shade asked.

"The puppets," he said, "they've breached."

"Where's Frost?"

"They left. Him, Graves, Colonel Bain …"

"And everyone else?"

"All dead."

Shade paled. "Cavanaugh? Is he—?"

"He's alive. He's the one shooting."

She nodded, unable to do anything else, too tight in the chest. She handed the woman to Edward. "Take her," she said. "To the colonel's apartment. Stay there until I arrive."

"Yes, your Highness."

On the fourth-floor platform, Cavanaugh was reloading his pistol. His shotgun lay on the floor. On the stairs past him, zombies fought with barbwire brambles. Shade was glad to see his finely crafted face, his hazel eyes.

"Your Majesty," Cavanaugh said. He saluted her, arms forming an X. "I was worried."

"No reason," Shade replied. She checked her bullets: only a handful. "I see our general has left us."

"He said we're leaving tonight. Is that true?"

Shade inserted the magazine. "Shoot with me."

They ruptured a few cerebrum boils, blotting the staircase with clots and pus.

In between shots, Shade said, "Can you handle them?"

"Yes."

"Good. When the general returns, apprehend him." She lanced her last boil and put away her gun. "He and I need to speak."

She began to walk away, and Cavanaugh called out to her.

"Where will you be?"

Shade stopped to look back. "Bain's," she said. "Conducting an interrogation."

Then she followed Edward downstairs.

In the colonel's living room, Edward had tied the redhead to a pinewood chair. He had placed another seat nearby and had lit candles. Rodents of light licked the blood that marked the woman's body. Waifs of shadow panicked on the walls.

Standing guard behind the woman, Edward saluted as Shade came in.

"Go," she told him. "Cavanaugh needs ammunition."

Once Edward left, Shade sat in the empty chair. The redhead stared at the carpet. A bite festered on her neck, discernable from all the cuts. Fishhooks decorated her hand, arm, and ear.

"Where did you come from?"

No answer.

"I'll torture you if necessary."

Nothing.

Shade twisted a fishhook in the woman's knuckle. Silent tears streamed from the woman's eyes. Shade twisted harder, yet not a peep. Nothing to satisfy the Beast.

"I could tear them out. Perhaps that would loosen your—"

In another room, something thunked: a spy. The redhead seemed not to notice.

Shade snuffed the candles. She moved toward the noise, toward Bain's bedroom, as stealthy as a mouser. She stopped at the door to listen.

Thunk, thunk.

Shade drew her gun. She burst into the room, moving fast, keeping low.

Empty.

The room stank of blood, smoke, and human excrement. The mauve bedcovers were strewn. Along with yellowed fluid stains and cigarette burns, russet dots speckled the sheet. Red cast-off trails striped the ceiling, and a head-shaped discoloration splotched the rug. It had soaked into the paper shreds, lint, and other rubbish on the floor.

From there, smears led to the closet.

Shade opened the door.

On the floor inside, Bain's slave lay with her legs bent beneath her. Blood dyed her sandy hair and matted it to a crush on the side of her skull. Her eye bulged, held only by veins. Next to her, Bain had propped a length of pipe. Blood and hair dirtied its end.

Convulsing, the slave's knee hit the wall: *thunk, thunk.* Someone had bitten her neck. Bain, presumably. Although the colonel preferred to feed off his slave's psychic energy, Shade had seen him use his teeth. She felt angry and sick. The slave had been beautiful, but Bain had wasted her, had smashed her like a Victorian vase.

Drawing her knife, Shade knelt. She pressed the blade to the slave's throat. The Beast frothed at the mouth, and Shade had to swallow an upsurge of stomach acids. She clenched her teeth and slid the sharp edge along the woman's artery and vein.

"May you rest in peace."

Like a fish gulping air, the slave opened and closed her mouth. Finally, the jasper dulled in her eyes, and she suffered no more. Shade shut the closet and left.

In the front room, she stood over the redhead. She, too, was beautiful, despite her wounds. That flame of hair, those emerald eyes. Petite and elfish ears.

Cut her, the Beast said, drooling and red-eyed. *Cut her and drink.*

Shade stooped over the woman and breathed her in. Oh, the iron of blood, the copper and salt; hunger mixed with nausea, frowning, trembling, mad.

Yes, the Beast panted, *eat her beauty. Cut it out and devour.*

Shade clenched her knife. She bent and cut the woman's ropes. "Come," she said, taking the redhead by the arm. There were better ways to make someone speak. "Come and join your sisters."

After securing their handlebars in another lockbox, Frost's squad ascended the apartment block that neighbored the Haven. Bain escorted. Frost took the rear.

Unlike that of the Haven, this rooftop was free of puppets, but beleaguered with rain. On the other end, a pole bridged the alley between apartment block and studio apartment. The Undertakers had arranged the pole as part of their skywalk, a series of extension ladders, steel beams, and other improvised catwalks that led from building to building.

As Bain crossed the pole, Frost hoped he would slip on the wet metal. The plunge would not kill the colonel, but the zombies below might. At the very least, the misstep would disable Bain long enough for Frost to reassume the lead.

Bain passed without falter. Victor and Graves followed, and Frost went, too. They toured the skywalk from brownstone to skyscraper, from church steeple to colonnade to hotel balcony.

On the building across from the automotive shop, they congregated, they schemed.

The shop, Mickey's Mechanics, had three entrances: two garage doors and a regular door into the reception area. Puppets milled in the parking lot around a few trucks and one sports car. None had broken into the shop.

Frost conferred with his squad, sub rosa in the downpour. He ended with this: "Victor is most important here. We are his defense. Do you understand?" He looked at Bain as he asked it.

The colonel smiled. Water dribbled off his lips. "Let's burn."

They lobbed hand grenades into the parking lot, loosing the bonfires of Hell. Puppet parts scattered, smoking and hissing in the rain. With his launcher, Victor deposited a high-explosive bomb into the cab of a truck.

The vehicle detonated, and cooked arms and legs landed on the pavement several yards away. The sky's sprinkler system worked to extinguish the firestorm as more explosions shook the night. Zombies crawled through heaps of slaughterhouse goulash, some trailing grilled intestines, others dragging leg stumps, all scorched, their clothes alight. New appendages began to sprout.

"Down!" Frost said. "Down, down, down!"

Into the parking lot they flew, monstrous bats broadcasting bullets like sonar. Cranial wombs miscarried embryos. Glutton skulls regurgitated lasagna.

Touching down, Frost's squad played the parking lot like an arena. Victor and Graves hurried up the center, weaving between puppets, panning their M16s. Bain went rogue.

Attracted by the uproar, a militia of puppets paraded from a side street. The colonel ignited his flamethrower and spread the Fuhrer's gospel, transforming zombie soldiers into Nazis of combustion. Rain sizzled in the flames.

"Bain!" Frost shouted, gesturing with his Uzi. "Fall back!"

The colonel grinned at him. Firebugs flickered in his eyes, and he continued to stoke the masses, waving a red banner depicting a swastika of smoke. Like reptiles, the Nazis molted, shedding charred skin. The Puppeteer redressed muscle and bone, clothing them in Teflon-colored rawhide, arming them for war.

Victor and Graves reached the main entrance of the shop. Victor sorted his keys while Graves and his rifle repelled the Gestapo of the parking lot.

Signaling the end of Bain's SS, Frost administered cyanide capsules in fully automatic distribution. His casualties amassed into a lake of fire, but Bain recruited faster than Frost's poison could terminate. The holocaust incarnate pushed them into the parking lot.

Victor found the right key and inserted it into the lock. He turned it the wrong way. Graves went to change his magazine, and a tentacle lassoed him. The Gestapo crowded forward.

Frost yielded to Bain's army. He sprinted toward Graves and shot with his Glock, Uzi dangling inactive.

Lying on the ground, a girl attempted to trip Frost with her tentacles. A grenade had claimed her lower body and had melted the pink cotton-candy fabric of her nightgown. Her legs had failed to regenerate, resulting in a mishmash of black gristle, rubbery veins, and disjointed bone. Faces grew in the mess, dermoid cysts with teeth, hair, and thyroid glands, idiotic eyes blinking in the rain.

Frost sympathized. He shot her in the head.

While Graves struggled with his captor, battling off nooses and fists, Victor slid into the shop. Before he could shut the door, a puppet ripped it open. Victor fired his M16, turning the zombie's back into an open grave. But more puppets shoved through the door. Victor's rifle discharged twice, then fell silent as the zombies took him.

Frost shot the puppet that was attacking Graves. He swapped his handgun for his Uzi and sprayed the zombies that obstructed the doorway, tagging Graves on accident but not really caring. He definitely didn't stop.

Holding Victor's M16, a zombie exited the building. The ghoul shot back, a triple-burst staccato. Had Frost reacted sooner, he could have dodged the meteors. They struck earth in his chest, and quakes stunned him. Numerous volcanoes erupted on his breast, and magma flooded his lung.

Coughing up lukewarm lava, Frost staggered back. He aimed, but the zombie sent its last meteor shower. One of the stones struck Frost above the brow. It knocked his head back, and his skull distended. He had just enough time to welcome the dark. Then everything exploded—first red, then black.

He fell, and the darkness claimed him.

He never hit pavement.

Thirty-Nine

When the raven lady said, "Join your sisters," Ann rejoiced. *I'm coming, baby. I'm coming. Michael can't hurt you anymore.* She followed the raven from the interrogation room to the stairwell, even though her hip had stiffened into a burl of wood, even though her cuts opened with every move.

On the platform in the stairwell, a man was shooting zombies from behind a barbwire fence. Ann averted her eyes as sneers splattered and heads popped, trying not to gag on the tang of blood and guts.

The raven shouted something, and the man answered. Ann's ears were ringing, and she couldn't make out the words. The raven pulled her down a corridor, away from the gunfire. Ann caught her breath, smelling gunpowder and dust, thankful to be gone from the reek of death. She recognized this hall, recognized the hole in the floor, the one through which she had fallen. Her Auschwitz.

And in room 404, Ellie jabbered and swung in her hammock. *I'm coming baby. Everything's going to be just fine.*

The raven went to a different door. Michael snickered in the darkness.

"No, wait," Ann said. "It's that one."

The raven ignored her and turned the knob.

"Please, this is the wrong room. It's *that* one, right over there." She wanted to say, *My sister's in there*, but stopped herself. She would not give her enemy collateral.

The raven led her into the room, and Ann tried to jump away.

"This is the wrong one! Where are you taking me?"

The raven shut the door. Michael laughed one last time, and then his grin faded to black.

"Ellie!"

The raven twisted Ann's arm and drove her into a room full of rocks and barbwire. A ladder led up to a catwalk running through a crisscross of rafters.

"Climb," the raven said, nudging Ann with a gun. "Unless you want me to leave you in the brambles."

Ann glanced at the door, toward Ellie. She grabbed the ladder, put her foot on a rung—and then pushed off, thrusting her shoulder toward the raven's chest. She missed.

The raven whirled behind her and cracked her across the back of the head. Something trickled inside Ann's nasal passages. She knew she was falling, but couldn't stop it. Then, the abyss: nothing—dark.

Minutes later, she woke with a headache. She woke to voices and darkness. She was in a different room. Someone was in there with her.

Ann whimpered and curled in one corner, listening as the inhabitants whispered. No lamplight revealed the speakers. They smelled human—a mix of body odor, fecal matter, urine, and fear—but smell alone never qualified. Neither did sight. Ann's Mistress had feigned humanity so convincingly that Ann and Ellie had trusted her. Panic had tricked their conventional senses, as well as their intuition. And Mistress was far from human.

Muddled with pain and fatigue, Ann distrusted her ability to detect a charade. To her, the tenants were Morlocks, cannibals, troglodytes. She rocked herself and hummed a lullaby, blocking out her inmates' conspiracies.

After much discussion, one of the Morlocks stepped forward and imitated a female voice: "What's your name?"

Ann huddled deeper into the corner.

"We won't hurt you. We're prisoners, too."

Such a throaty voice, so soothing, like sand shifting in the surf.

"My name's Carly," the Morlock said. "What's yours?"

She spoke before she could stop herself. "Ann."

Carly the Morlock was silent for a moment. "I had a cousin named Ann. Well, she wasn't really my cousin, just the daughter of my mom's best friend. I knew her for so long I just called her my cousin."

"I . . . I was named after my grandma," Ann ventured.

"I was named after the family dog."

Behind Carly, a few nervous titters fluttered from the group, each one feminine, except for the chirrup of a boy's laughter. Ann giggled too, like hiccups, unable to stop.

"So," Carly said as she knelt, "did you come from outside?"

"No. I've been here. In the building."

"There's more of us then? In another room?"

Ann thought of Ellie and Frank, of limbless bodies swaying. "Yes. But—they're hurt."

"What do you mean?"

"They're … I'd rather not—" Ann stood up, dizzy, hurt. "I have to go. I have to get out of here." She felt around the room, steering clear of Carly and her company.

"What's happening?" another woman asked. "What's she doing?"

"Ann," Carly said, "there's no way out, Ann. We've tried."

"He's going to kill her," Ann said, more to herself than to anyone else. She stifled a sob. "Oh my God, Michael's going to kill her."

"Ann, who's Michael?"

Mumbling, searching, searching for an exit, finding nothing but plaster.

"Who's Michael?"

Turning now, locking onto a shape that might have been human, might have been Morlock. "He's going to kill her! He's going to kill my baby!"

The tears came from nowhere. She sagged, and Carly hugged her, held her up. Ann stiffened at first, dreading the albino creepy-crawl of the Morlock, but Carly had the swaddle of human skin, warm and peach colored, not alien white. Ann's cuts burned, but she let them and relaxed. She could not remember her last hug. Had it been with Ellie, or Michael?

"He's torturing her," Ann said, blubbering. "He's going to kill her."

"It'll be okay. Everything will be okay."

"No," but she was graying now, weakening. "No it won't."

The women enfolded her, and a child's arms wrapped her waist. Finally, after the Iceman and Auschwitz, after Victor and his bag of pain, Ann let go; it was okay to let go.

In the rafters above, Shade eavesdropped. The redhead's name was Ann, and she was fretting about someone called Michael. Shade knew no one by that name. Perhaps he was a torso; Ann claimed to have come from the warren, so the speculation was reasonable.

When the women dissolved into tears, Shade left, disgusted by the salty smell, disgusted by the slight burn in her own eyes. She thought about visiting Grace in the warren, to ask a few questions, but Cavanaugh needed help. Shade went to the stairwell.

Edward had just returned with a shipment of ammo. He furnished Cavanaugh with magazines and shotgun shells, and Shade refilled her gun. She stocked up on spare magazines and ordered Edward to keep putting up the fence. He nodded and left for more wire.

"Where did the woman come from?" Cavanaugh asked as he prepared his gun.

"From the warren." Shade shot a naked blonde with three tits, one black. The blonde hung herself on the barbwire. "But she looks as if she has climbed through a snare, and someone has decorated her with fishhooks."

Cavanaugh shot a tramp clad in greasy rags. "Victor's a fisherman. He'd have hooks."

"Why would Victor keep her in the warren?"

"Maybe he and the nurse have some sort of tryst."

"Likely," Shade said. "Perhaps I should speak with him as well."

Using its tentacle like a grapevine, a puppet swung along the balustrade, sneaking around the snare. More followed suit. Shade stopped the first one, and its carcass disappeared down the shaft. She didn't have enough rounds to stop them all.

"Lieutenant! On the left!"

Cavanaugh handled most of them. Two made it to the landing. Shade thrust her knife through the leader's eye socket, and when she retrieved the blade, the zombie fell.

The next puppet flogged her with a tentacle. It hit her temple. Cavanaugh repaid the favor with a face full of lead.

On the stairs, the zombies parted, and a man wearing a flak jacket and a helmet approached the barbwire. He had handheld wire snips and a riot shield. He blocked Shade's bullets and pruned the wire.

A dozen zombies came forward, armed with clippers. Even as Shade and Cavanaugh cut them down, more picked up the tools and resumed work.

Shade aimed at a pair of clippers. Her slug divided the tines, which clanged to the stairs, useless. Cavanaugh replicated the feat. The riot guard remained untouchable. He alone had clipped halfway through the snare.

From the handrail, Shade vaulted over the shaft. She sprang off the opposite wall and grabbed the balustrade higher up. The riot zombie looked over at her. Shade shot him. His helmet was a poor skull, dumping brains out the back. He dropped the snips, and a Latino zombie picked them up. Others enveloped the Latino and warded off Cavanaugh's assault.

With their tentacles, the puppets tried to knock Shade off the balustrade. One restrained her arm. Another jousted her with a wooden pike. Shade let go, hanging from the tentacle.

Cavanaugh killed the jouster, and his stake tumbled down the shaft.

Shade swung onto the staircase. She hauled the zombie off by the tentacle and shot it as it dangled. It released her and plummeted.

"Shit," Cavanaugh said, pointing.

A procession of zombies came to the fore, each with a weapon: a few pistols and a shotgun. Shade doubted that zombies could employ weaponry. But Cavanaugh grasped her shoulder and pulled her to the floor just as Remington beetles whizzed by. A lucky insect nestled in Shade's shoulder. Her body quickly ejected it.

Cresting the platform with a shipment of wire, Edward sustained the shotgun blast. Like meat-eating termites, the buckshot devoured his thigh to the bone. He crumpled, falling victim to his own bristly web.

Bullets munched through the floor around Cavanaugh and Shade. The lieutenant shot back, but missed.

With the sentinels to safeguard him, the Latino zombie clipped through the snare, growling and hungry for flesh.

A rose bloomed in the void. As the blossom opened, it disclosed a postmortem sky, weeping embalming fluid. The plates of Frost's skull began to interlock.

Beneath him, the ground rumbled and thrummed. Graves uprooted him and dragged him across the lot. Through rosy, transparent petals, Frost could see puppets chasing him. They mingled with Bain's progeny, who were still aflame. Bullets reduced their heads to splatters, and Frost smelled gunpowder. He was deaf to the shots though. He could hear only the fizz of rain.

Behind him, the Redhound crashed through the garage doors, dragging metal and shooting sparks. It stopped, and Graves carried Frost to the passenger entrance. The door folded open, and they climbed backward up the steps, still fighting off zombies.

As the door shut, a tentacle snuck in and grabbed Frost's ankle. It dragged him down the stairs towards the puppet's mouth, pressed in the crack of the door.

Graves hewed the lasso with his machete, and it retreated.

The door shut. The bus began to move.

Two seats remained inside: Victor occupied the driver's seat, and the passenger seat was empty. The rest of the commuter seating had been replaced with a cage, encircled by an aisle and several gun ports to the outside.

Graves potted Frost in the passenger seat and leaned over him, dripping water. His lips moved, and his words became gradually louder, as did the Redhound's growl.

"Can you hear me?"

Frost seized Graves' throat, choking off the inquiries. "Where's Bain?" His voice was mushy and swollen, so he tried to bolster it by clenching his teeth. "Where is he?"

"He disappeared," Victor said, steering out of the parking lot. The vehicle jostled through a throng of zombies; the tires bounced. "He just fucking disappeared."

Frost released Graves and stood. He stumbled forward and braced himself against Victor's seat.

Still alight, Nazi hellions charged the bus. The plow steamrolled most, leaving fiery smithereens. Some of the fascists clung to the bus's exoskeleton. Their dictator had deserted them. He had left them to simmer in his inflammatory rhetoric.

"Graves," Frost called, tightening his hand on Victor's seatback. "Kill them."

Graves put his handgun through a porthole and removed the clinging bigots. The surviving Nazis lumbered after the bus, left behind as Victor accessed the street.

Aside from a few clusters, no zombies obstructed the road, and most of the cars, police cruisers, ambulances, fire trucks, and Humvees now rusted beneath the Haven's barricade, no longer roadblocks.

Frost sat in the passenger seat and held his head, allowing himself to heal.

During the combat, he had misplaced his Glock but not his Uzi. He switched out magazines. Puppets would surround the Haven. The building itself was now undoubtedly a hive. Parking the Redhound and getting inside would be no easy task.

"Graves," he said, "take Victor's M16 and his grenades. When we arrive, you will be bombardier. You will guard the Redhound while Victor and the others fetch our herd."

"Yes, sir."

Soon, more zombies filled the street. Graves kept them off while Victor plowed them under. Through the buildings, the Haven appeared, a grave marker for Roman's regime, a giant crypt of narrow halls and dusty rooms.

Frost gritted his teeth, and his chest began to tighten with that old claustrophobia. He looked through the windshield, up at the building tops, glimpsing a flap of someone's cape.

Bain.

Frost pulled a box out from beneath him, a store of handguns, ammunition, and two Uzis. He prepped one of the submachine guns for Victor and restocked his belt with spares. Across from his seat, a flamethrower hung from a hook. Frost donned the canister beneath his cape, then set the Uzi in Victor's lap.

"Drop me off here," he said.

"What? They'll swarm us. They'll—"

"Do it, soldier. Open the door."

"What about the Haven?"

Frost said nothing. He didn't have to.

Victor looked back at the road. "As you wish." He slowed down and waited for a safe spot devoid of zombies.

"You're in charge of the torsos," Frost told him. "Grace has prepared them."

"Fine." Victor opened the door.

Frost saluted his subordinates. "Long live the Haven." Then he stepped down the stairs and jumped into the rain.

The women finally calmed down and disengaged from the group hug. Carly led Ann to a blanket and helped her sit. Ann's hip complained, but all she could do was grimace.

One by one, the women came to her and held her hand, her good one. They introduced themselves, giving nothing to identify but the texture of their skin and the quality of their voices. They all sounded young, or at least not much older than Ann. She forgot most of their names, but she remembered the boy. Carly stood by him, encouraging him to speak.

"Tell her your name," she said.

"Payton."

"Hi, Payton." Ann took the boy's hand. It felt small, almost like a seashell. His arm tensed, wanting to pull back, but Ann rubbed her thumb across his knuckles, and he stayed. "My name's Ann."

Payton was quiet.

"Can you tell her hello, Payton?" Carly asked.

"Hi."

Ann smiled and continued to massage his knuckles. "Old enough to ride a bicycle yet?"

"Mom was teaching me."

"His mom's name was Nina," Carly explained.

Ann's eyes stung, and she had to bite her lip to keep her smile. "Well, I bet you were doing great," she told Payton.

"I hurt my knee once. I had to get stitches."

"But you didn't stop, did you?"

"No."

Ann squeezed his hand. "That's good." Her voice had grown thick and ropy. Her eyes stung more. "Never give up. Never ever."

"I won't," he said.

After the introductions, Payton and Carly sat next to Ann. The others gathered around, powwow style.

"I know you're tired," Carly began, "but we have to know: what's going on out there?"

Even in this prison, the gun battle was heard. During the introductions, the women had whispered about it, but they had been polite enough to wait.

"I don't know," Ann said. "I couldn't see very well, but—I think those things are inside."

"What?" a woman asked. "The zombos?"

Ann recognized the southern accent, the African American baritone. She thought it belonged to a woman named Dominique, a preschool teacher who secretly moonlighted as a stripper.

"I think so," Ann replied.

The women talked amongst themselves. Ann felt bad to bring such terrible news.

"You said there are others in the building," Carly said. "How many?"

"I don't know. Ten … maybe twelve?"

"Are they in danger?"

"Yes. They—they can't walk. And my sister, she's one of them. She's pregnant."

Carly's hand found Ann's in the darkness. "And this Michael, the one who's going to hurt your baby, is he one of them?"

Ann sighed. She knew she was going crazy (from the stress, from the shock, from the pain), but to have her insanity brought back to her like this … it made her realize just how many bolts were loose.

"I don't know what I was talking about," she said. "My husband—Michael—he died saving me and my sister. I thought he'd come back to … to hurt us."

Carly's grip on her hand wavered, as if she thought Ann was lying, hiding something. At first, Ann wanted to redouble her hold, but then she couldn't care less. How dare this woman judge her? Even if Ann still thought Michael was out there (and some part of her feared he was), it wasn't this stranger's place to play lie detector.

"You've been through a lot," Carly said, reaffirming her grasp. "We understand."

Ann hung her head. "Thank you."

Another woman piped up. Ann thought her name was Ginny or Jenny. She had a whiny voice that cracked on the high notes: "What're we going to do? We're trapped in here. And those monsters are right outside."

The group debated the issue. They talked about breaking the wall or prying open a window.

Dominique rejected the idea. "What're we going to do, Spiderman down the brick?"

No one could argue. The fire escape was nowhere near their room, and the building formed a sheer cliff, no real ledges or convenient drainpipe. Just a four-story plummet to barbwire and stone.

They fell silent, shifting on their blankets, listening to the gunshots from down the hall.

Ann thumbed her ring. "Couldn't we—do you think we could boost someone to the door?"

Dominique: "Been there, done that."

"It's locked," Carly explained, letting go of Ann's hand. "There's a guard."

"Not when I came through. There wasn't a guard then."

"But it's still locked," a nameless woman contributed.

"Well, we can't just sit here." Ginny again. She was making Ann's headache worse. "If the zombies don't kill us, the vampire will."

Dominique said, "Wish I had a crucifix. Or at least some damn garlic."

Several women agreed.

"No," a new speaker said. Ann didn't recognize the voice. It sounded as if the woman were exhaling cigarette smoke with every word. "She won't kill us all. She needs us. But you go out there and you die for sure."

"Meet Shirley," Dominique quipped, "vampire psychologist and fortuneteller extraordinaire."

"How do you know she won't kill us?" Ginny asked. "Last time she took Mary, remember?"

"Mary was a bitch," Shirley said. She sounded serious.

"Carly's the one who's named after a dog," Dominique teased.

"You're a bitch, too." No teasing from Shirley.

"That's right," Dominique said with ghetto girl attitude, that swivel of the neck and cock of the hip. "When I go into heat, I attract a man. Your skinny white ass draws nothing but flies."

"Ladies, ladies," Carly interrupted. "Young ears hear, you know. And it doesn't help us to bicker. Ann has a good suggestion. We could at least try it."

"Go ahead," Shirley responded. "But shut the door on your way out."

Dominique chuffed. "See. Told you she's got bugs up her ass."

Payton giggled, and Carly allowed it. Ann was glad. She loved the singsong of the boy's laughter. She almost smiled herself, but those gunshots. And Michael.

"So what're we going to do?" Ginny persisted.

Carly said, "We're giving it a try."

"But how will the last person get up?"

"I don't know. Good question. Any ideas?"

No one offered suggestions.

Carly sighed. "Well, I guess we'll figure it out when we get there."

"Carly-momma?" Payton asked.

"What is it, doll?"

"We could make a rope, couldn't we? With the blankets?"

"That's brilliant, honey. That's just what we'll do."

Ann started to get off her blanket so they could use it, but Carly advised her to rest.

"Here," she said to Payton. "Stay with Ann, okay? Keep her company?"

Payton sat next to her. She put her arm around him, relishing the warmth and sturdy feeling of another human being.

Within minutes, the women had knotted the quilts into a rudimentary rope. Dominique volunteered to tie it to the rafters, so the others began to boost her up.

"You're hurting my shoulders," Ginny whined.

"And you're a pain in my ass. Now go higher."

Eventually, Dominique grabbed a beam and pulled herself up. "Got it."

"You're going to die," Shirley said, low enough so that only Ann and Payton could hear. "You're all going to die."

Payton returned Ann's hug. She glared toward Shirley. She put her mouth to the boy's soft, angelic hair, the smell of butter. "Never give up," she whispered. "Never."

But as she said it, a saying popped into her head, something from a cartoon about cats, mice, and America—"Never say never." She held Payton tighter, hoping he wouldn't notice her quiet sobs. He said nothing and nuzzled under her arm, as if she could keep him safe.

Shade took a bullet to the biceps. It shattered bone. "Retreat!" She and Cavanaugh rolled from the landing into the hallway. With a demolished leg, Edward stayed on the steps, allowing himself to heal.

Cavanaugh bent Shade's arm. "You're hit."

She pulled away and started to reload. "When did they learn to shoot?"

"Recently." Cavanaugh replenished his own gun. "They know about stakes, too."

Shade stepped onto the landing and fired. She missed the Latino zombie's clippers and ducked away as the shotgun boomed.

"How?" she asked.

Cavanaugh shook his head. "Maybe they remember. Or maybe they learned from us."

"You speak as if they're intelligent."

"Well look at your arm," Cavanaugh said.

She glanced at it. The wound was closing up nicely, but he was right. Aggravating, but right. Still, he could've found a better way to present his case. Instead, he had used her injury to further his agenda, his view that she should sit this out. Not because she was royalty (he had fought beside her father without telling him what to do), but because she had long hair, big breasts, and soft lips.

Shade took another shot at the Latino zombie. She hissed. "Damn it! They're almost through."

Cavanaugh held her arm and looked deep into her eyes. "Let me greet them, then. Let me smite them upon our doorstep."

Shade clenched her teeth. She met his gaze and nodded. "Together then."

Cavanaugh searched her face, and for a moment she thought he would try to stop her. But then he nodded too.

"So be it."

Cavanaugh went first, and they stormed the landing, gunning. The lead spores of their enemies zoomed past. Shade's own spores rooted in the brain of a pistol-bearing zombie, cultivating toadstools. Her second fungus engendered death cups; yet another shooter expired. Cavanaugh shot the Latino, though too late. The puppet had trimmed enough wire for his comrades to wrestle through. And with each trespasser, the crevice expanded, like brush beaten back from a path.

Staying behind the snare, the zombie infantry resumed bombardment. Buckshot eroded the side of Shade's face, from neck to lower jaw. She did not relent, regulating illegal aliens even as rounds punched through her chest, even as blood stained her tongue and leaked down the back of her throat. Cavanaugh grabbed her arm and towed her back to the hallway.

"There are too many!"

Shade's face was a twitching slaughter of muscle, chewed-up tongue, and tooth shards, one eye popped and runny. She could not speak. She could only salivate sanguine.

"Jesus, look at you!"

More gunfire broke out in the stairwell. Edward, flat on the stairs, had replaced Shade as border patrol. Black locusts wrecked the step above his head, showering his hair with splinters and debris. Unharmed, he sent the infernal migrants back to Hell.

No matter; the immigrants immigrated. A pizza delivery boy in a blue windbreaker raided the hall. One of his tentacles had grown a mutant hand: three fingers, one thumb. It tried to whack Shade. She blocked it, and Cavanaugh fired, topping the floor with anchovies and feta from the delivery boy's head. The lieutenant ushered Shade farther down the corridor, hounded by zombies and bullets.

Halfway to the refectory, a corpse lay in the passage. Cavanaugh stopped by it and expended ammunition on their pursuers. He went to squire Shade deeper, but she stood her ground.

"Come," Cavanaugh said. "You shouldn't be out here."

Shade held up the pentagram. Though her mouth was still in repair, she managed to say, "I fight."

Cavanaugh let go of her arm. "Very well. This will be our final stand."

He tried the door to the warren, but it was locked. He and Shade took cover in the doorway of apartment 403, the empty room. The puppets came. Countless had mutated: multiple arms; a fetus developing from one zombie's chest, twitching but comatose. They forced Shade and Cavanaugh into the adjacent snare, out onto the rocks and wire. The puppets began to climb the ladder to the catwalk, to the refectory. Shade and Cavanaugh picked them off.

Grabbing the rungs with his tentacles, a bicyclist clambered over the others, black and purple spandex bulging over malignant growths. He made it to the catwalk and demonstrated excellent balance. Shade disrupted his performance. The bicyclist toppled, no helmet to protect his head, no brain with which to think.

Other gymnasts attempted the beam. Many fell, either downed by bullets or overthrown by competitors. Legs shattered upon the rocks. Bones broke through skin. Zombies thrashed in the barbwire, their flesh fusing over the steel. They tried to stand, but the wire pulled at their skin like meat hooks.

Three zombies reached the portal into the refectory. The forerunner reached for the deadbolts.

"The door!" Shade yelled, pointing her gun.

Cavanaugh pointed too.

The zombies shielded their leader, and he unbolted the first lock.

Shade took out one of the disciples, plastering gobs and tentacles on the ceiling and wall. Cavanaugh's barrage trashed the other disciple's back, popping holes in his blue raincoat.

The leader threw the second bolt. Shade zeroed in on his head, but something grabbed her ankle: a zombie from the snare, shriveled face, eight black tongues, an ear growing from its cheek.

It bit her leg, teeth clicking shin.

Shade roared and gunned the zombie through the eye. Luckily, its teeth had not pierced her leather pants. Luckily, they had not pierced her skin.

The leader opened the hatch. Shade shot at him, but he ducked inside. His disciple followed. Screams shook the room.

Spraying zombies with his Uzi, Frost cut a path toward the closest building. An Italian restaurant occupied the building's first floor. It had a red-brick façade, and its olive-green awning dripped rain. The words "Il Ristorante Migliore" were frosted on the glass, garnished with grapevines. A narrow staircase led to the apartments above. Frost headed upstairs. The zombies pursued.

He wanted to arrive at the Haven simultaneously with the Redhound, so he could ensure that his men accomplished their objective. The legions outside the building would slow the bus and give him enough time, granted Godspeed.

He also wanted to catch Bain.

At the stairwell's apex, Frost booted the white door. Wood cracked but did not give, secured with a deadbolt.

Uncurling like fiddleheads, zombie creepers came for him. He kicked the door again. The black vines found him.

With one last kick, Frost opened the door; it slammed into the wall of a dark hallway.

Frost wheeled, saturating the puppets with lead, leaving some behind. He bolted through the door and shut it. The zombies smashed through.

In the hallway, blood defaced the left wall in swooshes, spatters, and chunks of dried flesh, graffiti, calligraphy, and cursive. Apartments lined the right. Most doors gaped, emitting putrefaction, and as Frost dashed past, residents emerged. He had expected fewer zombies. Nothing lived in this building, so the puppets had no provisions. And this close to the Haven, the majority prowled the streets. Nevertheless, twenty to thirty ghouls surrounded him, mostly Italians, as if an entire generation had lived here above the family restaurant.

Each corpse displayed advanced mutations: tentacles unraveling from an open mouth; a cognizant but shrunken extra head; a functional third arm. Grace must have been right: the zombies were cloning with their own stem cells. How else could the Italians advance without a food source?

Hurdling over lumps of slippery offal, over bloated cadavers lying in ring after ring of fluid stains, Frost made for the only window along the hall. It opened onto the roof. As he bounded over the body of a fat, bald Italian wearing boxers, a tank top, and floppy socks, tentacles whipped up from the floor like striking coral snakes. They gripped Frost and pulled him down. He landed on his side to salvage the flamethrower canisters. The Italian wormed toward him, belching gravy and black tadpoles. Other tentacles groped for Frost's throat.

He minced the Italian's face into ground sausage and then rolled, stood. The zombies blocked the window, too many to obliterate. More came up from behind. They would close in and trap, bury, smother, worse than any walls.

Frost hurtled through a doorway, into an apartment. Water stains spread across the ceiling and dripped onto the floor. Paper plates littered a coffee table, crusty with spaghetti sauce, pizza, and fettuccini.

Someone had been slaughtered on the couch. No body. Just the stains, contrasting pea-green upholstery and white pinstripes. A naked girl lay on the brown carpet, skin shrunken on her bones and sucked into the hollows of her pelvis, temples, and ribs. Something had peeled her belly, and her intestines were dried to the floor and to the newspapers strewn about her. Excrement moldered between her legs.

In a recliner facing the TV (an old dusty box with knobs instead of a touchpad), a man had committed suicide. His brains had rotted to the seatback and to the blue shoulders of his bathrobe like ruined manicotti.

Frost hurried toward the window.

A zombie jumped in front of him, three penises dangling from his boxers, one gray, the others black. A tentacle hung from his eye socket, none from between the frayed strands of his comb over. He held a Berretta. He shot Frost in the gut.

Frost never slowed. He swapped magazines and redecorated the walls with the Italian's skull matter. He pushed the corpse over, went to the window, and threw aside the curtains.

On the sill, dead flies had accumulated. Cobwebs fringed the frame, and rain turned the glass into an obsidian lava lamp. The window sash had been painted shut. It would not open.

Bringing only their appetites, zombie neighbors paid a visit. Frost smashed the windowpane with the butt of his Uzi. He knocked away the scimitars of glass and started through.

Puppet strings grabbed at him. Frost ducked through the gap and hung from the brick ledge. The Puppeteers fettered him, each manipulating him into separate dances and fits, his arms flailing overhead. Rainfall sputtered in his face.

Chips of glass still toothed the window. Frost ran along the brick wall, back and forth, lacerating the puppet strings on the sharp fragments. The string tethering his right hand slackened, went flaccid. Frost flung it to the zombies assembled below. He scuttled along the wall once again, catching the gutter pipe that poured into the sewer.

Straddling the duct, Frost pulled on his last restraint, dragging the puppeteer's head through the window. With the Uzi, he kneaded the Italian's face into unrecognizable dough, daubing the brick with rotten tomato paste.

Kicking back more tentacles, Frost shimmied toward the roof. The drainpipe creaked and bent, pulling loose from its brackets, bursting into waterfalls. Frost kept going and finally made it to the top.

Zombies had peopled even this locale. Recently, as well; when Frost's squad had passed on the skywalk, this roof had been desolate. Bain must have attracted them. Or maybe he had let them out.

The corpses hobbled out of the rain, moaning like the survivors of a terrible car crash. Frost leveled a group and let the downpour rinse their sins. He crossed a streetlamp bridge to the roof of a neighboring building and followed the catwalks toward the Haven.

Distant explosions announced Graves' bombardment: the Redhound had reached the Haven. Frost hastened, flamethrower sloshing on his back.

After Dominique tied the blanket rope to the rafters, Carly climbed up. They were working on the door when the gunshots intensified. Payton trembled. He whimpered, and despite her stinging wounds, Ann held him closer.

"It's okay," she crooned, stroking his hair. "We're safe."

"Jesus," Dominique said from the rafters. "Sounds like they're right out—"

Hinges shrilled as the hatch opened.

"Shit!" Dominique made a short yelp, as if slugged in the stomach.

Carly shrieked and tumbled from the rafters. When she hit the floor, something cracked. She began to wail. Dominique was silent, but under Carly's scream, under the gunfire, someone was slurping; a wet mass plopped onto the plywood.

Michael, Ann thought. He was eating her. He was eating Dominique.

The women scrambled around, shouting, colliding. Someone kneed Ann's shoulder and she cried out. More legs pushed her to the ground, and she had to roll away, away from the blanket, away from Payton, afraid of being trampled.

She hit the corner, safe.

Then Michael landed in the room.

A woman yowled. Flesh ripped and cartilage split.

"Payton!" Ann called, competing with the uproar.

He didn't answer.

Ann didn't shout again. Michael might recognize her voice. He might come for her, pieces of Ireland still stuck between his teeth.

Holding her hand out in front of her, Ann scooted away from the wall, cringing, expecting a stampede. There were more ripping sounds and a *gluck*,

gluck, gluck. She gagged on the raw smell of blood, meat, and feces, the brackish fumes of piss.

She couldn't handle it. She had to call out. She had to make sure the boy was okay.

"Payton!"

She stretched her arm farther, scooting, scooting—and then she touched someone.

Michael, she thought. *Oh God, Michael.*

But then the person cried out and shied away. And through the smell of slaughter, Ann caught the boy's buttery aroma.

"Payton," she said, "it's me! It's Ann!"

She found him again and pulled him into a hug. He tried to get away, but Ann murmured in his ear: "It's okay, it's all right—*shhh*." She took his hand and scampered back to her corner, away from the turmoil. She huddled over him and tried to pacify his sobs.

"Help me!" Ginny squealed, so close that spittle misted Ann's back. "Help!" Then Ginny gurgled as her enemy garroted her and dragged her off.

Payton bawled, and Ann rocked him, uttering prayers and ignoring the caterwauls of her new friends, ignoring Death, though he knocked, though he loomed, wearing Michael's face as a mask.

Shade leapt onto the catwalk. Two of three puppets had infiltrated the refectory. The third Shade had killed. As she strode toward the hatch, more zombies came up behind her. Cavanaugh covered her from the snare, shooting the zombie nearest her. The monster's cheek ulcerated, expectorating blood and tongue. Its body collapsed into the barbwire.

From below, a tentacle wrapped Shade's ankle and wrenched. She fell, catching the catwalk. The edge cut into her fingers. The zombie tugged, trying to drag her toward its hungry mouth. Other zombies balanced down the catwalk, headed for the refectory.

Cavanaugh killed the zombie that shackled Shade. She lifted herself onto the bridge and blocked the oncoming puppets. She kicked the first one, snapping its breastbone and knocking it back. Cavanaugh cut down the second, turning its head into a science project volcano.

Shade turned to the hatch.

At the mouth of the refectory, the first intruder had detained a black female. Its fattest tentacle elevated the woman, and its skinniest tunneled behind her eye. Another tentacle routed down the female's esophagus, an endoscope paired with a vacuum. Seizures wracked the woman's arms and legs. She was drooling, and her single eye roved in its socket.

Shade shot her. She shot the zombie. Both fell into the darkness.

In the room below, someone bellowed in anguish. Someone else driveled a rosary, and beneath that, Shade could hear the glug and suck of liposuction.

She descended into the refectory. The second intruder had pinioned a brunette to the floor. The brunette's neck was crushed, and the zombie explored her guts with its tentacle. It hissed at Shade. She shot it. She put a bullet in the woman's head.

There was one more fatality. She had been rent open at the ribcage, and a fatty lobe hung from her deflated breast. Shade dealt a bullet, a bribe to keep the dead from walking, a coin for the ferryman of the river Styx.

Except for three women and the boy, Shade's flock had been decimated. The third woman, the boy's surrogate mother, had broken a leg. Bone jutted from her calf. Shock glazed her eyes. She was sweating, mewling, crying. Agony had stretched her face tight, except for the furrows that quivered around her mouth and eyes. So fragile, so pathetic, bones of porcelain, organs overripe.

Let her suffer, the Beast said, wallowing in her fear. *Let her cry.*

"Please," the woman said, hitching. "Please—help."

Shade pointed her gun. The Beast roared, displeased, and the woman suffered no more. Now only the boy and two women were left. Their laments could pierce the thickest skin.

"Your Majesty!" Cavanaugh called, voice as loud as his pistol. "I can't hold them!"

As he said it, three zombies jumped down from the hatch. Two of them looked normal, but one suffered severe abnormalities. His stomach had patched an evisceration, but instead of a bellybutton, he had formed a penis, infant-sized and hooded in foreskin. His testicles had not dropped into their scrotal prune, and the penis dribbled urine onto his belt. The zombie's right cheek had been slit up to his molars, and his lips had healed that way. A crop of miniature tentacles wriggled on his chin.

His cronies rushed forward; he went for Payton and Ann.

Dodging a tentacle, Shade sidestepped one of the minions, a female. With a quick kick to the neck, she snapped the zombie's spine, paralyzing her. The other cohort lunged. Shade fired, and the puppet's carcass smacked the ground just as the woman's spine rehabilitated.

Useless penis flapping, the mutant pounced on Ann. Shade spackled the plaster with his gray matter and with pieces of his cranium, pieces of his face. Ann shuddered as the zombie slid off her. She continued to ramble, sheltering the boy from the carnage. The child had pissed on the floor. He blubbered, traumatized. Shade's eyes prickled with tears.

Biting down, she let the Beast consume her. She emptied her magazine into the last trespasser, the woman, tenderizing her head.

"Your Majesty!" Cavanaugh yelled.

Zombie reinforcements shambled down the catwalk.

Shade rocketed into the rafters.

Tentacles.

She cleared a path, reloaded, slashed with her knife, gun ablaze.

In the antechamber, Cavanaugh hopped from rock to rock. His pistol barked. His bullets mauled zombies. Innumerable corpses piled below the footbridge, a body dump from the plague. Some of the bodies foamed at the mouth, still animate. They struggled beneath their fallen comrades, tentacles demented, painted with gore.

Bolting the refectory hatch, Shade stayed on the catwalk.

A new wave of zombies swamped the room.

Cavanaugh exhausted his ammunition. Shade's was diminishing.

Trampling the flesh and bone that cushioned the barbwire, a battalion attacked the lieutenant. Batting away creepers, he joined Shade on the overpass.

"Fall back," Shade commanded.

He unbolted the hatch, but stopped. "Are you coming?"

"Fall back. Guard our flock."

"I will not," Cavanaugh said. "Not without you."

Shade shot an approaching zombie. Tentacles began to reach from below.

"I said fall back, Lieutenant. Someone must lock the door."

"Then let it be me. Let it—"

Shade's Glock interjected. A peephole opened in Cavanaugh's forehead, and all his thoughts blew out the back of his skull. Shade tried not to see his face (mouth agape, eyes like open wounds). She tried to picture Frost instead.

Cavanaugh fell into the darkness, fading like a ghost, down, down, down into a Stygian well. Shade locked the refectory behind him. She howled, freeing squalls, unleashing tempests. She fired at the zombies and blinked back tears.

Forty-seven

A circus sideshow capered after Frost across the skywalk, three-legged men and triple-nippled girls, faster than the humans they impersonated, accelerating through the crackle and screen of rain.

From a tenement, Frost teetered along an extension ladder toward a window washer's platform, rigged to an office building. The freaks performed the high wire act with equal agility.

Frost made it to the platform and began to climb its cables. Fleshy whips captured his leg and pulled. He used his Uzi, and a quadruplet of acrobats cartwheeled over the railing. More climbed after him to the top of the office building.

Up here, fans, exhaust pipes, and cooling units had colonized. In the night beyond them, Graves' bombardment continued: poppies burgeoned from volatile seeds, nurtured by the rainstorm, fostered by the blacktop. Each flower telecasted audio blooms, overlapping explosions and concussions.

Frost sped to the building's edge. Many smaller buildings came into view. The Haven towered over them, its boarded-up face lit by explosive flowers, a rose in death's twilight kingdom.

Behind him, circus freaks gamboled onto the building. They flexed extra arms and wheezed through various nostrils.

Frost jumped over the edge, disregarding the rope that led down to the next bridge of the skywalk. He soared, cape open in a giant wing, Uzi pendent on its strap. Rain pelted his face, and the wind buffeted him.

Zombie aerialists dove after him, plummeting to their messy deaths, splattering on the sidewalk. One smashed the roof of an Impala and shattered the windshield.

Frost alit atop the apartment block that neighbored the Haven. His legs buckled and he rolled, trying to distribute the impact. He stood up. His heels hurt, but his legs weren't broken.

No circus performers harassed him on his way to the fire escape.

In the street, zombies rallied around the Redhound like ants surrounding a caterpillar. Graves bobbed out of the roof hatch, scattering poppy seeds from the M203 grenade launcher attached to his rifle. The flower petals scintillated, brilliant orange, brilliant red, and nearby insects burst into crimson vapor, into innards and limbs. In its wake, the Redhound's plow left blood meal and bone.

The ants scaled the bus, burrowing under its exoskeleton. Some tried for Graves, but they tangled with the crown of concertina wire. Graves exterminated them with the M16.

The Redhound veered into the clearing of grenade-scorched pavement and potholes. It reversed over the cemetery gate, which had fallen completely, and the bumper met barricade, pushing against the Bloodhound's conduit. The engine cut off, and Victor emerged from the hatch. Chucking bug bombs, he scurried across the roof to the barrier. He sprang over the concertina wire and ascended the boulders and steel beams, rising toward the Haven.

Graves operated the machinegun mounted to the roof, eliminating zombies, a hailstorm of shells.

Satisfied, Frost retrieved his handlebar from the lockbox. One pair was missing. Only Cavanaugh and Bain owned extra keys.

Frost inspected the Haven's fire escape. No sign of the colonel. Just zombies hiking the stairs. Down in the barricade, a chauffer had taken the place of the police officer and was lifting others to the escape.

Frost whizzed down the cable to the Haven, his final flight before reentering the tomb. Leaving the handlebars attached to the zipline, he eliminated the chauffeur and mowed through the zombies toward the top. They were thick with tentacles, growing up the building in vines.

With his Uzi, Frost cut a zombie in half and threw the foliage overboard, intestines running out in stillborn snakes. He cut until his bullets ran out.

He cursed. He couldn't use the flamethrower, couldn't encircle himself with fire. The jungle closed in, ready to tear him open like a bag of compost. Frost pruned back creepers with his knife. He booted a knot of them over the guardrail, slashed one at the tip and watched it bloom into black flags.

Vines knotted around his arm. Some dangled from the platform above, questing for his face. He grabbed one. It grabbed him back.

Planting off the handrail, Frost swung high on the grapevine, grabbing the railing on the next platform up. The tentacle pulled at him, suctioned to his arm. He severed it with his knife and leapt up another story.

No zombies choked this level. Frost went over the railing and continued up the stairs, vines growing after him. He awakened the flamethrower and burned them back.

On the roof, Bain had left a surprise: a gaggle of blazing Nazis clubbing the stairwell door. The supremacists turned on Frost, their faces mere crisps on a skull. He skirted them, luring them away from the entrance, doubling back to the door.

It was unlocked. He left it open.

He let the Nazis enter behind.

Rousing the flamethrower, he assisted the bigots. Some say the world will end in fire, some say in ice. Frost thought both. He decked the walls with Hitler's red flags and spread propaganda all down the stairs.

Aside from Payton's sniffling, the room was quiet. Carly had stopped bleating. Dominique no longer joked. Outside, the gunfight continued. The door was shut. Ann raised her head but could see nothing.

"Hello?"

Nobody answered. No Ginny, no Carly, no Shirley. No one.

Ann caressed Payton's cheek. "I have to get up, honey. You have to let go."

"Huh-uh," he said, shaking his head and clinging tighter. "No."

"I have to," she said. "I have to see if ..."

If everyone's dead, Michael finished.

"I have to see if everyone's okay. I have to help them."

She pried away from him and crawled along the floor, knees grinding against the wood. Her hand bumped into something—a body. Long hair, small nose. Warm lips, but no breath; warm neck, but no pulse. Ann jerked her hand back, chilled. She let out a small moan.

"Annie?" Payton said. "Annie, where are you?"

"I'm here," she replied, swallowing vomit. She wiped her hand on the floor. "I'm fine."

Payton's feet scuffed plywood, and Ann glanced back. She held her hand out like a stop sign. She knew Payton couldn't see it, but maybe he would feel it subliminally.

"Stay there," she said. "I'll be back."

Payton didn't say anything. The scuffing sound stopped.

Careful not to touch the body, careful not to nudge it, Ann went farther into the room. Several feet away, she set her hand in a lukewarm puddle. She recoiled. She put her fingers to her nostrils. Through her nose and down her throat, pennies melted, copper drizzled. She stifled retches and smeared the blood on the plywood. A residue coated her palm.

Stomaching the acids, Ann quested deeper until her fingers met flesh. The lump of meat neither reacted nor breathed. Ann backed away, still cleaning her hand on the floor.

"Hello?" she said. "Carly? Dominique?"

"Carly-momma," Payton called. "Carly-momma? Where is she?"

"I don't know." Ann tried to sand the warbles out of her voice, but it still sounded bumpy and warped. She listened for breathing, for anything. She heard only her heartbeat and Payton's accelerated respiration, the gunshots from right outside.

She allowed this body a wide berth.

Ahead, she found the quilt she had shared with Payton, rumpled from the mayhem. Ann used it like a hand towel, scrubbing off the blood. Bringing the blanket along, she found the wall and followed it, brushing against it with her hip and shoulder.

She stumbled on a third body, this one in leather. The hand of the corpse was cold but pliable. Ann checked for a pulse: none.

"He's not dead," someone announced from the nethers of the room.

Ann gasped and pulled her hand away. "Shirley? Oh my God, are you okay?"

Before Shirley could respond, the cold body grabbed Ann's arm and sprang upright. She screamed and tried to pull away, but the corpse held her. It croaked, attempting to speak. Its message was barely decipherable: "Where is she?"

"Please," Ann said, "I just—I was just trying to help—"

"Where is she?"

Ann thought he meant Ireland. "I don't know. I don't know what you mean."

"She shot you," Shirley told the corpse. "She shot you and locked you in here."

Groaning, the man used Ann to stand. He kept his hand on her shoulder, wobbling, top-heavy. His skin was cold.

Michael.

He leered down at her, white teeth glowing. Dark bits flecked the gaps between his teeth, and his breath reeked like a gutted deer, like the poor herbivores he hunted and butchered.

He had gotten to Ireland. He had eaten her, and now he would eat Ann too.

Michael hauled her to her feet.

"Please," she said. "I love you. I love you."

He slammed her against the wall and bit into her neck, that familiar pang of lover transcending hymen. Ann's nipples hardened. Acupuncture needles tingled down her spine.

She had been waiting for this—oh God, how she had waited!

Ann hugged him, hooked her leg around him, grinding. She put a hand on the back of his head—except there was nothing there but a pit rimmed with bone shards and mats of hair. She poked something squishy. Membranes and cortexes began to seal around her fingers like lips forming a kiss. She moved her hand, shuddering, now stroking the nape of his neck and his long hair, nibbling his ear, gnashing the lobe.

"Please," she said, holding him tighter, kissing his cheek, biting. "I love you."

He continued to feed, and the room grew darker.

The gunshots outside fell dead.

Tentacles shackled her. Shade spent her final bullet in a bellhop's cranium and tossed her Glock. The zombies had cornered her. Even if she fought, they would win.

Holding her pentagram, she pressed against the refectory hatch. She crossed her arms in salute and closed her eyes. "For the City of Roses," she said.

The tentacles began to mummify her. Suckers smooched leather and skin.

"For Roman."

Down the hall, automatic gunfire echoed into a crescendo.

"Your Highness!" Edward yelled.

"Edward!"

With her knife, Shade cut her constraints. More scuffled with her, but she beheaded the hydras and vaulted off the catwalk.

The puppets had overlooked a sector of the snare. Near the wall, a rock obtruded from the barbwire. Shade lit on it and snatched up the wire. Like a caterpillar, she spun a cocoon and suspended herself in the brambles. Most the zombies ignored her, coveting the morsels in the refectory. She managed to avert any carnivores, slashing with her knife through her thorny shell.

Edward arrived at the door of the snare. Puppets confronted him, and he sawed through them with his machinegun. He spotted Shade and threw a carbine to her. She disentangled herself and joined the extermination, killing the zombies nearest the refectory hatch.

Soon, Shade and Edward stood amid brain muck and twitching cadavers. The Sexton took Shade's hand and helped her onto solid ground.

"Hurry," he said as more zombies poured into the room. "There's a fire."

Shade stepped away from him. "Cavanaugh."

She climbed to the catwalk and threw back the bolts. Beyond the hatch, the refectory lay silent against the clangor of Edward's fusillade.

"Lieutenant," Shade said. "Rise."

Panting, someone shifted against wood, but Cavanaugh remained unresponsive. Maybe she had killed him. Maybe during his fall, he had broken a rafter and the splinters had impaled him. Or maybe he was lurking, waiting to attack.

"Cavanaugh."

"Your Highness," Edward yelled. "Please!"

Cavanaugh appeared at the doorway, brown hair windswept, hazel eyes wild. Shade embraced him, breathing in ginger and chives.

"Forgive me," she said. "I had to."

He pressed cool lips against her forehead and whispered absolution: "I know." His breath smelled of blood. He had fed.

"Your Highness!" Edward reloaded, stepping back as more puppets came into the room.

Shade handed her knife to Cavanaugh. "Come," she said. "Join us."

With her carbine, Shade helped Edward push the zombies into the empty room and then into the hallway. Divots and holes marred the warren door, but the barrier had withstood the pillagers. Somehow, Grace had fortified it.

With a massacre behind them, Shade, Edward, and Cavanaugh progressed to the stairwell. Smoke had filled the shaft, and the upper stories blushed ochre and orange.

On the staircase, they caught Victor ascending to the fourth-floor platform. Shade pinned him against the wall, driving the oaken stake between his ribs.

"Good evening, Victor," she said, grinning in his face. "Where's our general? Where's Frost?"

As his retinue of SS soldiers crumbled to smoldering skeletons, Frost entered the penthouse level. He stopped at Roman's door, at the roses. The light from the stairwell licked the flowers and trapped itself in the cellophane wrapping. Frost splashed the flowers with Cabernet Sauvignon, trapping the light in each petal, giving the corolla iridescent life. He saluted. Then he moved to Shade's apartment and kicked down the door.

Frost had never set foot in Shade's living room. No furniture or carpet covered the plywood. The room was free and open, the walls a comfortable distance. One wall featured countless bullet holes, cavities, and punctures. Frost imagined Shade, breasts heaving and glistening with sweat as she beat the plaster with her fists, as she gashed it again and again with her blade.

Shade's bedroom was equally Spartan, so unlike Grace's. Frost could have lived in here. He could have thrived.

To the ceiling, Shade had fixed a pull-up bar, from which she probably hung upside down. She had no bed, just a pentagram of votive candles melded to the floor with wax.

Using the ever-burning tip of his flamethrower, Frost lit the design. Luminous cardinals took flight from the wicks, darting and flitting about the chamber. Their scarlet plumage brightened the walls, where a surreal mural stretched in black and red marker, red for the roses and blood.

On the back wall, a monolith loomed from cement rubble, from rose-bushes made of barbwire and scraps of gory flesh. Wooden marionettes swarmed the streets surrounding the building, and human-sized bats swooped around it. A rose vine strapped a heart to the monolith's black stone, bruising the muscle, puncturing it, watering the flowers below with dark red rivulets. The marionettes too close to the rosebushes exploded into splatters of eyeballs, teeth, and brain, shot by the sentries atop the roof. The splatters folded into petals, into roses, a scarlet field around a dark tower.

In the corner of the left wall, past the zombie ranks, a human puppeteer peeked out, eyes bloodshot and sneering, hand extended, fingers strumming the puppet strings. On the right wall, beyond legions of the undead, Shade had illustrated the Elizabethan theater. A single rose grew from it, its spine twisted as if arthritic, its leaves threadbare and papery. Its bud mirrored the monolith's bleeding heart.

Frost aimed his flamethrower at the Haven's caricature, prepared to anoint the building with flame. But light and dark metamorphosed into the nude human form, into Shade, her pallor slick with candlelight, shadows sashaying like hair over her shoulders and breasts. She worked in fast-forward, skittering from one section of wall to the next, inking in the maws of the puppets, pigmenting the roses of blood.

Frost lowered his flamethrower. He left the spirit to her art and canvas.

In the living room, he vented his own ire on Shade's punching wall. The fire curled like a fox, razing the lath and plaster with its teeth. Frost coaxed the fox to the other walls and wheedled it into the corridor, watching its ridgeback bristle, watching its tail wag.

Canine and master crossed into the stairwell. Frost united the fox with its parent blaze and let it frisk and frolic and tear up the stairs. Puppets braved the man-eating dogs of fire, stripped of their flesh, now just charred vertebrates, walking bones, the strings of their manipulators nearly incinerated, simmering in pressure-cooker skulls.

Frost led them downstairs. Near the sixth-floor landing, he encountered corpses intact, waiting in queue as the ones ahead of them went through the barbwire border. The illegal immigrants were too dense to navigate, so Frost sicced his foxes on the stragglers and bounded into the shaft. He flew over the puppets that crowded the fifth-floor landing and touched down in the seer's hallway, where specters chanted hexes to repel the zombies. Puppeteers tested the hall with tentative feelers, but cringed at the chill of ectoplasm. The puppets dismissed the passage and went to meet the guns of the border patrol.

Flamethrower in remission, Frost fanned away the phantoms. He stalked down the corridor, boots clopping in time with the firefight below.

Slumped against the wall, Ann wept. Michael had drained her vigor, had siphoned it from her neck. She hated herself for giving in to him.

"Annie?" Payton called from across the room. "Annie-momma?"

Ann could only sob in response, a suppressed sob, all the wind knocked from her, her solar plexus seized.

Payton's knees clonked against the floor, as if he were crawling.

"Annie-momma?"

The clonking stopped, and Payton gasped. When he spoke, his voice trebled high, like water tension about to break. "Annie-momma, I found someone. She's—she's all sticky."

"She's dead," Shirley said from her corner. "They're all dead."

"Payton," Ann wheezed, "please. Get away from there."

Finally, his small hand found her. He hugged her, rankling the fish-hooks in her arm; numbness dulled the barbs.

"I warned you," Shirley said. "I said what would happen."

Ann mustered enough strength to cover Payton's ears. "Go to hell," she said.

Shirley chuckled, dry as smoke. "Look around, hon. Where do you think we are?"

"Why didn't you help? Why didn't you help us?"

"Because. I didn't want to end up on the floor like Carly."

Ann sat upright, dependant on the wall for balance. She cradled Payton and combed through his hair, glaring through the dark toward Shirley. "You're already on the floor."

"Yeah," Shirley said, "but at least I'm alive. You should be glad to say the same."

"Why are you like this?" Ann asked. She didn't really expect an answer. It was just the only alternative to slapping the bitch. "What the hell happened to you?"

Shirley didn't answer, and Ann began to doubt she ever would.

"I had a husband, too," she said. "Steven. I wanted to stay at our apartment—we had food, water, cigarettes … booze—but he said it was best we find other survivors. So we did. A whole apartment of them. Women, children, men with guns. Then *they* showed up, the vampires, and that's how I lost my eye."

She fell silent for a moment, and Ann thought she was finished. But then Shirley continued. And now there was something different about her voice; the smoke had thickened. "That's how I lost Steven."

Another pause. Shirley cleared her throat and went on. "He tried to protect the others. Tried to attack the vampires with his Swiss Army knife. His *Swiss Army knife*, for Christ's sake." She laughed, dry and humorless.

Ann could almost see her shake her head. Then Shirley's voice went flat and cold. Ann knew the woman was looking at her, and shuddered.

Shirley said, "One of them shot Steven in the face."

Ann waited a full minute before deciding the story was over. "I'm sorry," she said, a little chilled by the temperature of her voice, a little vindicated too. She did feel a prick of empathy for the woman, but she could easily ignore it.

"Nothing to be sorry about," Shirley said. "Steven was an idiot. We were fine by ourselves, but he had to drag me into it. I should have let him go by himself. Because that's the only way to survive in this world. By your own damn self."

Ann tightened her arm around Payton. His breath puffed softly against the outside of her breast, small and warm. "I'd rather be dead than alone."

Shirley chuckled. "Hon," she said, "that's where you and me differ."

"Where's Frost?" Shade repeated, pressing the dagger deeper into Victor's ribcage. On the landing above them, Edward and Cavanaugh shot the puppets that slipped through the barbwire. Cavanaugh had picked up his shotgun, which, surprisingly, the zombies had ignored.

Smoke continued to fill the stairwell.

"General Frost left us," Victor said. "He sent me to deliver our sheep."

"He set this fire, then. He caused the outbreak."

"No. Colonel Bain had the flamethrower. He abandoned us."

Shade recalled the colonel's slave, pulped and stowed in his closet. For some time, Bain's underpinnings had been rusting, deteriorating, his eyes always jittering as if barely contained in their sockets. His worsening cigarette habit exemplified this breakdown. Still, this havoc did not stink of Bain. It stank of Frost.

"Your Highness," Edward said, looking back over his shoulder. "The fire! It's spreading! It's getting worse!"

True, flaming hunks of wood dropped and sowed new blazes. Cavanaugh swatted coals out of his long black hair. And the firelight now evoked shadow play, black snakes flicking black tongues, waves breaking upon a beach—all things from Plato's cave. There was a world beyond this, a whole world!

"We'll all die," Victor said. Though unsmiling, he was ever the hyena, that predatory gleam of teeth, that hint of a grin. "We've got to leave."

Again, Shade appraised the fire. Before long, the upper stories would collapse and destroy those below.

A dark figure flew past overhead. Not just another shadow. Frost.

"Edward," Shade said, staring into Victor's eyes. "Escort Victor to the refectory. Round the humans into the warren and wait for me there."

"Yes, your Highness."

Shade spoke conspiratorially, so only Victor could hear. "I know about the woman," she said, noticing the slightest tic in his lip. "There will be a trial. Obey my orders, mine alone, and your punishment will be less severe."

"Yes, your Majesty."

His lip had curled, and Shade could see he was probably beyond rehabilitation. She considered killing him. But he had valuable skill with a wrench. Besides, he was close to Frost and could have information, answers to Shade's many questions.

She withdrew the stake from his ribs. "Go," she said. "Edward will lead you."

Victor saluted her and marched away, Edward following.

On the stairs, Edward had left a shipment of barbwire. Shade carried it to the landing, where Cavanaugh blasted zombies, corking the breach with the dead.

"Allow me," she said, and she stuffed the wire into the gap and entangled it.

"They seem to have declined," Cavanaugh observed. Less than half a dozen tussled with the snare, weaponless, unable to trim the brush.

"The fire," Shade explained.

"Of course."

She avoided his eyes, for her gunshot might have still echoed there.

"Help them corral the humans," she said.

"Are we leaving then?"

Shade blew away a firefly. "We may have no choice." She stepped to the balustrade and placed her hand upon it, as if to hurdle it.

"Where are you going?"

Shade looked back. She did not answer, and Cavanaugh did not press. Evidently, the gunshot *did* still echo. All through his head. Through Shade's, too.

She planted off the balustrade and bounded upward.

Her pentagram reflected infernos.

So did her eyes.

Fifty-Three

The wraiths thickened near the seer's apartment. Frost waded through the murk, through the screeching faces and writhing torsos. He shivered. His testicles shriveled up into his pelvis. How he craved the high mercury of his blaze.

The ghosts tried to absorb his thoughts, but he locked his secrets beneath the ice of his eyes. The specters could not thaw the vault.

Frost opened the seer's door.

She was snoring, chortling, a bullfrog. The room smelled of pond scum and sewage. Black seaweed floated around the seer's sleeping bulk, undulating on imperceptible currents, much like the feelers that surrounded Colonel Bain: not tentacles, but psychic antennae and siphons.

As Frost stepped into the tendrils, the seer grumbled and stirred. She opened her eyes, and around the room, candles flared on end tables and stands. Light urinated upon her flaps and folds. On her chins, slobber glistened. It seeped down her neck, webbing her nest of moles. It ran all down her shoulder.

"You," she said, gurgling algae. "I know what you've done."

Frost came closer, and the seer's ghostly vines knotted into a shield around her.

"Stay away!"

Yellow fluids drenched the seer's futon mattress, tinting the air with sodium and humid ammonia. Pus slimed the khaki fabric. It stank of an infected wound.

Frost readied the flamethrower. He moved forward, colliding with an invisible membrane. The sac enveloped him, and its capillaries hemorrhaged. Ruby ink infused the film, unfurling into a rose bud, a heart. Frost's vision reddened, and then drained into darkness.

A moon leered down at him, empty eye sockets, lipless grin. It was his reflection. He was the moon. Below him, black, silver-frothed waves lapped a gray beach. Two sets of footsteps disappeared on the horizon, one big, one small. Salt lingered on the breeze, alchemized into blood.

The Sitka spruces opposite the ocean curled over and clawed away the sand. The waves gnawed at the shore, and the beach began to crumble. Waves swept the footsteps off the beach, and then swept the sand into darkness.

Frost's moonlight dimmed.

From the center of the void, a wine stain unfurled. It pulsed, and red rivers scriggled across black silt, spilling and spilling until Frost bared his fangs. He activated the flamethrower, and the wine began to gray. The psychic membrane wilted, decomposed, revealing the seer.

The flame engulfed her. She clamored and flapped her arms, fat slapping fat. Thunderheads materialized above her. In the black and purple heavens, chain lightning buzzed. Dazzling bolts struck. The clouds began to leak, but the fire endured the supernatural rain.

Frost distanced himself from the pyre, reveling in its nimbus, admiring its core.

Lard bubbled and boiled from underneath scorched flesh. The seer's eyes burst like cysts, and she piped at a dangerous boiling-tea pitch, raking away the fried skin of her jowls. Her keen amplified, honed into a spike. It rose to a tremolo. The seer vibrated and began to crack. And at the highest soprano, she fulminated, a flash of fire-spawned pterodactyls, vultures, and crows. Shedding feathers of combustion, the birds molted into soot. The candles waned, and the room darkened. Other than the char on the futon, nothing remained but the smell of singed hair and barbeque.

Frost kindled the khaki mattress. He converted the entire front room into a furnace and continued into the hall. The seer's phantasms dissipated and became smoke. Only one lingered. A star glittered on the apparition's breast, and night-spun tapestries of hair parted around a granite-chiseled face.

Frost crossed his arms over his chest in salute.

Roman stared at him. He turned and walked into the flames.

The general returned to his ritual of fire, and the building griped, suffering heartburn, an ill not even the rain could cure.

Fifty-Four

The door opened in the rafters above, letting in a beam of blinding light. Payton cowered against Ann, and she defended him with her arm.

Shirley surfaced in the light: gray hair, though her face was a peach, no wrinkles. Her left eye hid in shadow, probably the one she was missing. She sat against the wall with her legs crossed in front of her. Like Ann, she was nude. Her breasts pointed in opposite directions. A big mole flawed her neck.

Ann looked away, not because she feared the other woman's gaze, but because of the murder scene between them. No matter how much she blinked, a snapshot had imprinted her retinas. Blood stood out the most—blood, and the exit wound left by each victim's scream.

Two men lowered into the room, bringing smoke. The light concentrated on Ann. She covered her eyes and tried to quell Payton's trembles.

"Well, well, well," Victor said, standing over her, penny clinking against teeth. He was so close that Ann could smell motor oil. "What happened to this one?"

The other man stepped beside Victor, just an outline. "We found her in the stairwell. Have you seen her before?"

"No."

Victor seized Ann's good arm and lifted.

"Annie-momma!" Payton clung to her, scrabbling for a better hold, but Victor booted him in the chest and he sprawled on the floor.

"Payton!"

Victor pulled Ann away. "Grab the other two," he told his accomplice. He grappled Ann from behind and launched into the rafters, where he muscled her through the hatch.

His flashlight surveyed the corpses below. They all had tentacles. Some had extra body parts, extra eyeballs and ears. The room sweltered with smoke, gunpowder, and blood. And another smell. Something like castor oil, only clammier, more organic, maybe coming from the black goo that stained the bodies, from the chunks of black and red organs heaped on the rocks and dangling from the barbwire.

Something moved in the body pile. Victor's light passed over a corpse with no head, and Ann thought she saw Michael, grinning from behind the body, mouth rimmed with gore, brains between his teeth. Then the light moved away, and Michael disappeared. Ann could still hear the wet smack and squish as her husband devoured the slop.

In the empty room after the snare, Victor turned to Ann, his voice low and menacing. "Is that your boy in there?"

Ann tried to look oblivious, dazed.

"Well, if you don't want me to cut his pretty little throat, you'll do as I say. Do you hear me?" He wrenched her arm to the breaking point. "I said *do you hear me*?"

"Yes," Ann said, biting down to stop her tears.

"Good." Victor peeked into the hallway and shined his light both ways, illuminating smog and several bodies, all dead. He turned back to Ann. "There will be questions," he said, "an inquisition. You will say that you broke into the building. Your wounds? Inflicted by another human. If you say one word about our little bit of fun—one word at all—the boy dies. Horribly."

Ann remembered Victor's story about his grandfather—*I cut out his eyes and put him in a room full of broken glass.* She shuddered.

In the snare behind them, the catwalk creaked; Payton blubbered.

"Come," Victor said. He steered into the hall.

Cotton wads of smoke clogged Ann's lungs. When she coughed, the cotton turned to burdocks, prickly and hard. Something squished beneath her foot. She fixed her gaze straight ahead, swallowing, swallowing, because thick saliva suddenly filled her mouth, because her stomach suddenly churned with the smell of raw meat and that castor oil stink.

As her foot pulled free from the muck, she gagged, doing her best to clean her sole on the hallway's cardinal runner. But even the carpet was soiled with dumplings of gore and toothpicks of bone.

Down the hall, Victor pounded on apartment 404. "Grace! Open up! It's Victor!"

The door swung inward. Mistress peered out. Her eyes had sunken into bruised sockets, and her hair, usually lustrous filigree, now resembled straw. She noticed Ann, but acted like a stranger.

"What's going on?" she asked Victor. "Where's Frost?"

"He's coming. Have you done—?"

"Yes."

"Good. Let me in."

In the warren, lanterns revealed no harnesses. The torsos now hung from a set of costume racks, like those from a movie set. Ellie swayed in the center of one rack. Mistress had not removed her eyes, and Ellie was looking around with the amazement of a child. Her belly still swelled with Ireland.

Ann wanted very much to go to her sister, to stroke her hair and sing her a lullaby, to feel the bulge and warmth of life inside her. But Victor had already threatened Payton, and Ann would not endanger Ellie as well. She forced herself to look away and to quit fidgeting with her wedding ring.

Another knock at the door.

"It's Edward," the caller said.

Mistress let him in, along with Shirley and Payton.

"Annie-momma!"

The boy tore away from Edward and dashed toward Ann.

Victor latched onto his fragile arm. "Take the women," he said, pushing Ann toward Edward. Payton reached out, but Victor lifted him. "I'll watch the brat."

"What are we supposed to do?" Grace asked.

Victor caressed Payton's cheek, leering at Ann. "We wait," he said. "Frost will come."

Fifty-five

The stairwell was a snow globe gone volcanic. Molten snowflakes spiraled down, and the air rippled with heat. The staircase groaned. With her back against the wall, Shade waited by the hallway where Frost charmed fire from his dragon. His demons cackled as they axed support beams, doorframes, plaster, and lath, replacing the seer's phantoms and waifs.

He had killed her. He had killed the seer. Shade could feel it, some weight lifted, some electrical current gone, like electrolytes flushed from the body. No more magnetic poles. In some ways, the seer had been their gravity. Without her, they would drift into space, doomed to darkness and chaos.

Shade fingered the oaken stake and shut her eyes to the stinging heat. In the sunrise behind her eyelids, the final ramparts of Roman's castle slipped into the sea.

Frost's footsteps came closer.

Shade held her breath. She had to disarm him; her pentagram retarded small amounts of fire, but the flamethrower exceeded its threshold. He would cremate her.

Backward, Frost emerged from the hallway.

Shade ripped the canister off his shoulders. He whirled and brought around the flamethrower's gun. Shade held it sideways. It spit fire onto the wall beside her, a hot and raging Satan.

Frost drove Shade into the banister. She nearly tumbled over.

"Your Majesty," he said, bowing his head in mock reverence.

Shade shoved him back. He threw aside the flamethrower, his face glimmering bloody in the flames.

"Traitor," she said, circling with him.

"The *island*, Shade." That old snake hissed beneath his words, and the lust began to smolder behind her breast. "The freedom, the hunt."

She saw it again, the beach, the man. And the blood—the *blood!*—such a red apple in such a green Eden.

She clutched her pentagram and shook her head. "Murderer."

Frost stopped suddenly, and the fervor dropped from his cheeks, leaving him pale, wintry, a corpse. "I—"

"I will kill you," she said.

He nodded gravely. "So be it." And then he lunged.

Shade dodged him. She kicked out, and his leg buckled inward. At the same time, metal seared across her throat. Her artery spooled out ribbons of wine, burgundy unraveling in pennants and flags.

Crippled, Frost cut her again, plunging the knife into her gut. He turned it, fashioning a red-lined orifice before pulling out. Shade staggered, gulping air through the mouth in her throat and muffling the one in her belly.

Frost threw his blade. Shade moved, but it still slit her face. Her cheek flopped open, revealing teeth. A crow's feather of hair floated to the floor.

As Shade reeled from the assault, Frost came in low, hobbling yet quick. He dug into her belly and plunged through intestines, burrowing beneath her ribcage, seeking her heart. Shade kneed him in the jaw. He fell, sputtering blood and pieces of enamel.

Through the snowing embers, Shade swooped, pulling out the oaken stake that had killed her father. Her hair streamed behind her, intertwined with the still flowing strips of blood.

Frost rolled. He held a broken baluster. Shade spitted herself upon it, felt it gore her stomach and probe beneath her ribs. It punched a grunt deep from her solar plexus.

Frost grinned, teeth fragmented and stained garnet. Shade looked down between their chests. Frost looked too. His grin wavered.

"Sturm, swung, wucht," Shade whispered.

She pulled the oaken stake from between his ribs, and fire ants scoured his face.

The vampires marshaled Ann, Shirley, and Payton into a line near the torsos, against the wall. Victor placed Payton on the other side of Shirley, so Ann could not comfort him. Shirley would not touch the boy, reserving half a foot of personal distance on either side, avoiding eye contact by staring into space, her head held high.

Cavanaugh had shown up. He, Edward, and Victor stood watch over the line while Mistress and Adia double-checked each torso's harness, checking the buckles and straps and the carabineers that latched them to the bar.

When no one was watching, Ann examined Ellie for any incisions or bruises, pleased to find her sister's skin milky and unscathed. In fact, Ellie waggled her leg stumps and sniggered, drooling but happy, aglow with motherhood.

Frank seemed less exuberant. He stared at Ann, his eyes the same natural gas flames. Partially hidden in the brush of his beard, his lips were pressed flat, incapable of smiling. Ann tried to ignore him, but his gaze burned into her breast, right where Victor had branded her. She crossed her arms over her bosom, careful to keep her pierced arm on the outside.

Someone knocked on the door.

"It's Frost," Victor said.

Cavanaugh opened the door. On the other side, the raven waited: Shade. Her cheek lay open, and the stomach of her corset had been gashed. Frowning with two flappy lips, her neck salivated down her chest and down the sleeve of her coat. A wooden dowel protruded from just under her ribs.

Cavanaugh pulled it out. He took Shade's arm and helped her into the room. He brought her to the line, to Shirley.

"Here," he said. "Drink."

Shirley tilted her head to expose old puncture wounds. Shade bit into her and licked. Her cheek began to splice itself. The grimace across her neck pursed its lips, turned white, and vanished.

Shirley's eyelids fluttered. She moaned and tweaked her nipple. Ann, too, felt the heat, that furnace above her bosom, warming her brain and sending sparks all through her nervous system, vibrating in each filament like notes on a violin. She could still feel Michael's mouth close over her throat, could still feel him penetrate her. He was feeding from her, even now, even though his touch had cooled from her skin.

Completely healed, Shade pulled away from Shirley. The woman slouched against the wall with a smile and a sigh, heaving from some mysterious orgasm. Pale, so very pale. Her empty eye socket flickered with shadows. And though ecstasy swelled inside her, Ann shivered. That eye, that terrible missing eye—looking into it, Ann felt very cold and very much alone.

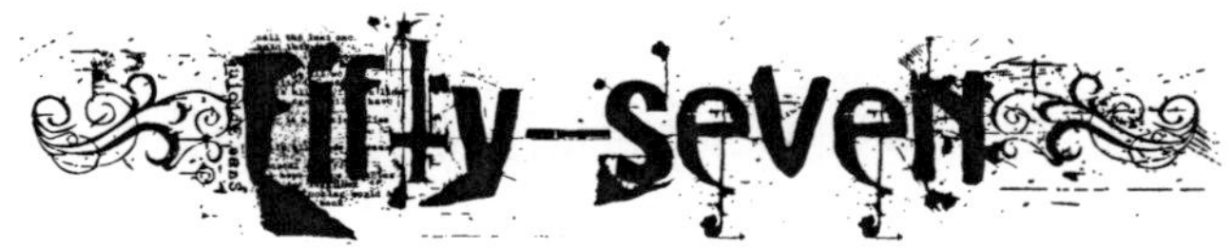

Fifty-seven

Shade felt better, repaired. Blood always sped up the healing process, giving cells the necessary nourishment, and the one-eyed woman—Shirley, her name was Shirley—her wine was nearly vintage. Shade's organs mended around the hole that Frost had dug, but still she felt empty, as if she had lost something, something that had burned up with her enemy, the man who made love to her atop the Haven (yes, it had been love; Shade knew that now), the very man who murdered her father. She supposed this hole would never heal.

She turned to Victor. "Where's the Redhound?"

"Outside. Graves is guarding it."

"Good. Open the tunnel. Cavanaugh, accompany him. Edward will gather the arsenal."

The three men left, leaving Shade, Grace, and Adia.

"Where's General Frost?" Grace asked.

Shade studied the bellies of the female torsos. "How many are pregnant?"

"Two. Where is he?"

"Bring just those two. And one man. We can carry no more."

"Where is he?"

Shade faced her. She recognized the feel of her own expression: it was Frost's mask of ice. "General Frost is dead."

Grace crossed her arms. "You mean you killed him."

"He betrayed us."

"He was *saving* us. You would've kept us here to rot."

Shade stepped close, locking eyes with the midwife. Grace kept glancing away, but the scowl never left her face.

"I made a promise," Shade said. "My father told me to protect our home, and I have. At the expense of my own men, I have. Anything less would have been sacrilege."

Grace still looked defiant, but she kept her mouth shut.

Shade stepped away. Twitches wracked her mask of ice, and she tried to stop them. The hole inside her sagged and deepened. Had Frost suffered these same tremors? Had he fought to hide them? Perhaps, Shade thought, but only in the beginning, only before murder chilled his heart.

She finally suppressed the twitches and straightened her back, a little sickened by her slouch, that pitiful human posture. "Prepare the torsos," she said. "The pregnant women and one man."

Grace said nothing. She and Adia consolidated the pregnant torsos on one costume rack, and Shade looked at the humans standing against the wall. Ann was there, still upright despite all her wounds. She glanced away from one of the torsos and looked at Shade.

Soon, Edward returned with a box of flashlights, firearms, ammunition, and concussion grenades. Three machetes hung from his waist.

To the crossbar of the costume rack, Grace had strapped a duffel bag of medical supplies and instruments. Edward doled out weaponry and added the spare guns to the bag.

"It's time," Shade said, fitting some grenades into the loops on her belt. "Let's move."

Edward and Grace each hefted an end of the costume rack. Adia shepherded the humans from behind, and Shade took point, leading everyone to the stairs.

The stairwell sweltered with smoke and flame. Logs of the staircase clunked down all around, and the heat baked Shade's face.

From the second story landing, Victor and Cavanaugh had lowered an extension ladder to the first floor. They had also positioned planks from boulder to boulder, rebuilding the old walkway along which Bloodhounds had goaded their prey. Both soldiers stood next to a culvert pipe fitted into a window frame. Usually, plywood sealed the exit. Victor had removed the barrier. The pipe coursed under the barricade, to the street, straight to the back door of the bus. The Bloodhounds had used it to import their refugees.

Automatic gunfire resounded down the tunnel: someone was firing the Redhound's machinegun.

"Is the way clear?" Shade asked Cavanaugh.

Victor directed his light into the passage, revealing corrugated metal and emptiness. He nodded.

Shade told Victor to lead, and he stooped into the pipe. As the others filed in, Shade gazed back toward the stairwell, toward the smoky firelight. Finally, after years of upkeep, the castle was destroyed. Her father stood in the smoke, his hair flowing. Shade crossed her arms in salute. He returned the gesture, and though he did not smile, that hole inside Shade felt shallower. Not gone—no, never gone—but not quite as deep.

Roman wafted away with the smoke.

Shade lingered a moment longer, breathing in the incense of burning wood. Then she relaxed her salute and entered the pipe, footsteps echoing forever.

Ω

At the tube's end, Victor unbolted the steel plate. The Redhound's back door had been rigged to slide open to the left. Victor unlocked and opened it. Zombies banged on the bus's exoskeleton, but none had occupied the vehicle.

Victor scooted around the bars and headed for the driver's seat. Cavanaugh opened the cage, and Edward and Grace began to unload the torsos inside, lining them up on the floor in front. Shade, Adia, and the mobile humans waited in the tunnel.

With Victor at the wheel, the bus rumbled to life. Grace transferred the last torso. She would have to stay in the cage to prevent the bodies from rolling around and injuring themselves.

"Move," Shade told the humans.

Shirley entered first. But before Ann and the boy could enter, Graves screamed atop the bus. Dozens of feet tromped across the roof, and the machinegun stopped.

There was clamoring.

Then just the growl of the motor.

Shade nodded at Victor, and he peered out the hatch, pointing his Uzi upward. Graves' head fell through.

Victor caught it and stepped back. Flesh oozed between his fingers, red with blood and stringy with hair. Graves' eye popped out and dangled, dripping humors through a rupture.

Victor sneered and threw the head aside. It hit the wall and left a splatter, hit the floor and left a smear. Victor raised his Uzi just as the puppets dropped down. One of them wore football gear, the helmet dented and full of bullet holes. He tackled Victor, and bullets *ping-ping-pinged* along the ceiling. Victor began to scream.

More zombies started around the cage, toward the rear.

"Out!" Shade commanded. "Out!"

"The babies!" Grace cried. "They can't eat the babies!"

She and Edward each grabbed a torso: she, the redhead; he, the bearded male. Shirley pushed past Grace, escaping into the tunnel.

Grace tried to exit too, but a tentacle seized her ankle through the bars. It tripped her, and she dropped the redhead on the floor. A tentacle snaked into the pregnant woman's vagina and began to suck like an abortion vacuum. More feelers molested the other female torso, and as they fed, the puppets grew new tumors and limbs. The other zombies plugged into the spines of those who were dining and shared the deformation.

Edward made it through, minus his captive.

Grace was caught up in tentacles. "Help!" she screamed, reaching out to Shade, eyes desperate and imploring. "Help me!"

"Shut it," Shade said, looking straight at her. "Seal the hatch."

Cavanaugh replaced the steel plate and went for the drill. Two zombies hit from the other side. The plate slipped. Tentacles and arms came through. Cavanaugh could not hold them. The plate clanked to the corrugated floor.

"Run!" the lieutenant yelled. He opened fire.

In the bus, Victor kept screaming. So did Grace. By now, their skin had started to drip from their bones.

Ann saw everything. She saw Mistress pick up Ellie. Then she saw Shirley shove past, and the next thing she knew, Mistress and Ellie were on the floor, harassed by tentacles. One began to rape Ellie. It pushed straight inside her and pulsed, as if sucking something out. Ellie's stomach began to shrivel.

It was Michael. He was the rapist. Wedding guests howled around him, helping him. Michael leered up at Ann, and she knew he had won. He was the abortionist, feeding on new life. Cavanaugh closed the pipe, and Ellie was gone.

Ann screamed and ran forward to save her sister, her Ireland. Cavanaugh rammed his shoulder into her ribs and forced her back down the tunnel.

"Let go!" She pulled his hair, pulled until strands uprooted, until she plucked away patches of scalp.

Gunshots, screams. Scissors of flashlight cut puppets from the dark. The zombies sported black and dripping Siamese twins, perfectly formed, tentacles instead of mouths. They pawed at Adia, tearing away her shirt. Tentacles wrapped around her throat and strapped across her breasts. They yanked her back, out of the light. Her squeals ended with a rip.

Cavanaugh forced Ann onto a rock mesa inside the building. He forced her away from her sister, away from her family.

Finally, Michael had won.

Somebody stood at the head of the pipe: Colonel Bain, biting a cigarette. He held the plywood seal, and Shade worried he would shut them in. But Bain waved them on. She yanked the seal away from him and turned to the tunnel.

The one-eyed woman emerged first. Then the boy. Cavanaugh pushed Ann out, and Edward was last. He fired at the onrushing zombies. Some were completely black and nude, as if the Puppeteer had cloned its host.

"Move," Shade told Edward. She positioned the shutter, pinching tentacles between it and the wall. "Cut them!"

Edward chopped them with his machete. A head poked through, and he hewed it from the spine. The head dropped. It began to grow new shoulders. Its tentacles looped around Edward's leg and pulled itself closer, biting at his boot. Cavanaugh lifted a rock and crushed the head into sticky membranes and fragments of bone.

Once Edward cleared the entrance, Shade pushed the shutter in place. Zombies bashed the other side. Edward drilled it, fastened it, but as soon as Shade relieved pressure, the screws began to pop out.

"They'll break through," Edward said, but Shade wasn't listening.

She turned to Bain. "Where were you?" She grabbed the collar of his cape and shook the cigarette from his mouth. "Where the fuck were you!"

Bain put his hands on hers, but didn't pull them away. "I was tracking Frost," he said. "I knew he betrayed you, your father. I was going to stop him."

"They're breaking through!" Edward announced.

Shade glanced at him, suddenly aware of the situation, aware of Ann screaming and resisting Cavanaugh.

"The boat," Bain said, locking eyes with Shade. "We can still get to it."

"How?" Edward asked. "The puppets … those things—"

"The sewer," Shade interrupted. She narrowed her eyes at Bain, and he smiled. "We'll go through the sewer."

Ann struggled against Cavanaugh, bucked against Cavanaugh, calling for Ellie, crying for Ireland. Shirley just stood there with that dead face of hers, that empty eye and empty look.

"I hate you!" Ann screamed at her. "You selfish bitch, you killed her! You killed my sister, my baby!"

Shirley avoided her eyes, unflinching and totally unaffected.

"I bet you watched as they killed him, didn't you? I bet you let them kill your husband!"

This time, Shirley's face changed, tensed. Barely, but it did. And her eye began to gloss. Ann felt a stab of bitter triumph. It wasn't enough.

She lunged, ready to punch Shirley, ready to make her bleed, make her feel something, some kind of pain. Make her share the misery. Ann told herself it was to teach Shirley empathy, but she knew the truth.

Cavanaugh didn't let her get that far. Suddenly, he was behind her, yanking her arm up and straining the bone. He said something, a warning, but his words were lost. Ann lunged once more, and her arm cried out.

A hand, cold and little, touched her side.

"Annie-momma," Payton said, gawking up at her, blue water trembling behind his eyelid. "Annie-momma, please."

Edward held the boy's shoulder, but had let him come to her.

"Please," Payton said, "I'm scared."

All the deer fled from her muscles, and she slumped, feeling small and selfish. "I'm sorry," she told the boy. "I'm so sorry."

She didn't have the energy to weep, or the tears. She looked at Shirley and found that the woman's eye was watering. Just a little. Ann felt another stab of triumph, dulled by remorse. Shirley avoided her eyes, and Ann slumped farther. She did not fight when Cavanaugh pushed her along, through more barbwire, through more stone. She didn't have the strength. Or the will.

At the front door and its shattered windows, Shade removed the desktop that covered the pipe. "Be careful," she said. She glanced at the boy, then to Ann. The woman had stopped crying, but tears still cut through the dirt on her cheeks.

"One mistake," Shade warned, "and the junk will crush us." She told them this, and some part of her hoped they committed sabotage. No more hassles.

She slid into the compartment and ducked through the broken window, making room for the others. Bain came next, then Ann and Cavanaugh. Shirley, Payton, and Edward arrived last.

"Step where I step," Shade said, and they entered the labyrinth of concrete and steel.

The blaze in the Haven reddened each droplet of rain, as if the building's arteries had sprung a leak, showering the barricade, water trickling through crooked gutters, droplets ripening on snarls of barbwire, waterfalls rushing off concrete ledges; puddles, lakes, rivulets and streams, all Egypt's rivers converted into blood.

Through nets of fencing, Shade spotted the hydrant. "This way!" she called, ducking beneath I-beams and a rusting chassis.

Something clashed behind her.

Edward called out: "They're coming!"

The puppets had finally broken through the pipe and were hurtling after them through the maze. The ones in front had black skin. They loped and ducked and dashed, muscles flexing and shimmering in the firelight, perfect specimens, perfect beings. Aryans.

Shade sped up, but Edward, Shirley, and the boy lagged behind. Cavanaugh and Ann moved slower, too. Naked, barefoot, the humans had to avoid broken glass, nails, and jags of metal. Getting them beneath the bus would be difficult.

"Bain," Shade said. "Take the rear. Keep them off us."

Bain nodded and ducked into a crevice to let the others through the narrow stacks of rebar and highway dividers. Once Edward passed, Bain ran behind him, firing at the oncoming spawns, which took the bullets and kept coming.

Bain nailed one in the head.

It didn't stay down.

Shade reached the hydrant, along with Cavanaugh and Ann. Shirley tripped on a signpost. She hit the ground, and when she looked up, her forehead vomited red through a newly formed mouth. Her palms had also formed maws of raw pink. Above her, a fossil of car parts, iron benches, concrete rubble, and barbwire groaned and shifted ancient bones.

Shirley looked up, blinking back red rain.

"We have to get her," Ann said. "We have to help her."

Cavanaugh held her back.

Shirley lifted herself onto her hands and knees. The fossil gave, dropping metal bones and mortar organs. She became the organic smear underneath.

The cave-in created a hill of bones between the hydrant and the rest of the group. Bain was still firing on the other side. Edward had started to fire, too.

"Payton!" Ann screamed.

"Go," Shade ordered Cavanaugh, pointing to the crawlspace beneath the city bus. "The manhole's on the other side. There's a crowbar in the bus, just through the window."

Cavanaugh pushed Ann toward the hole. She wrestled him.

"Payton!"

"Crawl," Cavanaugh told her. He forced Ann down, and she finally went through. Cavanaugh followed, and Shade was alone.

She drew her gun and started up the heap of industrial bones, up the ledges and shelves. Through the opening above, the Haven burned like a massive torch. Embers blew down into the barricade, mixed with the rain.

Scaling the side of the hill, Edward and Bain shot down into the master race of black puppets, the Aryans. Payton was at the foot of the pile, trapped behind a windshield. He had crawled through a crevice to get behind it, and now tentacles wriggled between the bars and the scrap metal to lick out the morsel.

Still attached to the car's steel frame, the shield could not be easily lifted. The superhumans pummeled the glass, crunching it like the shell of a hardboiled egg. Edward and Bain could barely keep them off.

Sprinting down the hillside, Shade passed the colonel and Sexton. Their bullets zipped by her, leaving jet streams in the rain. Shade's own bullets formed similar contrails.

Hitler's children fell away from the windshield, bullet wounds popping like pustules. Shade flipped into a diagonal kick, bearing down upon them with a hail of lead. Her boot fractured an Aryan's jaw. The puppet fell away, and Shade lit on the windshield without making a crack.

A regular puppet lashed out with his tentacle and grabbed Shade's arm. She pulled him down onto a broken PVC pipe. The pipe punched through his eye and out the other side, slick, black, and skewering a chunk of brain.

Shade turned to the windshield. With one punch, her fist went through the glass. She tore a hole in the pane and dragged out the child.

Bain and Edward had started down the hill, still firing, still holding off the super soldiers. But the enemies groped for Shade. They groped for the boy.

Sidestepping tentacles, she ducked into a narrow pathway through the junk, carrying Payton through the throat of the fossil. Her foot caught a lever, and a V-8 engine fell. It crushed a pursuing superhuman, squashing its head like a rotten jack-o-lantern.

More garbage dropped as Shade's misstep resonated through the barricade. Highway dividers, parking meters, and truck tires shifted downward, chasing her through the steel labyrinth. She ducked and jumped and swiveled, holding the boy tightly. Wires whipped her face. Switchblades of metal gashed her arms.

Rounding back toward the fire hydrant, Shade stumbled again. A rock rapped the back of her head, and asteroids exploded across her vision. A shiv punctured her stomach and broke off inside. Her shin butted a lead pipe. She tripped.

Spiraling to land on her back instead of the boy, Shade lurched forward, hoping to clear the deathtrap as it closed its jaws of metal and stone. One last blade opened her scalp, and she was through. She hit pavement with a thud.

Fortunately, an Ionic pillar braced the cave-in, preventing spillage into the main path. The fossil lay dormant. Shade stood up. She grabbed the boy's hand and ran toward the hydrant.

Wriggling through the bricks beneath the bus, Ann scraped her elbows and bashed her knees. Her hip hit the edge of a brick. Pain screwed a bolt into the joint and tightened it down.

On the other side of the bus, she tried to stand, keeping her injured leg straight. Her whole pelvis had bloated with the ache. The marrow in her bones had bruised.

Cavanaugh was still crawling.

Ann reached through the bus window, feeling around for the crowbar. Something poked her finger. She recoiled and kept rummaging. It had to be there. Shade had said so.

Wood, upholstery—metal!

Ann grabbed the shaft and pulled it out. Like a hammer, the crowbar had a claw. Ann held the opposite end and stood over the crawlspace, waiting. She took huge breaths. Water trickled down her body, painting her red.

Cavanaugh poked his head out and looked up at her. "Stand back—"

Before he could finish, she bashed the crown of his skull. He deflected with his hand, but Ann struck it and cracked the bone. She beat his head again, and his skull began to cave. Ann kept braining him, her tears mixing with the rain, her growl chewing through the gunshots and the wet smacks of steel against flesh. She pictured Michael, she thought of Ellie, and she hit so hard Cavanaugh's head was now mashed lasagna: tomato paste and noodles of skin.

He stopped moving. His blood blended with the rain.

Ann threw the crowbar and pulled at the shoulders of Cavanaugh's coat. Her fingers slipped on the drenched leather. She grabbed his hair, but the scalp peeled off. Black strands stuck to her hand. She worked her fingers into his mouth and tried to tow him by the upper jaw, but all his organs had hardened into lead. Tired muscles stood out in Ann's neck. The body scooted, then stopped.

She cried and hit him. Her back groaned. Her hip bitched. But she clenched her teeth, leaned back, and pulled. Cavanaugh did not move. Then he did, leather scraping and scuffing across the road. Ann wanted to drop him and catch her breath, but if she did, she would never start again.

She left Cavanaugh against the postal drop boxes. He twitched, and his skull began to inflate. The cranial plates relocked. Skin grafts grew on his scalp.

Ann picked up the crowbar. She started to beat him again.

"Stop!" Payton yelled.

Ann looked up, heaving, blood-spattered.

The boy stood by the bus, soaked and dripping. His lower lip trembled. He was crying.

"Payton," Ann said. She must have looked scary, all bloody and wet, pieces of scalp hanging off her weapon. "Payton, I—"

"Stop. Please."

Ann nodded and swallowed, wincing at the pain in her throat. "Okay," she said. She dropped the crowbar and took a step forward. "Okay."

Payton hesitated. He glanced at Cavanaugh.

"Payton?"

He hugged her. She hugged back. God, she wished they could stay like this.

On the other side of the bus, guns emulated thunder.

"We have to go," she said.

Into the slot on the manhole cover, she inserted the prying end of the crowbar. The muscles in her neck and shoulder strained as she levered open the lid. Her legs quavered. Her arms quaked. Slowly, the cover lifted, but only a crescent.

"Payton," she said, gritting her teeth. "Help."

He pressed down with her, and the lid opened more, releasing the sound of rushing water.

"Turn it," Ann said. "Flip it over."

They tilted the bar, and the lid shifted with a deep scrape. Payton's strength began to flag. Ann held the lid by herself.

"Don't stop now! Don't you ever stop!"

Payton's muscle returned, and with one final heave, they ejected the cover. It clattered and thunked on the concrete.

Ann tucked the crowbar underarm. No time to catch her breath. Cavanaugh would wake soon, and the others would come. Either that, or the zombies would. Michael would be at the fore, still energized from his fetal supper.

"Come on," she said. She guided Payton into the hole and followed close behind, down into the subterranean river. The water washed over her like the Iceman's breath. It stung her cuts, and Ann prayed she wouldn't catch an infection from all that fecal matter and waste.

Clinging to the ladder, Payton stood nearly chest-deep in the stream.

"Can you swim?" Ann asked.

He nodded. "Kind of."

"We have to swim, okay?"

He nodded again.

"Stay by my side."

She took his hand and held the crowbar in the other. As she immersed her upper body, her breasts shriveled and numbed.

Ann pushed off the tunnel floor and towed Payton along. The current surged them forward. All they had to do was stay afloat and pray for the sun.

After sending the boy beneath the bus, Shade joined Edward and Bain atop the ruined fossil. The Aryans scaled the bones, black flesh wet and red in the firelight. The labyrinth teemed with them, a nest. A few inferior zombies intermingled, a minority among the superhumans.

"Keep shooting their heads!" Bain shouted. "It takes a lot!"

Shade obliterated one superhuman's skull, leaving only the lower jaw and a nub of brainstem. Only then did it fall.

The enemy forces began to crest the summit.

"Fall back!" Shade said. She took wing and glided to the pavement. Bain and Edward followed.

Like nightfall, the raiders came over the hill. No amount of bullets would stop them. Shade and her troop paced backward, firing. Soon, they pressed against the bus.

"Quickly!" Shade said, reloading. "Crawl!"

Bain went first, then Edward.

The Aryans approached the fire hydrant.

Like a tropical snake, a bright orange extension cord dangled from a thatch of rebar. Shade pulled it. The bracket that supported the rebar gave way. Steel bars rained down and crushed a few Aryans. Shade dived under the bus, barely escaping the avalanche.

The rods blocked the entry to the crawlspace, clanking, clattering, and making noise.

On the other side of the bus, in the arena of blue mailboxes, Edward was cradling Cavanaugh. The lieutenant's head was pulped but mending nicely.

"She hurt him," Bain said, smoking a wet cigarette. The smoke was diluted in the rain.

Shade knelt by Edward and placed a hand on Cavanaugh's chest, sighing with relief as she found his pulse. His skull had restructured in many places, but it still suffered soft spots. Hair sprang from a plot of recently sowed scalp, and his left eye bulged, rooted in its socket with red veins. His other eye ticked back and forth behind its lid, blinking against the rain, dreaming.

Shade wiped away the hair plastered to his face. "The woman did this?"

"Yes." Bain blew out smoke. "She escaped into the sewer. She took the boy."

Cavanaugh murmured. His eyelid fluttered open for a second. Shade waited to see if he would say anything else; he remained unconscious.

She turned to Edward. "Carry him," she said. "We have to catch the woman."

In the sewer, Shade dropped from the ladder, into the water. It pushed against her, almost waist-high. She shined her flashlight upstream. The water reflected the flashlight, setting fire to the ceiling and walls. No escapees, neither upstream nor down. They were too far to see.

Bain shined his light, too, and Edward supported Cavanaugh.

"They went downstream," Shade said over the sound of the water.

"How can you tell?" Bain asked.

"I can smell the woman's blood."

Bain sniffed the air. He was smoking another cigarette.

"Put that out," Shade told him.

He took another drag.

"I said put it out."

He grinned and flicked the cigarette into the water. The smoke remained, smothering Ann's coppery scent.

"Come on," Shade said. "They're not far."

Searching with the lights, they waded onward.

Slowly, Cavanaugh came to. "Where are we?" he asked, his voice mushy and drugged.

Shade briefed him. She started with how they had found him, beaten and unconscious. "How did it happen?" she asked.

Cavanaugh rubbed his temple, still purple and swollen. "She caught me under the bus. I was crawling."

In a better situation, Shade might have smiled. Ann had overpowered one of the strongest Undertakers. She had subdued him and had slipped away unnoticed, child and wounds notwithstanding. And she was a woman, no less. A strong and capable woman. Yes, in a better situation, Shade might have teased Cavanaugh about this.

She clenched her jaws and woke the Beast. It sniffed the air and growled, drooling and ready to hunt. She tightened the chain around its neck, though she knew it would do little good. Still, precaution was best. She wanted the woman and boy alive. She and her kin would need their blood.

"I apologize," Cavanaugh said, wobbly but standing on his own.

Shade put a hand on his shoulder, partially to stabilize him, partially to stabilize herself; he had very sturdy shoulders. "No need," she said, offering him a smile that was more like a wound, letting her eyes welter in tears. "We will move on."

He nodded. "We will move on."

His one eye was still bloodshot, but it transfixed her, that hazel iris, a mixture of madrone leaves and earth. Something could grow there, she knew. Something already had. A sapling, a plant they had germinated together. Given time, they could water it and watch it grow, let the roots grow deep and bind them.

Perhaps Frost had been right about the island. Perhaps it would set them free.

Shade squeezed the lieutenant's shoulder one last time, and they continued into the tunnel, guided by flashlights, two north stars in impenetrable space.

Sixty-Four

Lights lit the tunnel behind them. Ann glanced back, frozen in mid-swim. A beam probed the tunnel, an oncoming train, roaring and swift.

She tightened her grip on Payton's hand. "Hold your breath," she said, trying to be quiet. She wasn't sure he heard her over the flood, but it didn't matter. She pulled him underwater and kicked off the floor, propelling them forward.

Payton's hand began to slip from hers. Her lungs burned. She tried to redouble her grip on him, letting go briefly to grab higher up; his arm glided along her palm. She clamped down, dropped the crowbar, and reached with her other hand. Their fingers interlocked. And then Payton slipped away.

Years ago, Michael had taken Ann rafting. She had fallen overboard during a rapid, and the river had whisked her downstream. She fought it, tried to swim ashore, but the rapids forced her downriver. Rocks loomed, and panic swept through her, faster than any current.

Now, in the sewer, that panic returned, a childish fear that she would be swept to sea, far away from everything she loved, into the jaws of a shark.

Ann popped her head up and gasped. Resisting the current and the slippery floor, she stood and felt around for Payton. The pursuing flashlight did not reach this far; Ann could see nothing.

"Payton," she whispered, afraid to yell. She could barely hear herself. *"Payton."*

She thrashed the water, feeling for soggy hair. Or cold skin. She found nothing. He was gone, swept out to sea.

"Annie-momma!"

She flinched.

At first, she wasn't sure what had happened. Then Payton called again, and his cry resounded through the tunnel.

Still far away but quickly bearing down, the flashlight fixated on Ann.

She splashed toward Payton's voice. Was he downstream and to the left? She didn't know. The tunnel played ventriloquist, throwing his voice around the passageway. Ann groped through the darkness. She bumped into something with her knee. She grabbed it. A metal bar.

"Annie-momma?"

"Be quiet."

He was latched onto an iron ladder, trembling and cold. Ann looked back at the light. No longer a ghost, the beam began to pierce the darkness around her.

"Climb," she said.

"What?"

"Climb."

She pushed him upward, and he mounted the ladder. Ann followed. The rungs were slick. Payton's foot slipped, and she had to boost him.

Their pursuers splashed closer, the light beams gleaming off the water. Ann expected a claw to seize her ankle, some creature formed from the shadows and the stink, chortling as it tore her off the ladder, its eyes glowing green.

Payton stopped climbing. Ann thought, *No, no—higher, he has to go higher*, but he had reached the top. She put a hand on his leg to comfort him, hoping he would be quiet. She trembled and tried not to pee.

Someone emerged in the chamber below them. It was Shade, the raven.

She's going to look up, Ann thought. She could feel it. And when she did look, it would be over. The vampires would shoot them like they had shot Shirley's husband. Or they would suck them dry, and damned if Ann didn't wish for that the tiniest bit, even though the thought shivered her to the marrow.

Shade slowed, scanning the ladder with her flashlight. The beam seemed to burn at Ann's heel. She had to move, had to climb higher. She had to shrink into a microbe, microscopic and witless.

Don't look up, she begged. Then she realized Shade might be able to hear her thoughts, snatch them from the very air, and that darker part of her—the part that resembled Michael—it said, *No, do look up*, because this was tiresome, wasn't it? Running and hiding and staying alive. *You need somebody—you always have. You need somebody to take care of you.* And feeding the vampires wasn't that bad. In fact, it was good. *Really* good. Just thinking about it stoked that old furnace behind her bosom, a strange sensation contrasted with the chatter and grind of her teeth.

Yes, Ann thought. *Anything. Just send me back to my Ellie and Ireland.*

But Shade turned her flashlight ahead and kept walking. Her men did the same.

Ann waited until the splashing faded, then let out a shaky breath. The heat faded from her chest, and she was cold. Relieved and a little sick. Sick at what she had been about to do. She thought she might vomit, but the nausea passed, leaving a queasy slick of self-loathing at the bottom of her gut.

"Payton," she said, swallowing thick bile and saliva. "Can you lift the lid?'

He tried to push it, but couldn't.

"Let me try."

They switched places, climbing around each other on the ladder. Ann pressed on the lid. It lifted, barely. She grunted, tried again, but it was too bulky. It clunked as she let it down. Ann cursed and struck the ladder, then rested her head against her arm.

For some reason, she thought of Shirley. Not Ellie, not Ireland, but Shirley, standing up just as the junk crashed down. And that's when the tears came.

Payton calmed her with his kind little hand. She had nothing left inside. Nothing but a stone in the pit of her stomach, a resolve to save this little boy.

"Annie-momma?" he asked.

"I'm here," she said, taking his hand. "I'm fine." She sniffled and took a deep breath. By the time she let it out, her head had cleared. "Climb down and hold the ladder, okay, honey? We have to find another way out."

Payton started down the ladder, and Ann waited. Then she went down, too, and they reentered the flow together.

The flashlight had disappeared, leaving only the roar of the underground river. Ann looked upstream into the darkness. She wanted to travel away from the vampires, but the deluge would tire them out, like a treadmill. They had to go *with* the current. To the ocean, if fate willed it.

"Hold my hand," she said, and Payton took it.

Yes, she would save him, because that's all she had left. This hard little stone in her stomach, a calcified fetus. They took the first step toward freedom.

A flashlight blinded their path.

Sixty-five

The Beast smelled its quarry as Shade approached the manhole chamber. It slobbered, growled, and strained against its chain, ready to lunge into the shaft, to gnash flesh and to crunch bone. Shade reined it in. They would need stealth, subtlety. More like a cat, less like a dog.

She put a hand against Cavanaugh's chest. He stopped. So did Edward and Bain. Shade whispered her plan in the lieutenant's ear, purring and panting, hyperaware of his scent, ginger and chives, sensitive to the strands of hair that tickled her eyes.

"Walk past," she said. "Turn off the lights and wait."

Cavanaugh nodded, face white and solemn. He relayed the message to Edward and Bain, and the troop moved forward, into the chamber.

Look up, the Beast growled. *I smell her. I smell her fear.*

Shade could smell it, too. Adrenalin, aluminum and batteries mixed with propane. And beneath that, blood, always blood, that rich arterial wine. She paused in the chamber and scanned it with her flashlight, wondering if she should tree the humans.

Yes, yes, look up. Let me take her, let me eat her.

Shade clenched her jaws and left the chamber. When they were a ways down, she and Bain shut off their lights. They listened for noises beyond the blast of water.

She thought about finding Cavanaugh's hand in the dark. They would entwine their fingers and let the roots grow between them, tingling in veins of light. How unprofessional, though, how juvenile. Save the seduction for later.

Shade clutched her pentagram and shut her eyes, ears attentive, nose in tune.

Down the tunnel, the woman whispered. Something clunked. Probably the manhole cover. Could they get out? Was Ann strong enough to lift that circle of cast iron? Maybe.

The lid made no more noise, and Shade feared they were gone, back into the world. If so, they would not get far. The puppets, like common garden slugs, would foul the last roses of blood. Shade almost convinced herself they *were* gone. But then the woman began to sob, and the young boy soothed her.

The Beast rumbled at the smell of Ann's grief, and Shade grimaced, feeling acid reflux more than pleasure, the bile that ate away inside her, that hole, that never-ending void. Would it be so terrible to set them free, to leave them behind? Shade and her brethren had caused the woman enough pain. They had been the death of someone she loved, and Shade knew the taste of those tears, bitter and cold.

Ann and the boy eventually descended the ladder. They stepped forward, splashing in the water, making so much noise, so damn careless and helpless and yet so resilient.

Shade turned on the flashlight. Ann shielded her eyes with her arm, fishhooks glittering. The boy hugged against her. They did not run.

"A bit dangerous to wander by yourselves," Shade said. "There are things worse than us, I assure you." She cocked her head toward the colonel. "Bain, escort our wards."

He moved behind Ann and placed a hand on her shoulder. Ann ignored him, her eyes fixed on Shade. How this woman could still function with all her lesions and bruises, with all her internal bleeding of the heart, how she could defend herself and still lock eyes with Shade was amazing. Sure, Ann believed she was used up—Shade could see that in the way the woman's face sagged with new wrinkles and fatigue, in the way her shoulders slumped beneath her responsibility—but there was iron beneath all that worn out flesh, an indestructible kernel of will and resolve, like the ball at the center of the earth, tempered in magma. No wonder she had bested Cavanaugh. This one was not to be underestimated.

"Let's go," Shade said, never breaking Ann's stare. "To the river, to the boat."

They progressed through the tunnel, through waterfalls and shafts. The orange ribbon of shirt appeared in the dark, and Shade stopped at the ladder.

"Bain. This sewer leads to the river. Get the boat, look for our flashlight along the bank. Edward, you assist him."

Bain gave his flashlight to Cavanaugh, and then he and Edward climbed to the street. With a scrape and a clatter, they were gone.

Cavanaugh herded the humans, and the troop moved on, silent in the rush of water. Again, Shade thought about finding her lieutenant's hand, but did not. Their time would come. At the island. The Island of Roses.

Ω

A sound echoed through the tunnel. A clunk, then splashes: something was coming. Shade searched upriver, but her flashlight found only water and stone. The splashing disappeared. Then the draft hit her, carrying the concrete of the city, the minerals of rain. That, and the strange meaty stink of Hitler's children.

Shade grabbed Cavanaugh's arm. They shared a glance, and she motioned for him to go, *run*—they've found us! She moved to the rear and drew her 9mm, predicting its trajectory with the light. No one in the tunnel. No sprinters with tentacles for mouths. Nothing but that smell.

Judging by the distance of the sound, by the degeneration of sonic waves, the superhumans had entered the manhole to the theater, the one that Bain and Edward had used. Very likely, the Sexton and colonel were dead, skeletons simmering in stew. Else they would have protected the sewer. At least Edward would have.

Where the hell were the puppets? Had they gone upstream?

"Shade!"

Cavanaugh had stopped several yards away, holding Ann and Payton by the arm. Shade held up her hand, hoping to silence him. The tunnel was a confusion of waterfalls and floods. Still no ambushers.

"I don't see anything!" Cavanaugh called.

Had it been a false alarm? Had she imagined it? She thought so. Just her tired mind projecting dreams.

Shade relaxed her grip on the gun, and something wrapped around her leg. A tentacle.

She cried out, and it pulled her underwater.

Dark liquid pummeled her, and the tentacle anchored her by the leg, pulling her back. Another feeler tried to wriggle up her pants, but she bent her knee and reached out. Her fingers found a face, a nose, an eye. She dug her fingers in and scooped, feeling the ball eject and float out on its nerve. She pressed her thumb through the back of the socket, cracking bone and jiggling the brain. The tentacles loosened, and Shade resurfaced, gasping.

"Run!" she screamed. "*Run!* They're underwater!"

More Aryans rose from the sewage, black as golems of silt. Shade shot the first two, the reports resounding. The back of each golem's head burst like a dirt clod, dumping sediment into the flow. They fell and floated down.

Shade ran.

The superhumans gave chase.

She turned and grabbed a grenade off her belt. She pulled the pin and tossed the bomb, using her flashlight like a laser scope. Her target caught the grenade. He reared back his arm, as if to lob it back. Shade dived into the stream.

The water muffled her ears from the detonation, and concussive waves rolled her along. The roof collapsed, crushing Aryans. Chunks of concrete fell around Shade, displacing water. A chunk hit her shoulder and broke it, pushing her arm out of socket. Ligaments ripped. Muscles tore. Bone cracked and fractured.

A boulder pinned Shade's arm to the floor, rocking on the metacarpals in her hand. She tried to lift the anchor, but it weighed too much. She tried to yank her arm out, stretching it farther from its socket. Her lungs began to burn. The roar of water turned to fuzz in her head, a nice, numbing fuzz beckoning her to float and to abandon all thought.

The boulder rolled away, and somebody lifted her into the air, the harsh, clammy air.

"Breathe!" Cavanaugh told her, and she did.

She wanted to clutch at him for support, to hug him and thank him, but she had to stand strong and push away. She wasn't weak. She stood heaving, dripping, her arm dangling useless, her hair drizzling ink. Behind them, rubble had blocked the tunnel. Pebbles and debris whisked past. Bigger chunks thumped around their boots.

"Nice shot," Cavanaugh said.

Shade grunted a laugh. The humans waited, huddled against the left wall.

"Bain'll be waiting," Cavanaugh said. He offered his hand to Shade. "Shall we?"

She smiled. At last, he wasn't being condescending, just purely kind. "We shall."

As she reached forward to accept his companionship, something black rose from the water behind him. Shade went for her gun—she had lost it underwater. Her knife, then.

The tentacle moved faster. It cracked Cavanaugh's skull and plunged into brain matter.

He gawked at Shade, eyes glazed. He opened his mouth to say something, but the tentacle pulled him under.

Shade dived after him, certain it was too late.

When the zombies first attacked, Cavanaugh had pushed Ann and Payton against one wall and had turned to shoot the attackers. Ann hugged the boy against her, submerging as the grenade detonated, a deafening fireball that shook the tunnel. She didn't hear the cave-in, not really. Not underwater. She felt it, though, could feel the ground rumble and the tunnel quake. Debris sprinkled the water.

She and Payton rose up, dripping. Cavanaugh called Shade's name and dashed through the water. No gunshots, no intruders.

Ann grabbed the boy's hand, ready to flee.

Cavanaugh called for Shade again and splashed in the water.

"Annie-momma," Payton said, looking back, "are they hurt? Are they okay?"

Ann looked back too. And though she wanted to run, she waited to see if Cavanaugh would find Shade. He did. He pulled her up, and said, "Breathe!"

Shade was alive. And the chance to run was gone.

Ann pulled Payton close and leaned against the wall, watching Shade and Cavanaugh, watching for another escape. So many times, her muscles twitched toward the exit, and she almost went with them. But something stopped her. Maybe it was seeing those black monsters and realizing she had no way to guard Payton. She had no gun and no fighting skills, had never taken women's self defense. And the tunnel ahead was so dark. More monsters could lie in wait, Michael incognito. Venturing without the vampires would be suicide.

Cavanaugh held his hand out to Shade. "Shall we?"

His flashlight highlighted her face, and her hair spun a dreamcatcher from the water drops. Shade smiled at him, and Ann recognized the look.

She had shared similar smiles with Michael, back when he was breathing. So much was communicated in that single smile, the lips pricked in one corner and plumped in the other, the eyes sparkling with mischief and desire. And trust.

Ann found herself smiling, too, a subtle upturn of the mouth. She quickly flattened her face into a non-expression, snipping the blossoms in her breast. Payton brushed her leg, and she cursed herself for not running, despite the dangers. Because there was one thing she knew about relationships based on power: they were the real vampires.

Shade reached forward to take Cavanaugh's hand, but their pact was never sealed. The zombie burst from the water and dragged him under. Shade dived in after him.

Cavanaugh's flashlight floated down, still functional and spinning like a lighthouse. Ann swiped for the light. She missed and swiped again. This time, she caught it.

Behind her, Shade splashed around, tentacles lashing at her from the water, a giant squid combating her from undersea. Cavanaugh was somewhere in the middle.

Ann seized Payton's arm. She shined the light downstream, finding neither monster nor Michael. She had no choice.

She ran.

Shade grasped Cavanaugh's hair with her good arm. She grabbed a tentacle with the other and let it pull her shoulder back into socket. More tentacles slapped at her, little mouths gnawing at her leather sleeves. She slashed them with her knife. Shade went to hack the tie that held Cavanaugh, but the sea monster pulled him away, leaving Shade with a handful of hair.

She thrashed through the water, trying to find him. She moved forward, backward, and spun around. He was gone, vanished, vaporized, some nefarious magic.

Down the tunnel, the humans were running away with the flashlight.

Shade punched the water. "Cavanaugh!"

Only an echo answered.

Then Ann screamed, and the boy yelped. Something was chasing them, a leviathan, bigger than the seer but rippling with muscles, mottled white and black. Glossy tatters clung to the leviathan's back. Shade recognized the material. It was the remains of Cavanaugh's trench coat.

Instead of killing him, the Aryan's bite had caused him to mutate. He had outgrown his coat during the change.

Ann screamed again and tripped. She went down with a splash, pulling Payton with her. Cavanaugh lunged—and Shade leapt onto his back.

The Aryan had melded into his spine, absorbed like a weak congenital twin, one arm dangling, the other melded around the leviathan's ribcage in a mulatto web of skin. Its tentacle still wired into the back of Cavanaugh's head, fused now into a hairy goiter that swelled his entire skull in a series of pulsating lumps. Even as she watched, the goiters expanded like elephantiasis. Cavanaugh's hair fell out, slick and stringy, and his muscles grew. His whole body threatened to clog the pipe.

Shade raised her knife to cut the Puppeteer's brain link, but the conjoined twin swatted at her with its free arm. It caught her wrist and tried to shake away the blade. She bit its hand and tasted the salt and grease of its sweat, the black gouts of its blood.

Heads began to surface from Cavanaugh's shoulder blades, formless knots shaking back and forth and stretching the skin. Their lips parted, snapping membranes and revealing white teeth in black gums. Eyelids opened into empty sockets, slowly filling with whites.

Cavanaugh sprouted more arms, now more like an arachnid. Shade warded off punches and protected her eyes from the claws. She cut with her knife, severing fingers, slashing wrists. One of the heads tried to bite her. She stabbed it in the eye, a hazel iris with a huge, irregular pupil. The head squealed and thrashed, crying white and black. Shade twisted her blade, grimacing at the crunch of bone.

A fist caught her bottom jaw. Another chopped her throat, and three more hands grabbed her cape. They flung her against the wall, cracking her ribs. She fell into the water and lost her blade.

Cavanaugh picked up Ann in a fist with too many knuckles and too many fingers. She tried to scream, but the sound was horribly compressed and winded. Her flashlight backlit the leviathan's head, strobing with the tentacles.

Payton cried Ann's name, pissing himself in the stream.

Shade staggered up. Ribs stabbed her lungs with each inhale. The knife, the knife—she couldn't find her knife! The cave-in had slowed the water flow, but the undercurrent must have swept it away.

"Help me!" Ann shrieked.

Shade pawed through the stream once more. Nothing.

She roared and flew onto Cavanaugh's back, planting a boot into one of the mouths, using its lower jaw as a foothold. The extra hands batted at her, but she bit the tentacle plugged into Cavanaugh's brainstem and shook her head. Black squirted out of the sides of her mouth. Cartilage squished between her teeth.

One of the hands pulled her hair, and a head chomped onto her thigh. Soon it would puncture the leather. The leather, and then her skin. She would melt or mutate like Cavanaugh. It didn't matter. She clamped her teeth deep in the tentacle and jerked back.

The head released her thigh and mewled. The arms clutched at her, shuddering, and the whole body thrummed with Cavanaugh's howl. He dropped Ann and stumbled forward, shoulders making craters in the walls.

With one massive arm, he reached around his back, groping for Shade, but the dozen fingers froze in an arthritic claw. The leviathan released one last bellow, a foghorn mourning lost vessels. He made a final pirouette, and then he collapsed, generating tsunamis. Shade jumped away before he could crush her.

She looked back at Ann and the boy. He was huddled against Ann's leg, hiding his face, and Ann was pointing the flashlight at the leviathan, the form afflicted with elephantiasis. Its chest was still rising and falling with breath.

Shade stepped up. "Flashlight," she said.

Ann threw it, and Shade caught it. She played the beam over what used to be Cavanaugh's face, propped against one wall. His skull had produced new plates, disjointing the old, and it had thickened with layer after layer of calcium, like the accretion of a pearl, his cheekbones now as large as fists, his jaw bigger than a shovel. Tentacles had grown from the left side of his face, and one had popped out his eye. But the left side was almost normal, his iris glinting like a tiger's-eye gem.

Cavanaugh blinked and drew a ragged breath.

Shade knelt beside him. She brushed back the few strands of hair that stuck to his forehead and cheek. He blinked again and focused on her, lungs flopping with erratic breaths. He tried to say something, but could only mouth the words.

"Shhh," Shade said, pushing a finger against his lips.

He coughed up blood and black mucus. Shade wiped away the fluids and tried not to let her face crack. Ann was watching, and Shade would not let her see any weakness. This was her Frost face.

Cavanaugh still wore his utility belt and the waist of his pants, the rest ripped away by goiters and malformed faces. Shade took the gun from his belt and pressed it to his temple. The shot would kill him. He was too damaged to regenerate, even if given human blood. The bullet would speed the inevitable.

Shade tightened her grip on the gun. Just once—and briefly—her lip trembled. The quake tried to spread to her entire face, but she froze it.

Cavanaugh met her eyes and nodded.

She nodded too. "May you rest," she whispered. "May you be free."

Cavanaugh blinked, and Shade pulled the trigger.

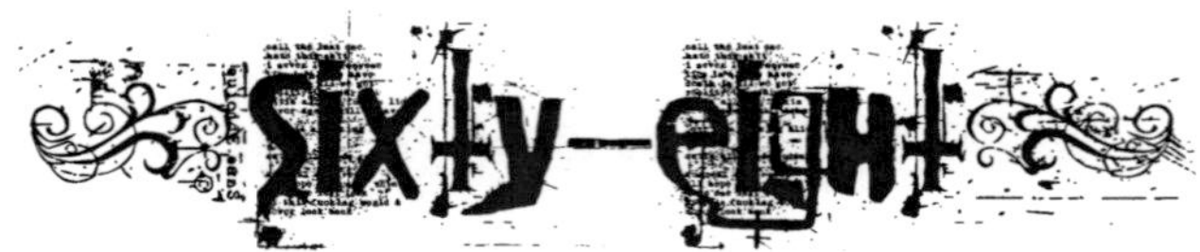

Ann held Payton close, and he wept silently into the soft spot beneath her ribs, warming her with tears and stinging her cuts. She was glad he hid his face.

Shade knelt beside Cavanaugh, the monster, and she did something unexpected. Ann had long attributed Mistress' cruelty to all her kind, but here she saw something very human. Shade brushed the hair out of her companion's face. She put her fingers to his lips and hushed the dying man.

She reached for his gun and pressed the barrel to his head.

Ann saw Shade's lip twitch and shudder, saw her bite down and harden her jaw. Then the emptiness returned. There was a brief flash, a boom (Payton flinched and held his breath; Ann felt the sucker punch in her gut), and then nothing but the gurgle and hiss of water, the voice of a stone throat.

Shade whispered a brief prayer and crossed her arms over her chest. She clutched the star that dangled around her neck, and after a short consideration, she took it off and laid it on the mountain of Cavanaugh's breast.

Ann tightened her arm around Payton. She fought the upwelling inside her, frowning and trying to scowl, trying to balloon a hateful blister that had been boiling inside her.

Shade looked up at her, face molded in blank concrete, eyes black, emotionless, and lost. She stood and holstered the gun. "Come," she said. "Watch your step."

Ann nodded, but didn't move. The vampire stared at her, stared *through* her. There were no tears in her eyes. So Ann shed them for her, mineral and salty as mourning mixed with anger.

They walked and rested when Ann grew tired, that old human fault Shade had come to understand, what with the lead and iron in her chest and legs. Eventually, they came to a place where the water spilled over a wall into a second pipe. This pipe, this outfall, led to the river, functioning as an overspill during periods of heavy rain.

Distantly, Shade wondered if Edward and Bain had reached the boat, if they had passed the outfall. The thought seemed more of a formality than anything, thin gauze to cover a cavernous wound.

She stepped over the wall and into the tunnel. She offered Ann a hand. The woman stared at her for a moment. She stepped to the wall as if to climb it alone, but then accepted the offer. Shade went to help the boy over, but Ann nudged her aside and picked him up herself. Shade expected another flash of respect for the muscles of this woman's arms and heart, but she felt nothing. She floated along, even though her body had turned to metal.

Soon, the smell of rain and river wafted into the pipe like someone's fresh sorrow. A blue orb materialized ahead of them, the light at the end of the tunnel. Shade led her prisoners to the edge and looked out.

Though the downpour had slowed to a sprinkle, a mini Niagara gushed from the pipe into the river, roaring and guttural. The night had faded to that blue hour before dawn, darkened in patches by partial clouds and the haze of distant rain.

Upriver, giant tombstones towered in the necropolis, the City of Corpses. Among them burned the Haven, the ultimate rose, undying in the eternal blue ambiance.

From around a bend, a boat motored. Shade held up the flashlight, but paused. *Let them pass*, she thought. She could kill the humans—the *Beast* could kill them—and she could let the sun pour red and orange upon her. She could die without seeing her failure reflected in the eyes of her men, without seeing their patronizing looks.

"What's going on?" Payton asked, his voice small and nearly dissolved in Niagara's roar.

Ann shushed him. "Everything's going to be all right," she said. "We're safe now."

Safe: Shade closed her eyes. Laughing at the absurd notion of safety, even offering a dry chuff, would have made her feel better. But even that part of her humor—the basest part that proves laughter is a defense against the darkness—even that part was dead.

Still, something in Ann's voice—the tone, maybe, or the feeling behind it—helped Shade open her eyes. It would have been so easy to keep them closed. There behind her eyelids, she could make any future she desired. The island, her father's castle, blood flowing in holy grails.

She sighed and pointed the flashlight at the boat. She flicked the switch on and off, broadcasting meaningless Morse code, a senseless SOS.

The boat approached, droning and shining a bright light, something to envy the sun. It stopped in the channel, unable to approach the shore where the water was shallow and the rocks were fangs. Bain tossed the life raft into the river and rowed toward them. Edward must have been in the cabin or below deck, hiding from the sun. Or maybe he never made it.

At the edge of the channel, still several feet away, Bain extended one fist in front of him and held the other by his cheek, elbow cocked back.

Shade squinted for a better look.

The arrow hissed past her, boring a hole into the tunnel's murk. It *splooshed* into the water and popped back up. It had a wooden tip, its feathers gray and white in the gloom. It floated over the falls and into the river, a strange bird to the lips of fish.

Bain nocked another arrow and pulled back. Shade drew her gun. Too slow. The colonel's shot pinned her hand to her breast. She stumbled, shaft deep between her ribs. The gun fell and disappeared in the rapids.

"Sturm, swung, wucht," Bain called, and yet another arrow struck Shade, this one in her stomach, piercing the void. The fourth missile went through her throat, and she tasted blood.

"When I was a Hitler Youth, the great Lieutenant General Erwin Rommel used to say that: sturm, swung, wucht—attack, impetus, weight."

A fifth, a sixth, a seventh arrow knocked Shade to her knees, barely able to stay up in the torrents of the waterfall.

"I repeated it before I sucked your father's blood."

The eighth arrow missed and disappeared into the tunnel. It had swished through her hair: that one had been aimed for her head.

"Now, I say it again: sturm, swung, wucht."

Bain docked the life raft at the water's edge, running it aground on the ax heads of shale. He stepped into the tunnel and cast a shadow over Shade.

An aura surrounded him, crimson flecked with red beryl, undulating with evanescent kelp. Psychic black streamers flowed from his body. They swam in the nimbus and curled around each other, sentient and aware, vile roundworms seeking a host. The tunnel filled with the smell of lightning and the rumble of thunder. Bain's thunder. He almost looked like a zombie, but his pure psychic energy generated the field.

One of the feelers wrapped around Shade, stinging where it touched her skin. His force nearly paralyzed her. Had she realized his strength before, had she seen this crimson thunderhead boiling beneath his wolfish grin, she would have killed him. Now, she could not move. The arrow in her chest would key her heart and unlock the deadly furnace.

Then she would wait. She would wait until Bain's teeth hovered over her neck, ready to sink in, and then she would pull. She would rake the arrow tip over her ventricle and burst into cinders and ash. She would cackle as the fire leapt up her throat.

"Traitor," she croaked.

Bain laughed, deep and predatory. "We all have our vices." He pulled her hair back and plucked the arrow from her neck. He lowered his face toward her artery, smelling of pure, singed ozone.

Shade tensed her hand. She was ready. Ready to pull the pin from this final grenade.

Bain put his lips to her ear, breathing the stale dust of cigarette smoke. "I admired him, you know." His voice was quiet and buzzing with the thousand wasps of his aura, strangely audible over the sound of the water. His eyes jittered, ashlar beneath eyebrows of dead brush. "Your father, my Fuhrer: I served him well. But he weakened in the end. I think that's why, out of all his capable men, he left you the crown. A woman. Because his mind was wasted, syphilis of the brain. So I drained him of what power he had left. I sucked it right out of him." The colonel flexed his aura, flaunting his stolen strength.

"Murderer," Shade said.

Bain's eyebrows went up in surprise. "No, *Frost* killed him. Your father asked him to. With his dying breath. He wanted to die with honor. So Frost used my stake. And he lied to you. Because he was afraid. But I, Shade, *I* am not afraid. I am a conqueror. I am your king."

"You conquered nothing," Shade said. "You're *king* of nothing."

The colonel sneered and tightened his grip on her hair. She could barely feel it under the sting and buzz of his presence, which grew between her teeth like fuzz and molded inside her veins. Her entire body whispered with the vibratory mold, each cell and blood platelet forming its own colony of fur.

"New blood replaces old, Shade, and now I rule the island, now I wear the crown. I am king of the mountain of corpses." He opened his mouth with a hiss and pressed his fangs to her neck.

Shade started to pull the arrow—but a blur shot past her face. A thud, a grunt, and then a wooden snap. Ann held the toothy end of another arrow. The end with the feathers. The other half protruded from Bain's chest.

He looked down at Shade, his eyes wide and ticking. "Sturm," he said, and then he breathed fire, incinerated from the inside. A breeze scattered him into the river, and he blinked out, extinguished and lost forever, sediment for the ocean.

Ann dropped the dowel, shaking. The boy ran to her side and nestled against her, and she looked down at Shade. So did Payton, those blue and green eyes, so beautiful, like the sea.

Once, Shade had longed to nurse him with her blood, to birth him into eternal night with new eyes of black. She could still do that. Rebuild what her father had started. But as much as the Beast wanted to, the sun was rising on a new day; it would leave no place for shadows.

Ann moved as if to help her stand.

"Go," Shade said, waving her away. "Live."

Ann's cheeks trembled, and a tear glistened in her eyelid. Then she brightened. She lifted her hand and unscrewed something from her finger. She looked at it for a moment and then held it out, concealing it in her fist.

Shade extended her palm. The ring thumped against her skin, heavy and lackluster.hyp

Ann smiled, and the tear rolled down her cheek. She seemed lighter now, and Shade didn't mind holding her burden.

Without a word, Ann guided Payton to the life raft, over the blades of shale. She pushed off and rowed into the channel. Before the currents swept them toward the ocean, she turned. She didn't wave, but her farewell whispered on the breeze.

Shade clutched the golden ring. She thought of Liam and Cavanaugh, of Edward and Frost. She thought of her father, a silhouette atop a dark tower, overlooking his land. No zombies, no death. Just endless roses black with night. She stood with him, watching the raft float into the horizon, watching the sunrise as it bloomed inside her, filling the emptiness with flame. And when the daystar flourished above mountains of slate, its blood trembled on the water and dripped from the ripples, vulnerable yet blooming, like flowers with thorns.

ABOUT THE AUTHOR

D.L. Snell is undead. Before the zombie apocalypse, he was an Affiliate member of the Horror Writers Association, a graduate from Pacific University's Creative Writing program, and an editor for Permuted Press. His horror stories appeared in anthologies such as *Potter's Field 2* from Sam's Dot Publishing and *Raw Meat* from the Carnival of Wicked Writers. Permuted Press planned to feature Snell's work in two of their future projects, *Elements of the Apocalypse* and *The Undead: Skin & Bones*, but the publisher was eaten by zombies. Snell's website used to be www.exit66.net. He still updates his MySpace from time to time, but only to send for more paramedics: www.myspace.com/dlsnell.

"[*Dying to Live*] put me on the edge of my seat from the opening scene of this apocalyptic thriller and never let up. Don't miss it."
—Joe McKinney, author of *Dead City*

Jonah Caine, a lone survivor in a zombie-infested world, struggles to understand the apocalypse in which he lives. Unable to find a moral or sane reason for the horror that surrounds him, he is overwhelmed by violence and insignificance.

After wandering for months, Jonah's lonely existence dramatically changes when he discovers a group of survivors. Living in a museum-turned-compound, they are led jointly by Jack, an ever-practical and efficient military man, and Milton, a mysterious, quizzical prophet who holds a strange power over the dead. Both leaders share Jonah's anguish over the brutality of their world, as well as his hope for its beauty. Together with others, they build a community that reestablishes an island of order and humanity surrounded by relentless ghouls.

But this newfound peace is short-lived, as Jonah and his band of refugees clash with another group of survivors who remind them that the undead are not the only—nor the most grotesque—horrors they must face.

"This is as bloody, violent and intense as it gets. An intelligent novel that will make you think and make you squirm with disgust in equal measure."
—David Moody, author of the *Autumn* series

Printed in the United States
215213BV00003B/24/A

9 780978 970710